What Feeds The Lake

J.C Hemstreet

Published by J.C Hemstreet

Copyright © 2024 J.C. Hemstreet

First Edition. All rights reserved

www.jchemstreet.com

No part of this book may be reproduced in any form or by any electronic or mechanical means, including information storage and retrieval systems, without written permission from the author, except for the use of brief quotations in a book review.

All characters and events in this publication, other than those clearly in the public domain, are fictitious or used fictitiously, and any resemblance to real persons, living or dead, is purely coincidental.

Editor: Cait Millrod

Cover Illustration and Inserts: Anastasia Poliakova

Cover Text and Interior Formatting: Valley&Vale

ASIN (Ebook edition): B0CVVBK3V6

ISBN (Paperback edition): 9798879934601

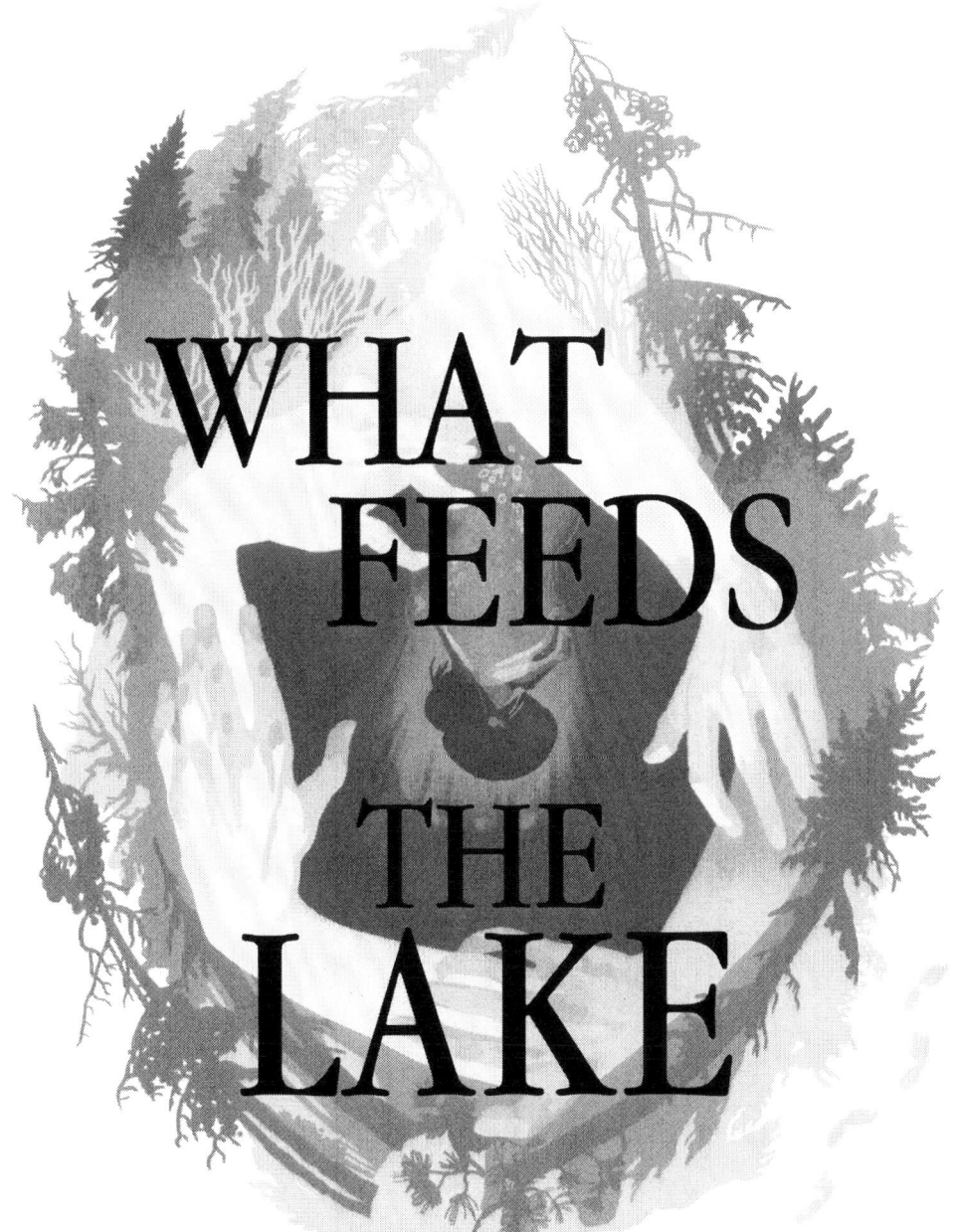

*For those who have gazed long into the abyss.
Tell me, what gazed back?*

Content Warnings

Dear Reader,

This is an adult horror romance novel. It contains dark and explicit content and deals with mature themes that may be distressing for some readers. It is important to prioritize your well-being while reading. The following list is provided for readers who want to know what to expect from the themes and depictions in this book. If you do not have concerns about dark content, and/or prefer to go into the story blind, skip this page. What follows may be considered spoilers.

Please be advised that the following topics are explored in this novel:

- Depictions of untreated and unresolved anxiety, panic attacks, addiction, drug-related withdrawals, suicidal ideation, self-harm and suicide.
- Mentions of child abuse and domestic abuse, both physical and sexual.
- Mentions of family member death including parents and siblings.

- Depictions of explicit sexual situations including themes of BDSM, unequal balance of power, and sexual encounters with a non-human.
- Depictions of drug and alcohol use.
- Depictions of verbal bullying.
- Depictions of physical violence and abuse.
- Mentions of religious trauma.

Your mental and physical well-being matter. Please do not read this story if doing so would jeopardize your health and healing.

An Invitation

In the late afternoons of autumn, the light in the atrium of Melrose Academy of the Arts could make a stack of medical records look whimsical. The light was deep gold and amber, filtering through three-story windows and scattering in prisms and sharp lines over the polished wood floors. As ordinary dust particles floated into the path of sunbeams, they were transformed into pixie dust, gleaming and sparkling.

It was the perfect place to hide out for a painting session between lectures, which Callan Lark had discovered within her very first week at Melrose, three years prior. But on this day, there was no easel at the center of the circular room, no fiery reds and oranges staining the wood floors as Callan pulled another destructive fire from the depths of her soul and smeared it thickly onto bone-white canvas. Today, the only paint she would touch was the midnight acrylic she picked nervously from under her fingernails, and the smudges of mustard flaking off her old flannel shirt. Today, the atrium held over one hundred chairs and an emotion that had always been blissfully absent from Callan's earlier visits: dread.

A professor she vaguely recognized stood at the front of the room behind a mahogany lectern, checking his watch as students filed in. They took chairs around Callan, but never the one nearest her. People moved around her like she was a rock jutting out of a river. A single cloud lingering over a sun-drenched field. An omen. When she had a canvas in front of her, that didn't matter much. She could almost pretend she enjoyed the solitude. But with nothing to distract her hands, she was beginning to wring them out in her lap, causing her arthritic finger joints to sting. Her ears started to ring.

She found a distraction in the Professor. The scowl on his face said that this meeting was as mandatory for him as it was for her. She guessed that scowl was the reason he'd been chosen for this role. None of her favorite sandals-and-socks professors would be able to stare down a room and tell them they might be homeless after graduation, six-figure Melrose degrees notwithstanding.

If she remembered correctly, this professor's classes were typically reserved for the most gifted and promising students, who had to be nominated for his exclusive roundtables or apply through a rigorous panel selection process for his studio time. Callan's attendance at this particular meeting was all the evidence needed that she didn't deserve a spot in any of those seminars. The Professor's mood only fouled as students approached him with eager smiles and hands extended for a sturdy handshake. He seemed relieved when the bell chimed and he was able to waive the line of students back to their seats. When he stepped around the lectern and into the pool of light cast by the tall windows, she realized why that line had mostly been made up of women.

His face was a careful juxtaposition of antonyms: feminine and masculine, warm and cold, boyish and ageless, soft and hard. A jaw cut from marble contrasted by bee-stung lips, the delicate column of a throat set against the harsh slash of high cheekbones. There was a wrongness to the beauty; as if all the natural luck tipping his direction evidenced some form of cosmic cheating or the covetous preference of a vain god.

"Good afternoon," he said soberly, fisting his hands in the green tweed of his pockets. His rough voice held none of the quiet, still beauty of his face. His accent curved sharply around the edges of his words, each one cut jaggedly from his tongue. "This is a meeting for graduating seniors. If you are not a graduating senior, leave now."

It was pin-drop silent as Callan craned her neck to see to the back of the room. Several students headed for the door with their shoulders hunched. When she turned back, the Professor was staring right at her. He seemed to realize himself, clearing his throat and pushing away from the lectern to pace in front of it.

"Right. There's more of you than I expected. Well, you're all here because you have yet to arrange post-graduation employment. Melrose prides itself on ensuring that all students have jobs following graduation." From the droning, bored way he spoke, he didn't really identify himself with Melrose or job placements. He was likely more concerned with the students who didn't even need Melrose. Who didn't need teaching jobs and side hustles, who might actually turn into capital "A" artists and make a living the way artists do.

"There are many options for employment following graduation, and your Melrose degree will take you far..." Now Callan was certain he was reading from a script. His deep, navy eyes glazed over as his mouth moved stiffly over the words. The longer he hunched over the lectern, the deeper the groove between his hawkish brows, the tighter his hold on the lectern's edges. From the primed hunch of his shoulders, he was becoming a flight risk. Callan could relate.

Speeding up as he neared the end of the page, he added, "There are forms at the front of the room that you should fill out based on your job preferences. You will be paired with a mentor for the winter term to work through the application process together." As his eyes rose from the paper they landed back on her. She squirmed under the weight of it for the split second it took the students to realize they were dismissed.

From there, the room descended to the chaos of squeaking chairs, voices layering and footsteps pounding. The Professor stepped back into the shadows to give the masses of students space to fill in their information on the forms. Forms Callan definitely should have been filling out if she had any desire to avoid homelessness the following May. Instead, she lingered at her chair, picking at her thumb cuticle until it bled. When she finally rose, it wasn't the front of the room her feet led her toward. It was the exit. By the time she was halfway to the door, she was running. She didn't stop until she made it to the fourth floor, where there were entire hallways of vacant, forgotten offices; another Melrose secret she'd been keeping for years.

The hallway of the administrative wing was dark with all the doors closed, but she found the one she was looking for by memory. Opening the door, she was greeted by a warm flood of light from the lamp she'd pilfered from the library, a stack of books that belonged there as well, and the thing she was really looking for—a half-finished painting still resting on the easel. Dropping her backpack at the door, she set about mixing paints and preparing her palette. Her mind still pulsed with nameless, jagged emotions that placed a hot, heavy weight at her sternum.

This particular fire was already raging away on the canvas when she came before the easel, but the emotions grew hotter and more unpredictable with each new brush stroke, descending to the blues and whites of the most destructive infernos. Her hands moved without much notice from her mind, which slowly but surely took to a staticky, loud silence the longer she stood before her art.

Some hours later, a prickle began at Callan's nape. "It's flat. Scraping would give it better texture," said a voice from behind her. Callan flinched so violently that her palette of expensive paints splattered her shirt in a Pollock-style masterpiece. The Professor from before was leaning against the door, his arms crossed. The shadows from the hall lingered in the hollows of his pronounced cheekbones, the smudges beneath his eyes, hung like a collar around his throat. He surveyed her room with twinkling, calculating eyes. "You aren't living in here, are you?"

She sputtered a denial as she wiped the paint away from her shirt, only managing to stain her hands and the entire length of her forearms. Finally, she gave up, shoving her hands behind her back.

"I just like the quiet for painting," she said, her voice tinny with rising panic. The Professor's eyes narrowed as he stepped further into her space. His appraising gaze landed on the neat bundle of blankets and pillows in the far corner under the desk, the neatly arranged clothes on top of it. He didn't comment further. He didn't need to.

He inhaled long and slow, clasping his hands behind his back. "I noticed you didn't sign up for any of the winter mentoring programs," he said. "Was there a misunderstanding about your employment status?"

"Well, um, no—"

"So, you presume that your art will have a sudden and unprecedented breakthrough this term? You'll hit the jackpot and never require gainful employment again? A Sotheby's auction will appear in the hallway and save you from poverty?" As he stepped further into the room, the air began to thin. The shadows that had been banished to the far corners by the lamp light crept forward, drawn to his presence. Maybe that was just the panic squeezing Callan's rib cage. When she didn't respond, the Professor lifted a single winged brow. The flames ever-present in her stomach flared.

"What does it matter to you?" She demanded. She flexed her hands into fists only to wince at the tightness in them, the way the paints further constricted the movement of the swollen joints. "I don't even know your name, why should you care whether I have a job or not?"

"I'm Dr. Ladon Cane, though you can just call me Professor." His drawling tone suggested that his name should have a profound effect on her. "And I don't care about you. I care about the reputation of this school. I'm on the Board of Trustees. Melrose prides itself on achieving full employment for—"

"Bullshit," Callan spit. Her chest heaved as the room returned to that staticky silence she usually only found with a brush in her hand. "I'm sorry," she added when the adrenaline had fizzed enough for her to realize what she had said and to whom. "But that's bullshit."

Those dark, calculating eyes were flicking over her features again, lips tightening thoughtfully. "Fine," he conceded with a sharp nod. "You're right. I don't give a shit about employment outcomes and job placements either. I care about the art, and making sure it gets made. And I'm sorry to say, Callan, but there won't be much room for making art if you end up at a temp agency."

"How do you know my name?" She asked, trying to avoid thinking too hard about the rest of what he'd said.

"I'm on the Board of Trustees," he repeated mildly. "And despite your very best efforts, you've been noticed. Someone even got the wild idea to nominate you for my winter term." He pulled an envelope from his coat pocket, extending it to Callan. She eyed it like it might contain anthrax. He sighed. "It's an invitation. One you definitely don't want to miss if that's the best you've got," he said, tipping the folder in the direction of her easel. She snatched it away from him but didn't open it. It felt weighty hanging at her side, especially with the Professor eyeing it so closely.

"Is that all?" She asked, indignant anger still sending pulses of electricity up and down her arms. Who the hell was he to offer her handouts? And what the hell made him think that she needed them?

"That depends," he said, dragging his attention back to her face. "Do you plan to attend my winter term?"

"That depends," she parroted, lifting a shoulder. "Do you make a habit of insulting your students' work?"

"Only the great ones." His eyes sharpened, lips curving up in a wolfish grin. Callan returned his even stare. "I'll see you at the end of November, Callan. I look forward to working with you through the term." With that, he was gone. The shadows of the hallway ate at him hungrily. Callan rushed forward to remind him that she hadn't agreed to anything. Yet.

But the hallway was empty and even darker than it had been earlier. She glanced over her shoulder to find dusk descending on the quad, the trees painted black by the peachy sky. She was late.

Ghosts

The night was unusually warm for early November, and the smell of sun-roasted dead leaves encircled her as she rushed across the grounds. The picnickers from earlier had dispersed, leaving the lawns empty and thick with shadows. She rounded a corner, heading past the labs at the north end of the campus, when movement in her periphery caught her attention.

She missed a step, her stomach lurching, but she didn't stop.

There was a hooded figure lingering in the shadows cast by a towering maple tree. The sight of the figure caused an arrhythmic turning over in Callan's heart, like a stalling car. It was always when she forgot about the figure that it reappeared, reminding her she would never be without it. Reminding her that she would not have the luxury of fully forgetting. It stalked her as her feet ate up the pavement, her pace and pulse quickening.

It never approached her, never spoke to her, never stalked her inside any building. But it wanted her to be aware of its presence, this she knew. It wanted her to be afraid. She refused to give it the satisfaction.

The jutting, gothic clock tower at the top of the quad began its low drone just as she crossed the street at the edge of campus and entered the glow of the bookshop window. The figure that haunted her shadows didn't follow her out of them, and she could almost, almost pretend this meant it didn't exist. But the memory of it wedged into the space between her lungs and her sternum. Waiting. Always waiting.

She hauled the cart of used, dollar books inside, finding the shop blessedly empty, save for one overfed, orange tabby cat who cackled at her as she set her things behind the register. His name was Schrödinger, owing to the fact that Callan had found him half-dead in a box in the alley behind the shop two years prior. He was certainly alive now, his tail swishing so vigorously on the checkout counter that it was sending invoices and receipts flying around the shop.

The bell tinkled as the door fell closed behind her. The space smelled like burnt coffee and bookbinding glue and the leaf litter that had blown in from the street. What it didn't smell like was dinner, which was unusual for a Tuesday night shift. Callan deposited her package at the register, which Schrödinger proceeded to maul as Callan drifted toward the darkened mouth of the stockroom.

"I'm here," she called. Edmund Warble grumbled a greeting, tottering out of the stacks as he pocketed his spectacles. He was a wraith of a man, all spine and arthritic joints and hair that looked like cotton balls stretched too far.

"You're early, Cal," he said, tugging at his wispy beard. His cloudy eyes wandered over the empty store, the dark beyond the window, a frown settling into his smile lines. Callan smirked.

"It's after five, Eddy. I'm late. Have you eaten anything today?" She asked.

"Oh yes, yes, I was just looking through an old Joyce that came in, seeing if I might be able to save the spine," he said, trailing off as he wandered back into the stockroom. The cat squawked again, turning in circles, telling Callan that he could definitely use some more kibble.

"I'm putting a dinner in the microwave, Eddy, and you're eating it," she called. Another grumbled response. The microwave dinners were nuclear-breakdown hot when she dragged them from the old microwave. When she'd first started working at the shop, she hadn't been able to tell the smell of his turkey dinners apart from the smell of the cat's canned wet food. But over the years, she'd developed a taste for them. Maybe it was just the routine of sitting in the mystery section with a single candle lit at the two-person table, Schrödinger twining his body between their legs as they shared a meal. There was a peace to it she rarely found outside of art.

"What's this package about," Eddy asked, holding the folder the Professor had given her aloft with two pinched fingers. He scuffed his way to the table and lowered himself to the chair joint by joint.

"Do you know of Dr. Ladon Cane?" Callan asked instead of answering, wincing around a bite of turkey.

Eddie hummed. "Oh, of course. I have at least one or two of his early works on art psychology over in the sciences section. He's gotten a bit esoteric in recent years, though I understand most of his work has been clinical. Shall I grab you one of his books after supper?" He stuffed a paper towel into his collar and rolled up his shirtsleeves.

"No, no," she said. Though she would definitely do some snooping while she worked on inventory that night. "It's just that I met him today. He gave me that package."

She went on to tell him about the whole strange affair, leaving out no details, including that the man looked more like a statuesque depiction of Adonis than human.

"I've heard of this retreat in the papers. Lots of great art has come out of them, certainly all the best of Melrose. Agnes Greer, Dominic Trent, I think he even hosted Theodora Del Toro a few years back. It's a bit like the famous summer at Lord Byron's Villa Diodati. A group of talented artists get together at a snowed-in cabin and work on their craft under his tutelage. Quite romantic," Eddy said wistfully. As he looked at her, his smile fell. "You're not considering saying no, are you?"

Callan shrugged, ducking her head. How could she tell Eddy, her very biggest fan, that she was ninety-seven percent confident she'd been invited by mistake? She now recalled Agnes Greer, who became a minor celebrity on campus last spring when she sold a piece at auction for six figures. But people weren't lining up to buy the pieces Callan had on display around the bookshop. None of her professors had taken an interest in her style or technique, or even, frankly, her. Her grades were good, but that had no bearing on her skill, only her perfectionism and talent for finding extra credit opportunities.

Eddy's heavy brows pinched as he chewed. "But you have at least looked in the folder, haven't you? Even just academically?"

Callan's stomach fizzed again, as it had every time she'd thought of opening the package since the Professor had dropped it in her hands.

"I was hoping maybe you would do the honors. You have a knack for sniffing out crap." She toyed with the envelope's bent edge. "I don't want to get my hopes up."

Eddy eyed the package as he tipped his head from side to side, chewing slowly, considering. "Alright, give it here." He wiped his fingertips on his bib and took up the package.

"Good sturdy hand," he said, commenting on the word printed on the front. "Expensive manila." He opened the folder and peered in. "Quite thorough for a prank, I must say." As he leafed through the stack, Callan's fingers began to itch with the need to steal them back, to know what his eyeballs were seeing with each rise of his eyebrows and soft hum in his throat.

"Alright, Eddy," Callan moaned, scrubbing a hand over her forehead. "Put me out of my misery."

Eddy nodded slowly, his eyes zigging and zagging, a finger tapping at his chin. Finally, his gray eyes met hers. Callan stole the papers from his hand with a loud snick.

"I think you need to go," he said. "I think this is exactly what you need, Callan. Honestly."

Callan flipped through the pages. There was a non-disclosure agreement, a medical consent form, more than one liability waiver and other legal papers from a fancy law firm with an ampersand in the name. There was a short list for packing, a long list of prohibited items (including every imaginable kind of art supply and electronics), an agenda, and a map.

"Pitch Lake," she said, glancing up. "Where is that? Any idea?"

"Not the foggiest," Eddy said with a chuckle. He took the map. "Ah, yes. Montana. Such wild terrain there are still plenty of lakes with no names. I'm sure he merely named it himself. Clever name, don't you think?" He asked, turning the picture to her.

Clever was one word for it. The lake, if it could even be called a lake, was oddly circular and jet black. It wasn't black in the way some bodies of water reflect their surroundings. This lake was black like tar. Densely black. But surely that was just the low-quality photo. It was surrounded by a jagged fence of towering pines that made Callan claustrophobic even from thousands of miles away. The lake leered at her, pulled at her in the same way the sidewalk develops a certain magnetism when viewed from a balcony twenty floors above. It made her dizzy. It made her curious.

"You really think I should trust this man?" She asked, still transfixed by the photo.

"What I really think is that you have more talent in your left pinkie finger than Greer, or Trent, or any other past graduate of his could scrap together in their entire life. I read the papers. I see what opportunities like this can mean for even mediocre artists. This looks like a golden ticket to me. If there's even a chance this could offer you a way forward, then go you must."

Coming from Eddy, it all sounded so logical, so sensible. Of course, she would go. They would be snowed in before anyone realized that Callan was a talentless fraud. And by then, what could they do with her except let her stay? It wasn't as if she had anything else to do over the winter break. If she stuck around campus, she'd eventually cave and submit all those teaching applications she'd been holding on to. And the thought of teaching cruel, pimple-faced teens how to draw a pear flooded her with dark, existential dread.

"What about the shop?" She asked. Eddy waved a hand dismissively.

"I need a vacation. The cold isn't good for these old hips. I'll visit Meredith in Florida. Close the shop while the kiddies are away on holiday. We won't sell a damn thing while school is out anyway. I'll save money not having to keep the heat on." What he didn't say was he'd save money not having to pay Callan minimum wage to eat dinner with him and manage the dwindling inventory for his failing shop.

"And Schrödinger?" They both looked at the overstuffed orange critter purring as it stretched its long body to cover both of their feet.

Eddy smiled wide enough to show his tobacco-stained gums. "I'm sure there will be plenty of field mice in Montana."

Callan plastered her chin-length hair against her head with two sweaty palms. The electrical sparks were back, zinging up and down her arms. "This is completely absurd, Eddy. You're sending me to the woods to have my skin made into a suit by a maniac posing as an art professor." There was no way he wanted her in Montana for her art. This seemed like the only plausible alternative at the moment. Maybe that explained his perfect skin as well.

Eddy laughed until it turned into a wet wheeze. "That would make for quite the biography. Every artist needs their tragedy, do they not?"

It was well past midnight when Callan locked the front door of the shop and made her way in the direction of the campus dorms. Though Eddy was already snoring in the apartment above the shop, she kept up the ruse of returning to her dorm room in case he happened to glance out the window.

She ignored the prickle at her shoulders that told her she was being watched, instead shoving headphones into her ears and turning up the volume. The more of herself she gave to her shadow, the more it seemed to grow. She starved it by denying that it existed, even if her denial was futile.

As she veered off the path leading to the dorms and headed back toward the administrative building, the prickle at her shoulders grew fingers. She yelped as she yanked the headphones from her ears and turned on the figure stalking her.

"I could have been anyone," Professor Cane said, his face swathed in shadow. "You should be more careful."

"What are you doing here?" Callan demanded, eyes darting around the dark, deserted quad. It didn't escape Callan's notice that her heart rate only accelerated upon realizing that her stalker was the Professor.

"Following a hunch," he replied, giving the quad his own calculating once-over. "Access to the academic buildings on grounds is restricted after hours for good reason, Callan. What if there was a fire and no one knew you were inside? I can't risk your safety. For that reason, I've had campus security check the locks on the administrative building."

Callan swayed on her feet. His stare held the same magnetism as the lake in the picture. She gripped the smoky tendrils of rage lining the bottom of her stomach and tugged.

"Thanks, ever so, for your concern, Professor," she said, acid on her tongue. "Would it be safer for me to sleep in the grass? The gym locker room, maybe? I've done it all before, so, which will it be?"

The tick, tick, tick of Professor Cane's jaw muscle was visible in the dark. He extended his hand to her; another offering she was loath to accept. The jangle of keys followed when she didn't give her own hand over.

"I don't have any courses this fall, so my home here is vacant through the end of term. You can stay there through finals." When Callan snorted, his voice rose. "Water my plants, make sure the pipes don't freeze, keep the place clean."

"Why?" She asked, all the bite from before replaced by dumbfounded shock. "Why would you do that for me?"

"I'm not doing anything for you." His voice was icy; annoyed. "I'm giving you a job. I expect that you'll be able to arrange proper housing come spring. If not, I'll have no choice but to raise the issue to the Registrar."

This time when the Professor jangled the keys, she took them. They were still warm from his touch.

"I don't have a car," she said, staring down at the keys. It was the last excuse she could summon.

"You won't need one. The house is on the edge of grounds, near the lake. Number 205. The lights are on for you."

"Thank you," she mumbled, finally daring to lift her head. The Professor was already gone. She was alone with the fog tangling through the trees of the quad.

Departures

If Callan had expected Professor Cane to materialize at his home during her month-long stay, she was both wrong and right. He never came through the door, but the house was haunted by him all the same. She had never felt so aware of a person that wasn't there, had never known someone so intimately without ever having a full conversation. Except, perhaps, the shadow that haunted her nights; lingering at the edge of the lake, barely visible from the kitchen window, from sun down to sun up. It never moved, never strayed closer, never stayed put when her nerves and anger got the best of her and she hunted after it in the dark with her flashlight. It was like Cane. There but not.

She had taken her job as housekeeper seriously, cleaning the home from top to bottom and back again. If she used the exercise to learn everything there was to know about him from the objects within his home, that was just a voyeuristic side effect. The more she uncovered, the less she understood Dr. Ladon Cane. He was a specter that existed at the edge of every frame, even within his own home. The longer she lived with his ghost, the further her obsession slipped beneath her skin and into her blood.

As she watched the last leaves of autumn scrape across the bleached and dying grasses of his lawn, she wondered if he'd be able to smell himself on her when they met again that day. The knowledge of him had only added to her desperation. She gripped onto the promise of his retreat with stinging, white-knuckled fingers that threatened to cramp before she even boarded the plane.

As the fog lifted from the lake's surface, Callan turned away from the fading image of her shadow at the lake's edge to check the locks on Professor Cane's doors for the fifth time that morning. Everything was in order for her departure, even if the inside of her head felt like a sandbox full of broken toys. Eddy was safely in Saratoga. Schrödinger was safely, if not a bit grumpily, tucked away in his carrier. Not a single paper or exam stood between her and the winter term. And yet, Callan couldn't help feeling like something was amiss. Like leaving Melrose was a grave mistake. One there would be no returning from.

But she'd grown accustomed to the familiar doom of her anxiety. She might have been more concerned about her impending travels if she was actually excited. A shiver worked its way up her spine, and she bounced on her heels and rubbed her mittened hands against her arms as she waited in the driveway for the airport shuttle Professor Cane had arranged for her.

She watched a distant beam of light become two headlamps as it slowly advanced down the deserted street. The shiny black SUV paused at the curb, exhaust forming a frothy cloud. Callan made to open the door, but it popped open before she could.

Professor Cane stepped out of the vehicle, so close to Callan that his misted breath tangled with her own. Her brain short-circuited as a wash of nerves sloshed around her already sour stomach. Regrettably, she hadn't mythologized him at all. He was, in fact, the most beautiful creature she'd ever laid eyes on. There wasn't any lust to the observation. It was a matter of artistic appreciation. The way the light fractured off every angle of his eerily symmetrical face, the palette of bone-white skin and fleshy, just-bitten lips and eyes the color of lakes known for drowning.

His hair was longer than she remembered and thrown back in a perfect mess of waves.

A surprised "hi," was all she managed, teeth chattering. Her fingers were numb around the handle of Schrödinger's carrier. She peeled them away one by one as Professor Cane took the load from her.

"Good morning," he murmured, glancing up and down the empty street before waving her into the vehicle. He held the carrier up to inspect its contents and Schrödinger hissed then growled low. "Cute cat," he said, handing the carrier back to Callan once she was seated. By the way he held the carrier away from his body like a stinking doggy bag, cute was the furthest word from his mind.

"Thank you for agreeing to let me bring him," Callan said. "I promise, he'll warm up to you. He's a bit distrustful of strangers."

"As he should be," Professor Cane said with a polite chuckle. He tapped the glass separating the cabin from the driver and the vehicle lurched forward. It only took a minute to clear the last street lamp in town and enter the dusky, night-swathed country. Professor Cane was so still and quiet beside her that it was almost like being alone with her own shadow. Callan sensed his eyes on the side of her face. With a slight blush, she let her short, dust-colored hair form a veil between them.

"Did you hand-gather all your students this week?" She asked, keeping her eyes on the midnight blue fields sparkling with frost. There was a tiny flutter of wings in her gut that told her she might not like his answer if that answer was yes.

"I was in the area attending to some business. I figured we may as well share a plane. I hope that's okay." Callan turned to stare at the dark space where his face was hidden. The whites of his eyes alone were visible.

"Of course," she said. As the miles stretched on, the silence began to itch. "Why aren't electronics allowed at the retreat?"

Callan felt rather than saw the slow shrug of his shoulder.

"The short answer is that I find them distracting, energy-zapping and annoying. The practical answer is that there's only a small generator and virtually no cell service at the cabin, which may be by design. And the somewhat longer-winded answer is that there are occasional electromagnetic disturbances on the property that tend to fry electronics at random."

The slush of the tires over wet asphalt filled the cabin. "It isn't because you plan to make skin suits out of us?" Professor Cane let out a sharp bark of a laugh. She heard the shift of the fabric of his pants as he crossed one leg over the other.

"A skin suit? No," he said, voice serious again. "But I am looking forward to peeling open that skull of yours and finding out what else is inside. Are all your jokes so morbid?"

"Yes," she answered instantly. Another quiet laugh the same frequency as the deep, raspy babble of a brook over moss-covered rocks.

"Is there any particular reason for that? A fascination with the macabre, an early experience with mortality, maybe?" His voice dipped an octave as it took on a professional tone. Callan knew that tone. She'd seen enough therapists to know when she was being spoken to and when she was being observed.

Her smile froze. "No," she said. "No, not at all." She sandwiched her hands between her thighs to keep from fidgeting. Professor Cane hummed and drummed his fingers over his leg. He was looking at her again. She could feel it.

"I apologize," he said. "My training gets away from me. I'm only curious, sometimes to a fault. You don't need to tell me anything you don't want to. That isn't the point of this term."

Callan nodded, forgetting that he couldn't see her in the dark. "It's fine, really," she said. "I read the course packet." And she had. Thirteen times from front to back. Yet in all those read-throughs she hadn't quite registered that the psychotherapy components of the term would be with Professor Cane. Terms like "group discussion" and "individual session" felt so much more monstrous when it was his navy eyes eating up every tell her face gave away. Not to mention, he made her heart beat off-rhythm. When he looked at her, her brain took on the blank, staticky quality of a radio between stations. She couldn't bring herself to imagine what it would be like to tell him things, important things. She'd rather strip naked in front of a classroom of people and tap dance.

"Where did you complete your training?" She asked, nearly choking around the idea of being naked in his presence. He never needed to know that she already knew every university he'd studied at, along with the fellowships he'd held and the awards he'd won. Or, for that matter, the cologne he preferred, and the brand of undershirt he wore. She could regurgitate his incredibly impressive and extensive curriculum vitae verbatim, both published and unpublished, at this point.

"Oh, the usual pretentious, ivy-infested suspects," he said, sighing as he wedged himself more fully into the corner, orienting his body towards her. "Can I tell you a secret though?" Callan nodded, and he must have seen because she felt the smile spread over his lips. "It's all bullshit. All of it. Every book, every lecture. I didn't learn a thing about people inside those classrooms."

"Sounds a lot like art school," Callan said. Then backpedaling so quickly she tripped over her own tongue, "Of course, that isn't to imply that your course is bullshit. I just meant, I just meant..." Oh god, she'd said "bullshit" to him again. Her cheeks were a near painful shade of plum.

"That learning is best done in the wild," he filled in for her, nodding, a smile in his voice.

"Yes," she said, breath hissing through her teeth with relief.

"My course is meant to challenge the curriculums that you and the others have already mastered. There's really no way to game this system. I suppose it's like life in that way."

"Any advice?" Callan asked.

"Don't pay attention to the others," he finally said. "Don't watch what they do. Don't try to keep up, or compete, or whatever else you've been taught to do since you first entered a classroom. Just feel your way through. I'm not here to teach you anything you don't already know. I'm just trying to help you piece it all together."

Callan's fingertips tingled with the urge to pick up a brush already. There was a heavy, near-painful sensation in her chest; an idle poking and prodding of her sternum. It was the tension of waiting, the fear of disappointing him, the dread that she would finally be sniffed out as the fake she told herself she was. But it was also the effervescence of excitement, the weightlessness of hope. They warred until all she felt was dizzy. Maybe that was just car sickness.

By the time they turned off at the regional airport, the landscapes had dipped from midnight blue to black with the wash of pinks and yellows across the sky. Callan began collecting her things, but the car didn't stop at the Departures terminal. It rolled along, past an unmarked hanger, and onto the oily black tarmac where a jet was waiting.

"When you said we'd be sharing a plane..."

Professor Cane's smile was pearly white and disembodied like the Cheshire Cat's in the dark of the cabin. "We would have needed three connections and a two-hour drive to make it to Paradise," he said. "It would be collecting dust if we didn't put it to use."

Callan's throat bobbed. So, he was private jet wealthy. It made sense with all the connections he had, the auctions she'd seen him photographed at, the one-of-a-kind art collecting dust on his walls. Still, it made her feel grossly inadequate. She had the sudden, violent urge to vomit up all the reasons he was wrong to let her onboard his jet, wrong to be hosting her at his estate when so many other artists were more deserving. By force of will alone, she managed to keep her lips sealed.

Schrödinger, who had been silent for the long drive, hissed with renewed zeal when Professor Cane took the carrier from Callan's lap. He sounded more like a back alley stray in a territory war than a pampered pet being loaded into a private jet.

"I swear he's not usually like this," Callan said, trailing after them, her cheeks hot. Schrödinger was a convenient scapegoat for her embarrassment, but it was more than that. She felt like a little kid again, with too-big pants hanging from too-scrawny legs and a stained shirt that smelled like the church food pantry and dusty pews. She didn't belong here. She watched the brittle smiles of the attendants wondering if they could tell it too. She didn't say that she'd never been on a plane before, commercial or private. But she didn't need to. She was so obviously out of place it didn't require any acknowledgment.

The seat squeaked as she slowly lowered herself into it, painfully aware of her thrifted pleather boots and polyester coat as she did her best to take up as little space as possible. Meanwhile, Professor Cane had thrown his jacket over one chair, tossed his laptop bag into another, dropped into yet a third chair, the one right next to Callan's, and kicked his legs up on a fourth.

"There's a bathroom and bed through there," he said, flicking a finger toward the back of the plane and then proceeding to loosen his tie. "The kitchen is stocked as well if you get hungry." Callan bobbed her head, swallowing thickly. She didn't know how to act, so she froze like a glitching computer. "It's a bit embarrassing to admit, but I tend to get violent motion sickness when flying. I won't be very good company to you, I apologize. But the flight attendants can help you with anything you need."

"I'll be fine, thank you." Callan smiled weakly and brushed her fingers over Schrödinger's carrier as he poked his cold, wet nose through the grate.

A flight attendant materialized behind Professor Cane's shoulder, letting him know that the flight was about to depart. He nodded slowly as she spoke and then murmured something in her ear too low for Callan to hear. The woman smiled slowly as her gaze jumped to Callan and away. She nodded and left, Callan's gaze unwillingly following her the entire way to the front of the plane, assessing every inch of her, from her perfectly smooth calves to her smoothed back bun. When the woman disappeared, she looked back to Professor Cane, finding he was already watching her.

"I'm sure your parents are proud to have such an even-tempered child," he said. His lake-blue eyes were churning with something like mirth, but more calculating. He reclined in his chair, spreading his lean legs wide. The flight attendant handed him a blanket and pillow before returning to the back of the plane. "Are they the ones that taught you how to suffer in silence, or did you teach yourself?"

Callan's mouth popped open involuntarily. She blinked. "My parents are dead," she said, repeating the simple script she'd been using for the last decade. It was bulletproof because no one knew what to say about dead parents. Usually, hopefully, they said nothing.

"I've read your file," he said casually, pouring ice water through Callan's veins. If she did have a file at Melrose, it was either empty or a mile long. She had fit well in the shadows there, staying out of the spotlight, avoiding trouble like her life and scholarship depended on it. But before... If her file said anything about her life before Melrose. She smoothed clammy palms over her corduroys as she searched Professor Cane's face for signs that he knew.

"Well, then you know everything you need to know," Callan said. If there was more breath to her voice than usual, she blamed it on the plane lurching into motion. She gripped the armrests as her attention swung to the blue lights on the tarmac.

"Not nearly," he said. The lights in the cabin chose that moment to flicker out, and the pale light from outside made his dark eyes depthless. Callan swore there was a tiny pinprick of glowing light in those depths. "Your breathing has changed. Are you afraid of flying, or is it that I know things about you that I'm not supposed to."

"I'm fine," she insisted. But her ears were ringing. The plane picked up speed as the lines on the tarmac went fuzzy with motion. Professor Cane pulled the blanket up to his chin and let his head recline against the pillow.

"With lies so pretty, I can't wait to meet your truths," he murmured. Her gaze shot to him but his eyes were already closed, his features softened. The plane jerked violently as they lifted through the low cloud bank. The turbulence didn't let up once they'd made it through the clouds. Every few minutes the cabin shook like they were inside a wrapped Christmas present as a child tried to determine what was inside. Professor Cane's eyelids didn't so much as twitch when the plane careened violently toward the earth in a three-second free fall before leveling out.

Things only worsened as they approached Montana.

Steel gray storm clouds swallowed the plane as it inched toward the earth, heavy rain pelting the metal shell and lightning strikes lighting up the cabin like camera flashes. The plane bobbed and weaved in erratic patterns as the black fuzz on the mountains became individual trees and the clouds parted revealing wisps of fog tangled among them. Still, Professor Cane remained dead to the world.

The plane continued to rock violently, even when they were mere feet from the rain-soaked tarmac. She held her breath as the tires screeched against the ground, sending her lurching forward.

"Welcome to Paradise," Professor Cane said cheerfully, clasping a hand over her arm as he sprung up from his seat. He didn't seem to notice her white-knuckled grip on the armrest.

Callan wasn't one for prayers or cosmic thanks, but she decided at that moment that she would not be testing fate again. Even if the art she made at the retreat turned her into a millionaire overnight. She would take her winnings and hitchhike.

Pitch Lake

Pitch Lake did not feel like paradise, even if it resided within Paradise city limits. 'City' was a generous way to classify a post office, a dingy bar doubling as a casino, and a single stop sign. There were no sidewalks; no people to walk them. Before she could blink, they were through Paradise and onto the pine-choked highway. The steel-tipped storm clouds racing across the sky leered closer as their car turned off the highway and drove up a steep mountain, gravel popping and gurgling under the tires. They went around and around; up, and up, and up.

As they climbed away from town, the mailboxes dotting the shoulder of the road grew sparse. Eventually, even the trees abandoned them, dwindling to nothing but spindly pegs poking out of the dark, wet earth. Professor Cane called them Tamaracks. He said they'd lost their golden needles and gone dormant for the winter. But they seemed dead to Callan. The rain blackened their bark, making them look charred and desiccated. And their uniform placement, the lack of any underbrush, was jarring.

They crested a hill and came upon the cabin tucked between slabs of granite and a few small, bushy pines with a higher, snow-dusted peak looming directly behind. The wind rattled the SUV, whistling through every crack. The cabin itself was larger than she imagined and rough around the edges like an unfinished sketch. It had a rickety wrap-around porch, two moss-dusted chimney towers, an assortment of sagging dormers and lopsided eaves covering its three stories, and a sloped, low-slung roof littered with pine needles. The yellow light pouring through the windows made eyes that tracked their slow approach.

"It's good we arrived when we did," Professor Cane said from beside her, his head angled so he could look up at the sky through the window. "This rain will be ice by nightfall and any more that comes will be snow. We could be snowed in by tomorrow." He sounded cheery about it.

"How will we get food and supplies up here?" Callan wondered aloud, craning her neck to view the steep, rocky terrain they'd covered.

"The pantry is fully stocked for the winter with everyone's favorites. And there's enough booze to kill us all ten times over," he said laughing.

"That sounded a lot like a morbid joke, Professor. Any skeletons in your closet?"

His lips twitched. Maybe she was making it up, but she swore his gaze kept dragging back to her mouth. It didn't seem he was going to answer her.

"The valet will bring up your things and get Schrödinger settled in your room. Why don't you go in and meet the others."

The others. Callan's gaze jumped back to the glow coming through the windows. She didn't like the idea of being the last through the door, of fitting herself into the social order after it had been established. She had already been relegated to outcast status; she didn't need to give them a head start.

She exited the vehicle and ran for the house, tugging down her hood to keep it from flying off. She was too stunned by the biting, blustery cold to wonder why Professor Cane wasn't following after her.

The pelting rain rapped impatient knuckles on the tin overhang of the porch. Callan shook off the water from her coat and pushed through the door. It squeaked and groaned on its hinges. Inside, flames licked up a wall-sized fireplace made of river rock, casting the dim, vaulted space in twisting shadows. The door fell shut behind her and it took several seconds of blinking to make out the shapes in the room. Overstuffed, tastefully mismatched and sun-faded furniture made up three sitting areas in the living room, all oriented around the large fire. The two-story windows facing the driveway were covered by plaid-patterned drapes and framed by wood paneling and built-in bookshelves crammed full of worn books, puzzles, and games. There were dim lamps on each table and a massive elk antler chandelier hanging above.

Three sets of eyes flicked to her and, realizing she wasn't the Professor, away. The students were dispersed in various stages of boredom. There was a willowy, fair-haired man stooped over a book in a regal, leather wingback chair, his fists smushed into his cheeks. Another with deep brown skin and broad features lay on a chaise near the fire, staring up at the wood-paneled ceiling and occasionally tossing a small, rubber ball. And the third, a woman of Asian descent with a slash of silver through her jet hair and tattoos crawling over every inch of exposed skin apart from her face, was carving down a small piece of wood with an aggressively sharp blade. It was her dark gaze that held on Callan.

"Last one in," she said. It wasn't a question, but Callan bobbed her head anyway. The woman disentangled herself from the lotus pose she'd been working in and sauntered forward on bare feet. "Fang," she said. "Veronica Fang. She/her pronouns."

Callan offered up her hand. "Callan Lark," she said.

"Callan?" Her name was a surprised exhale of breath coming from the far corner. The man with the light hair had finally looked up from his books and Callan recognized him immediately. He was at least a foot taller than the last time she'd seen him, and the braces on his teeth had been replaced with a megawatt smile, but he was the same ghostly pale boy that had haunted her around middle school art camp.

"Roth," she exclaimed, relief making her dizzy. She didn't realize how much she needed a familiar face until she saw one. He barged clumsily across the room, all elbow and knee joints just like she remembered, and sandwiched her in a hug that smelled like plaster and mint. Her ribs groaned from the pressure of his hug, her forehead barely touching his sternum.

"I didn't even realize you went to art school," she said into his faded flannel shirt. He squeezed her tighter, eliciting a staccato of pops from Callan's spine, before pulling away.

"Yeah, I've been hiding out at Pugh making my silly little sculptures. No bites from galleries yet, but I'm looking at internships. What about you? I thought you were dead." Callan laughed hollowly, suddenly realizing that everyone's attention was on her.

"No, not quite dead. Just at Melrose."

"So nearly dead then, at least of boredom," the other man said, coming up behind her shoulder. He had his hands bunched deep in his trendy herringbone pants. His full mouth lifted in what might have been a smile if his golden eyes weren't assessing her so mechanically. As it was, it looked a bit like a sneer. He bounced his ball once, twice against the polished wood floor. "I go to Pugh as well. You can call me Fray. I'm sure it'll be easy to remember."

Roth scoffed, gray eyes disappearing into the back of his head. "Do they hand out pamphlets on being a nepotism ass, or is that just bred into your blood along with the entitlement?" The question was directed at Fray, though Roth refused to look him in the face.

"What? I'm just stating the obvious. Half the buildings at Melrose are named after him."

Callan's brow crumpled. "Wait, are you related to Aemon Fray?" The imposter syndrome always waiting in the wings barged right back to center stage, tightening Callan's chest painfully.

Aemon Fray was the most famous living sculptor on Earth,

one of the greatest ever. Why would his son, or whoever this relative was, need someone like Professor Cane to help them find fame? Aemon Fray was fame and talent incarnate. She couldn't help the jealous perusal her eyes made over his body now that she knew who he was. Of course, he was beautiful in addition to being rich, and talented, and a shoe-in to the art world. The perpetual smirk-sneer on his face told Callan he was also an asshole, which tracked.

"I see you're all settling in well," Professor Cane said, materializing from the shadowy hallway beside the grand fireplace.

"Dr. Cane, hello, it's a pleasure to meet you," Fray preened, dropping his bravado like a masquerade mask and donning the one crafted for people who were actually important to him. He shook Professor Cane's hand vigorously, earning him a curious, appraising look from Professor Cane that wasn't altogether kind.

This brought a hint of a smile to Callan's lips. The two hadn't met before. She surveyed the others as they made introductions, trying to guess how well they knew the Professor. It was impossible to tell with Veronica, but Roth seemed standoffish, even shy. Professor Cane didn't give anything away either. He regarded all of them, Callan included, with a cool, unknowable aura. He hadn't been looking at her like that in the car. In the car, he'd looked at her like she was a painting he was dissecting stroke by stroke.

"I hope you've all had a chance to complete the pre-retreat reading list," he said, his eyes flicking from face to face before pausing on Callan. "There's a short writing assignment waiting on each of your desks along with your designated typewriter and journaling supplies. The first assignment should be completed and you should be prepared to discuss it at our noon meeting tomorrow." Callan's gaze slid to the others as she put on a polite smile and linked her hands. "We'll do better introductions over dinner this evening, I promise," Professor Cane continued. "But before the snow covers our path, I think it best that we visit the lake for the first time so you can all get your bearings with the property. Beautiful weather for a walk anyway." For the barest moment, his gaze flicked back to Callan and held. She was still wondering what that measly look could have meant when her boots hit the stoop, following closely behind Roth.

"Beautiful weather my ass," Roth grumbled under his breath, already shivering as the wind and wet ate through his shirt. The rain had stopped. But storm clouds were stewing and frothing overhead, the wind filtering the faint smell of snow through the wet pines in warning.

"It's a spring that feeds this lake, right Professor?" Fray called, shouldering past Roth to catch up to him. The heavy winds warped his voice, stealing it away like a piece of cloth torn from a clothesline, but Professor Cane seemed to hear him just fine.

"It's been quite the mystery," Cane said, turning around and walking backwards like a tour guide, missing every tree root and log in the muddy path. "Nothing lives in the water, and the mineral composition is unheard of, even compared to the most active thermal pools and hot springs. Scientists believe a mineral spring must feed it, but they've never been able to find the source."

As they left the cabin's clearing and made their way downhill, they began weaving through the labyrinth of barren, lifeless trees and mud. The wind was deflected by the peak behind the cabin, leaving the woods silent. Callan couldn't say why exactly, but as they carried on, that silence began to take on shapes, to grow teeth, to stretch its arms. It felt like the figure that haunted her shadows. She checked over her shoulder like it might be stalking them but saw only the disorienting mirage of perfectly arranged Tamaracks jutting from the earth.

In her distraction, she collided with Roth's back. They'd arrived at the lake.

There was no change in scenery to mark the lake. The fence of trees Callan recalled from the picture in the brochure was now as barren as the rest of the trees in the forest. There was no rocky shore, no steep embankment. The lake didn't even seem to have a shallow point. It simply began where the loamy earth ended. It was massive.

The water was black with a sickly green hue. It was as still and flat as the picture in the brochure; no ripples, no air bubbles rising from the depths. Callan had the urge to throw a rock in it to see if it would stick to the gelatinous surface.

Fray had the same urge but was unable to stop himself. The rock hitting the surface made a thick clunk before it was swallowed. The surface remained unchanged. Roth glanced back at Callan with a weary expression. Professor Cane, who had been carrying on a conversation with Veronica, finally paused.

"Welcome to Pitch Lake," he said. His voice was so much bigger in the silence. Even Fray, who was busy inspecting the lake's edge with a downed branch, stopped and listened. "This is where our journey begins and where it will end."

"Here," Fray said incredulously. "Like, right here. At this creepy lake?"

Professor Cane's jaw muscle ticked as his gaze made a slow path to Fray. "Creepy is just an uncreative word that uncreative people use for things they cannot understand."

Fray ducked his head.

"While you are here," Professor Cane continued. "I ask that you remain naked as the day you came." Fray snorted. Professor Cane shot him a look that could cut meat. "Not literally." Beside Callan, Roth chuckled nervously, shifting his weight between his feet. "While you are here, I want you to be naked of your pretense, naked of your shame, of your entitlement and expectation. I want you to cast off all the little devils clinging to your shoulders, telling you how to walk and think and speak and I want you to simply be. It's pretty easy in a place like this." He opened his arms wide to the forest. "There will be no one but us to witness you. For these next weeks, we stand apart from the world. And when we eventually return, well, we've all signed airtight NDAs."

He smiled then, and Callan finally released some of her

tension with a breathy laugh. Professor Cane's gaze snapped to her with hawk-like speed. As he appraised her, his smile fell, a divot formed between his brows. He turned his attention to the lake and Callan felt the absence of him like stepping out of the sun and into the shade.

"I hope you won't think me too eager if we start our lessons today," he said. "The lake seems to be in good spirits." He cut a path down to the bank. Veronica remained on the path, gaze zigging and zagging between Professor Cane and the rest of the group.

"You don't think we're getting in that, do you?" Veronica asked. The bite in her voice almost hid her concern. Almost. Her hands flexed at her sides.

"Of course not. What kind of art would you make as a frozen corpse?"

Fray snickered, already making his way up the lip of the lake to where Professor Cane was standing.

"Let this serve as your first and final warning," Professor Cane continued. "Do not go in the lake. No matter what. Sometimes the fog can become disorienting. Sometimes the water creates illusions that can be quite compelling. But under no circumstances should you enter the water."

Roth gave Callan an uneasy glance which she returned, keeping a wide berth from the edge. Veronica lingered beside the nearest tree.

"What's so special about it?" Fray asked, poking his stick at the surface again. Professor Cane snatched the branch from his hand and tossed it into the lake where it sank unceremoniously.

"The reflection of the lake will help you see yourself more clearly," he said.

Roth hummed, craning his long neck over the surface. "This thing doesn't seem to have a reflection. It's weird actually, how it absorbs the light from the sky."

"A keen observation," Professor Cane said, stepping close enough to the lake that the edges of his hiking boots became damp. There was no mirror of him below. Callan repressed the urge to pull him back from it. "But I do think that the more you look, the more you'll see. The more you'll find. Your predecessors certainly agree."

"So... you just want us to look in the lake?" Roth asked, still peering down at it. It seemed like a simple enough request.

"Essentially. Yes," Professor Cane said. He lowered to his knees at the lake's edge, glancing over his shoulder to see if they were joining him. "There's a meditation component to the exercise. We'll do our first session now. Here." He dug into his pocket, pulling loose a handful of plastic sacks and handing one to each of them. "To keep your knees dry."

Callan accepted hers and made a place for herself near the edge. Up close, she could see that the lake wasn't just black and green. It was rust and vermillion and emerald. The light from the sky didn't refract on the surface of the lake, or lend any insight into its depth. But it did illuminate the first few inches, making the water seem to glow, like sunlight through cola.

"Clear your minds and empty your senses," Professor Cane said from behind her, pacing slowly. His voice had taken on a low, melodic quality that scratched at an itch she hadn't noticed in her mind before. She wanted to listen, so she did.

He told her to soften her gaze over the water.

He told her to let her mind see what her eyes could not.

Then he wasn't speaking at all. His voice was just a suggestion, a gentle nudge against the walls she'd erected within her mind. He tried a door; one that was heat swollen and jammed with black char marks decorating it like lace. He wouldn't be able to get it open, at least not far enough to see inside. But just his presence there made acid pool in her stomach. She tried to back out of the meditation. It only tugged her deeper; a Chinese finger trap.

An insistent hand gripped her wrist, bruising her skin as it tugged her up a flight of stairs. There was so much black smoke she couldn't see the body attached to that hand, but she knew who it was by the way his touch made her skin feel swarmed with insects. He turned on her. He had no face. He didn't need one. She knew this memory, even if it stayed well hidden. He gripped her temples with soot-covered, blistering hands. The words he spoke were too garbled to make out but they existed in the gray matter of her mind nonetheless.

Callan blinked and she was back at the lake, staring up at the opalescent sky, the tops of the trees like eyelashes around a clouded, blind eye. Professor Cane's face came into view above her. She felt his thumbs at her temples, his fingers wrapped around her nape. She shot upright, but her mind dragged behind her like cold syrup. He was speaking, but his voice was far-off and distorted.

Then she noticed the stinging. Every nerve ending on her body burned white hot. She glanced down at herself, noticing distantly that she was soaking wet.

"Callan—" Professor Cane shook her slightly, catching her attention. He was wet too. His dark hair was plastered to his face; his long eyelashes heavy with water droplets. "I'm going to lift you. We need to get you warm. Now."

Proving a Point

Fray remained at the lake as the others rushed Callan back to the warmth of the cabin. The sky had gone from opalescent to gunmetal and crouched low among the trees, casting the forest in dingy shadows that made the lake look more like a pool of old, viscous blood than water. It asked to be touched, so Fray picked up another stick from the shore and did just that.

Even the way the water bent around the intrusion was wrong. He hunched back down on the plastic sack Dr. Cane had left at the shore to get closer to the surface, inhaling sharply. With the air so cold, it was hard to get a read on the smell of the lake. But even with his nose inches from the water, he didn't pick up on anything brackish or stale, nothing one might normally expect from such still, lifeless water.

He didn't know why the lake had piqued his curiosity. It was rare enough for him to take interest in anything, and usually those things at least involved pleasure or comfortable numbness. The lake offered him nothing, and yet he couldn't pull his eyes from it.

He sat back on his haunches and let the silence, the stillness, sink into his bones. It wasn't pleasant, but then again, sitting with himself rarely was. He wondered, not for the first time, what the hell he was doing wasting six weeks he could otherwise be spending partying his way through southern Spain in a drug-riddled haze. That's what his father expected him to be doing. Hell, that was probably *still* what his father thought he was doing, given his penchant for ignoring every word out of Fray's mouth, especially ones that involved Fray's own accomplishments.

Instead, he was surrounded by a bunch of try-hard nobodies hellbent on proving themselves. He wouldn't get into the weeds on what that said about him. He was here to prove a point. He was here because if he succeeded any other way, it would be his father's success, not his.

Fray's gaze snagged on a disturbance in the water near the shore across from him. He inhaled sharply, backing away so quickly he cut his hand on a rock. He realized it was only a pebble tossed in by none other than Roth Heller, the captain of all try-hards.

"Jumpy," Roth said, stuffing his hands in his pockets as he followed the path along the shore. The midwestern freak of nature was wearing nothing but a light flannel and jeans despite the plummeting temperatures. Every pale inch of him that was exposed glowed in the waning light, making him just as ghostly as the rest of the forest.

"What do you want?" Fray demanded, rising to his feet and dusting himself off. Roth's muted gray gaze fell to his palm.

"You cut yourself." His brows bunched together. "Is that your painting hand?"

Fray fisted the cut hand, wincing at the bright burst of pain it caused. "What does it fucking matter to you, Heller?"

Roth grinned, brushing his shaggy, nearly white hair away from his eyes.

"Look. Can we not do this?" He asked. There was a laugh in his voice, but the set of his eyes was serious, almost pleading. "It feels a little cliché, don't you think? We're the only two from the same school and we can't stand each other for more than five seconds. Well, you can't stand me. You haven't stopped growling at me long enough for me to decide if I like you or not." Fray made to cut in but Roth held up a delicately veined, pale hand. He shook his head. "Don't interrupt me."

He waited for Fray to concede. Fray rolled his eyes but eventually tipped his chin in acquiescence.

"I did some digging on the alumni of this program from Pugh. It isn't a competition. Almost everyone that comes out of this term goes on to insane success. We can both have a cut of the pie. You don't need to fight me. We've already won."

But that wasn't exactly true. At least the pit widening in Fray's gut told him it wasn't. Success was measured in degrees, and if his father had taught him anything, it was that the only success that mattered, the only success worth having, was the kind that came from everyone else losing.

"You think this is about competition?" Fray asked, taking a step closer as he pointed between himself and Roth. He sneered, making sure his gaze lingered on every piece of Roth's boyish body that Fray knew he must be self-conscious of. His knobby knees, his nonexistent waist, the oversized knot on his slender throat. "I'd have to think about you to be in competition with you, Heller. I don't think about you at all. You're nothing to me."

Another slow smile spread over Roth's face, eating up every inch of it until he glowed. "Did you practice that in a mirror? Very scary." Fray bared his teeth, but it didn't have quite the intended effect when Roth towered six inches above him. "Come on, get over yourself. It's colder than hell out here and I'm not going to leave you to drown like Callan. Let's go."

He jabbed a thumb in the direction of the trail but Fray didn't budge.

"I don't need a babysitter," he said through his teeth.

"No? Could have fooled me. You sure act like a toddler," Roth said, tossing the words over his shoulder as he meandered along the lake shore, staying a careful six feet from the edge.

Fray's hands flexed unconsciously and he hissed at the renewed pain in his palm.

"You should get some disinfectant on that hand," Roth called again. "I'll wrap it for you if you ask me nicely."

Fray grumbled a colorful string of curses as he stomped after Roth.

He was still a good fifteen feet behind, owing to Roth's freakishly long legs, when something crashed through the barren branches of the trees lining the trail. Fray turned just in time to watch a twig skid along the path and stop at his feet. It was wet and covered in hair-like algae, but Fray could have sworn it was the same one Professor Cane had taken from him and chucked in the lake. His eyes jumped back to the gap in the trees where he knew the lake lay, the cold air ripping the breath from his lungs.

There, at the lake's center, something dark bobbed just above the surface. From where he stood, it almost looked like the wet crown of a head. By impulse, he took a jolting step toward the lake. The branch that had fallen—or, perhaps, been thrown—cracked underfoot. He startled, blinking. In the span of that blink, whatever had been in the lake disappeared.

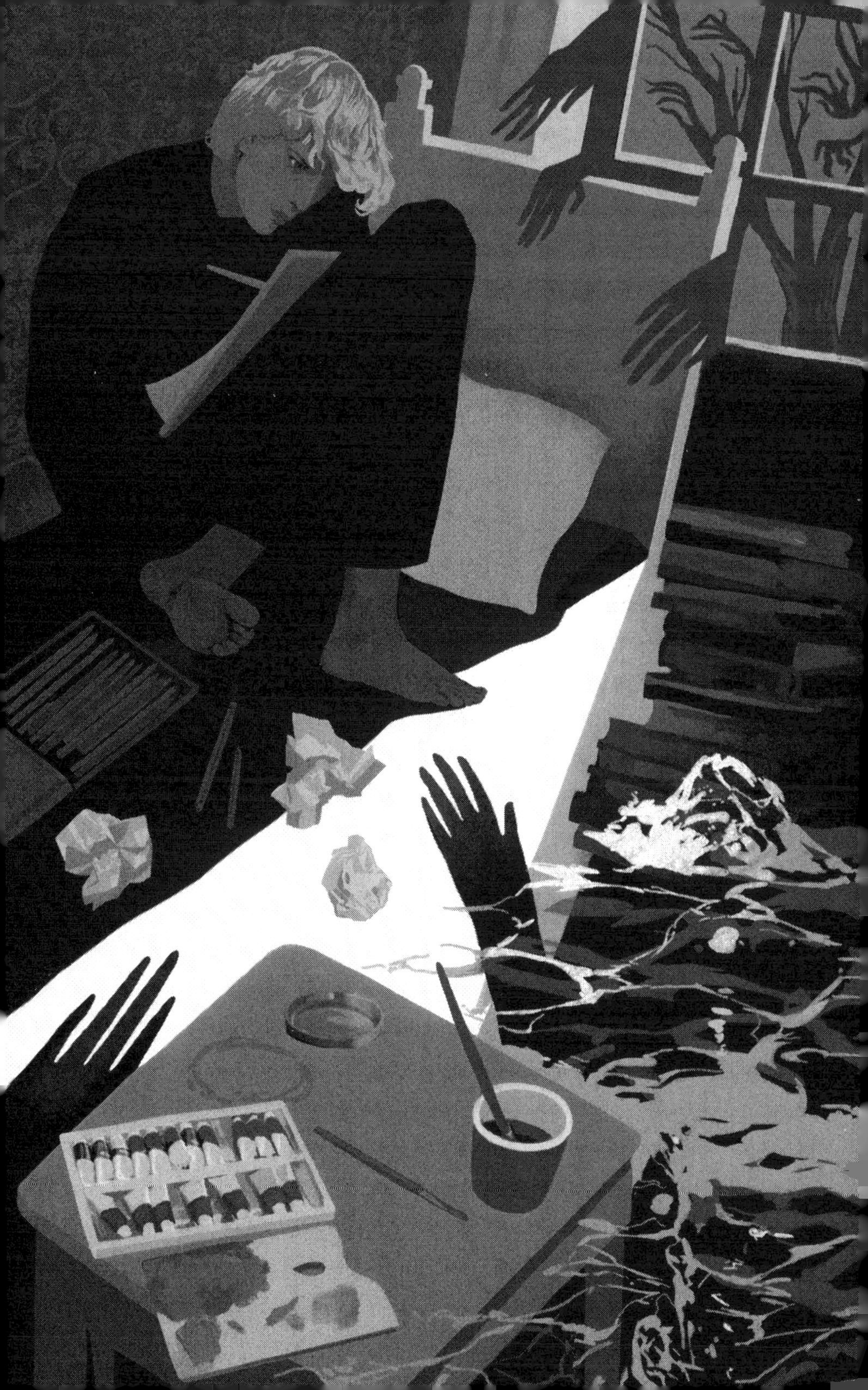

Silent Night

The cold of the lake had found a way through Callan's skin and into her bloodstream. Two hours and a long, hot bath later, she still felt the unnatural sting of the water. She'd thrown on her heaviest pajamas, crawled under the many layers of blankets on her bed, and Schrödinger was lying directly on her chest. But still, she couldn't shake the cold. She thought that maybe she'd swallowed some of the water and it was slowly freezing her from the inside out.

When had she fallen in? *Why* had she fallen in? It was good that the cold made her senses slower, otherwise she'd probably be having a panic attack. It wasn't a Freudian death wish that had pitched her forward. She'd been unconscious, or as close to it as was possible without being hit in the head or drugged. And she hadn't even felt the water while she was in it. Surely it should have woken her up.

Her thoughts paced round and round like a caged animal. A light tap on her door startled her out of it. The door snicked open. In a split second, Schrödinger was off her chest and under the bed. Callan pushed herself up against the headboard.

"I brought you some soup," Professor Cane said, carrying in a tray with an assortment of foods. From the way the contents tottered and slid around on the surface, he wasn't well-seasoned at meal delivery. "It should chase off the cold."

He set the tray on her bedside table. Callan thanked him as she snaked her fingers around a steaming mug of tea. Professor Cane watched her, his hands bunching in his pockets. His hair was still wet, and Callan hoped that was from a shower and not his rescue efforts.

"I'm sorry," he blurted. "I should have known you'd be exhausted after the flight. Sometimes meditation can drag us into sleep at inopportune times. I hope this hasn't frightened you."

Callan bit the inside of her cheek as the tea scalded her hands. From the warmth of her bed, it was easy enough to accept that what had happened at the lake was nothing more than a vivid dream. She really had been tired. And Professor Cane's voice had lulled her into a deep trance. There was no other logical explanation.

"I think I'll feel much better once I've eaten and slept," she said, meaning it. Professor Cane looked her up and down, his jaw tight, before nodding.

"I think the others aren't far behind you. It's been a long day, I'm sure we'll all be retiring soon. If you need anything at all, my room is the next over."

She watched his broad shoulders as he paced slowly toward the door. She imagined he hesitated there, long enough that she thought he might turn back to her. But then he closed the door and his soft footsteps retreated down the hall.

Not five minutes later, another, heavier set of feet were at the door. Roth snuck through and closed the door behind him without a sound. Schrödinger left his cave to twine around Roth's ankles.

"What did he say to you?" He asked, voice hushed. Before Callan could speak, Roth held a freckled finger to his pale, freckled lips, his gaze darting to the door. He crossed the room and sat on the bed beside Callan.

"Nothing, really," Callan murmured. "He just apologized for the meditation. He said I must have fallen asleep and tipped over."

Roth scoffed. When Callan's expression remained even, his face bunched. "You can't be serious." Callan shrugged. "Cal, I watched you. I'm absolute shit at meditating; ADHD and all that. I wasn't paying attention to what Cane was saying, I kept getting distracted by you three. You made a choking sound. And then you just..."

Callan turned, giving him her full attention. "What?"

Roth's translucent brows pinched. His mouth opened and closed like he hoped she might fill in the blanks for him. "Your eyes went back in your head and you fell forward. You sank so fast."

"I don't remember any of it," she said, shaking her head. She decided that might not be the worst thing.

"The weirdest part was that Dr. Cane didn't even hesitate. He dove in head first. It was almost like he expected it to happen."

This sent a chill twining up Callan's arms. But she refused to let her head fly off her shoulders on the first night of the term when so much was riding on it. "He probably just didn't want to deal with all the paperwork of a student dying in his class," she said. He must have felt guilty about putting her in the position. That much was clear from his delivery of enough dinner for three people instead of just her.

"I don't know," Roth said on a long exhale. "There's something weird about that lake. I don't think he's telling us everything. 'The reflection of the lake will help you see yourself more clearly.' What the hell does that even mean? That lake looks like nuclear runoff."

Callan shrugged. It was the same group therapy language she'd grown accustomed to as a teen; nonsense about finding symbolism in nature, understanding oneself through a different lens.

"It was a weird start," Callan admitted. "But I'm sure it'll get better from here. We'll probably start with real lessons and art stuff tomorrow. Maybe enough snow will come that we'll never make it back to the lake again."

"I hope you're right," Roth said, picking at the piling of the wool blanket. "Anyway, what have you been up to since art camp? Tell me everything."

Callan and Roth lounged on her bed and talked for hours, sharing her dinner and petting Schrödinger as he demanded. Callan was nodding off sitting up by the time Roth snuck back through her door and crept up the creaking stairs to his room on the second floor. Callan drifted off to the sound of the water pipes groaning, the wind rattling the timber siding, the creaks and cracks of the house settling around her.

She woke to silence.

The storm had settled, or perhaps they were in the eye of it. At first, she thought the loud, staticky silence was the reason for her waking. But then she noticed that her door was slightly ajar.

"Schrödinger?" She whispered groggily, rubbing the sleep from her eyes. When he didn't jump onto the bed, she tried again, this time pushing herself up against the headboard. "Hello?"

As if in answer, the door creaked on its hinges, swinging open further. There was no light beyond her door. The textured shadows only deepened. She strained to hear someone, something, moving beyond the threshold but the silence was like cotton balls between her ears.

She stepped into her fuzzy boots and crept down the hall, clicking her tongue in the hope that Schrödinger would materialize at her feet. Every step down the hall was colder than the last. Goosebumps prickled against her thick sweatshirt.

Turning the corner at the edge of the hall, she saw that the front door was thrown wide open, and a dusting of snow had accumulated on the wood floor. Realizing it was only a draft that woke her, her relief quickly devolved into panic. Schrödinger could have wandered out. He wasn't familiar with the area yet and could get lost in the storm.

Callan grabbed the flashlight from beside the door and stepped onto the porch, boots crunching in the snow. She glanced down and noticed another set of footprints on the deck leading out of the house. There weren't any others returning. They were about the same size as the tracks she was making and deep enough to almost obscure the tiny, perfectly preserved cat prints within them.

"Schrödinger," she hissed, continuing with the useless cat calls. Schrödinger wasn't one to hide or play coy. If he heard her, he would come. That's what made her take the first step down into the night. And then the next.

The snow was falling in fat globs that formed a layer on Callan's scalp within seconds. The snow added an additional hush to the still quiet. As her eyes adjusted, she noticed that the human footprints continued in a line heading directly for the trees and the path they'd traversed before. Dotted among them were Schrödinger's prints as if he had been twining his body between the person's legs as they walked. She fit her boots into the prints as she followed along the trail.

In the bobbing glow of the flashlight, the Tamaracks lining the trail looked strangely arachnid as they climbed toward the sagging sky.

Callan was at the lake before she'd made the decision to enter the forest. The snow around it made the tarry, flat surface all the starker. It looked little deeper than a puddle on the side of a road.

She startled when she realized she wasn't alone. Schrödinger sat on the nearby shore watching her, his eyes glinting a haunting, glowing green as Callan's flashlight passed over him.

"Schrödinger, come here." He didn't budge. He only stared at her, eyes occasionally catching that same eerie green glow. "Do you want a little treat?" Callan made kissy noises as she slowly rounded the edge of the lake, keeping a wide berth from the water and testing each step in the fresh snow carefully. Schrödinger continued to watch her every move, his body so close to the lake that Callan saw him in double, his reflection in the water warped and twisted by the lamp light. "Come on, Schrödinger, it's freezing. We need to get inside."

Finally, Schrödinger came unstuck. He chirped as he danced toward Callan and bumped against her fur boots which were now crusted in snow and ice. Callan set the flashlight on the ground as she scooped the cat into her arms. The flashlight caught every divot in the snow at the bank of the lake, projecting shadows across the uneven ground. She took a step forward, clutching the purring cat tight to her chest as she peered down at the snow.

The fine hairs on her flanks, her arms, and even the tips of her freezing ears all rose to attention at once. It wasn't just Schrödinger's prints on the lake shore. There were human prints as well. Handprints and bare footprints dotted the shore near the lake as if a dozen people had been swimming in it since the snow began to fall that night and had only recently pulled themselves out.

Callan's breaths shallowed, biting painfully at her ribs, as she surveyed the remainder of the lake shore. There were prints everywhere. The shore was more prints than undisturbed snow. The snow was glassy with ice from all the packing those footprints had done. The flashlight chose that moment to flicker and die, plunging the forest into blackness. Callan backed away slowly into the skeletal hold of the forest. The lake leered at her the whole time.

Once she found her way back to the trail she ran. The lake was not far from the cabin, but the run took a small eternity. The snow melting in her hair felt like fingers trailing through it, every tree branch and skeletal shrub tugged at her clothing was a grasping fist. By the time she made it to the cabin's stoop, her nerves were fried. She was whimpering like something that had been kicked.

"Callan?" A voice said from the shadowy porch. Callan gasped as she turned on the figure. Professor Cane squinted at her, a steaming coffee mug in his hands. The porch swing swung idly behind him as he walked forward. "Are you alright? What happened?"

"The door was left open overnight. Schrödinger got out."

Professor Cane stiffened, his dark gaze eating her up from snow-matted hair to nearly frozen toes and back again. "You went into the woods alone?"

"Just to the lake," she answered. Then, remembering what she'd seen, she added, "You don't know why there would be human footprints around the lake, do you? I mean, did the others go back after I'd gone to my room last night after the snow started? Are there other cabins up here?"

A pause. Callan shifted Schrödinger in her arms. He had gone from purring against her chest to stiff and silent.

"You shouldn't leave the cabin at night," Professor Cane said. "The woods are disorienting even in the daylight. And this area is a hotbed for apex predators. I'm sure the prints you saw were only an animal. You're lucky that's all you saw of them."

Callan's brow crumpled. The prints hadn't been animal. She'd counted five fingers and five toes, all grasping at the snow like they were pulling themselves from the lake. But the dark was disorienting, and she was too tired to wring out her mind convincing Professor Cane she was right. She decided instead that she would show him the prints in the daylight come morning. As it was, the snow had petered out. In the daylight, she would be able to make out the prints more clearly and see the expression on Professor Cane's face as he took it in. Now his face was swathed in shadows that made him skeletal and cold, alien.

"Why are you awake?" She asked.

A pause. "I'm a light sleeper. I heard you go out and wondered if I'd have to go after you. You were gone for a while. It's not long until dawn now so I figured I'd get a head start."

He was right. Though the sky was still sagging low and swathed in deep grays and blacks, lighter grays were beginning to weave their way through the fabric, causing the fresh snow to glow all the brighter.

Day came in a soupy mixture of grays and greens as the storm continued to churn, caught on the high peaks behind them. Callan returned to her room with the cat and feigned sleep until she heard movement overhead.

She followed the smell of coffee and pastries to the large kitchen across the main floor. Hilde, the home administrator as Professor Cane had called her, was flitting between pots and pans like a hummingbird, her apron and round cheeks dusted in flour.

"Good morning," she singsonged breathily, pushing a brimming cup of milky coffee toward Callan over the kitchen's island. "Mr. Cane said you preferred more milk than coffee. It's fresh."

"Thank you," Callan said, holding the coffee up to her nose and wandering to the breakfast table where Veronica was already bent over her wood carving. She had her legs pretzeled beneath her in a move that looked more torturous than pleasant. "Good morning," Callan murmured.

Veronica's onyx gaze flicked up. She straightened herself out. "Depends on your definition. I swear to god, there were little imps hammering on the siding last night. Every time my eyes closed, they started fucking tinkering."

"The wind was pretty crazy, wasn't it," Roth said, breezing into the kitchen with sopping wet hair and bare feet. He grabbed his mug from the island and went to the window behind the breakfast table. "Christ, we really are stuck now."

Callan glanced over her shoulder at the sea of blinding, sparkling white. The world was perfectly still, the sky an equally blinding robin's egg blue. The snow blanketed everything, even the spindly black branches of the Tamarack trees. It must have snowed another foot since Callan came in, if not more. There wasn't a chance that the prints she'd seen by the lake would still be visible. There wasn't even a chance of them getting to the lake today. Callan counted that as a blessing as she bit into a still-warm huckleberry scone.

Fray was the last to join them. He grunted a greeting and chose the seat at the table pushed furthest into the corner where he stooped over his coffee like he was trying to breathe it in rather than drink it. "This place is too fucking quiet," he grumbled.

"Are you serious?" Roth chided. "The wind sounded like a freight train rolling by all night." Fray glared at him through the steam of his coffee.

"The silence woke me up too," Callan said quietly. She'd moved onto a buttermilk biscuit smothered in gravy. "The wind stopped when the snow started." Roth bobbed his head as he bit into his biscuits. "Wait, were you the one that went for a walk outside last night?" She asked Fray.

Fray's heavy brows knitted. He spoke around a steaming bite of oatmeal. "You think I'd willingly subject myself to that?" He asked, hitching a thumb in the window's direction.

"Well, someone did," Callan said. "I woke up in the middle of the night and the front door was wide open and there were footprints leading to the lake. I found Schrödinger there."

"You went to that creepy ass lake by yourself in the middle of the night? Was one drowning not enough?" Veronica asked sardonically.

"Seriously," Callan said, glancing at each of the artists in turn. "Who was it? Clearly, it wasn't Fang. Roth?"

Roth looked up from his biscuits and gravy with a surprised "Huh?" He glanced around the table, realizing all eyes were on him. Even Hilde had paused her cleaning to listen, though she was doing a good job pretending otherwise as she wore circles into the same counter tile with her washrag.

"Wasn't me," Roth finally said. He crossed his finger over his heart and then raised three fingers in a scout's salute. "I was out like a light until the smell of bacon hit my bedroom this morning. And anyway, you'd never catch me out there at night. Do you see me? I'm the first to die in any horror movie."

"I have you beat on that front, actually," Fray said with a thin smile. "I think this tells us exactly whose prints you saw," he continued, directing the statement at Callan.

Callan was already shaking her head. "I saw him when I came back. It couldn't have been him."

Veronica hummed. "Maybe he was just coming back too."

Professionalism

Callan's neck hairs prickled with awareness just as she felt the quiet disturbance of Professor Cane's cat-soft feet against the hardwood behind her.

"Who's coming back?" He asked from the island where Hilde was pouring him another cup of coffee. He was dressed down compared to the attire Callan had seen him in before, but his wool blazer still looked wildly out of place surrounded by so much wood paneling and retro furniture. And compared to Callan's sweatsuit ensemble, he may as well have been wearing a tuxedo. She pulled her shawl tighter around herself as she shrunk under his gaze. No one had answered him. "Not a very talkative bunch in the morning, I see. That's okay. We have a soft start."

He pulled one of the high chairs from the island, scraping it across the floor so he could perch directly over the breakfast table like a tennis referee.

"Welcome to your first class," he said over his coffee. "I call this one 'show and tell.'"

Callan swallowed thickly around the crust of her toast. "I didn't bring a notebook," she said, ready to excuse herself to grab one.

"You won't need it. We're just talking." Professor Cane's smile was sharp as he jotted down a note in his own moleskin journal. Of course, he would be allowed notes. Talking, he'd said. Right. "Oh, and, Ms. Fang," he continued without glancing up. "I believe I was fairly clear. No art supplies or art creating unless specifically permitted. It's important to the progression of the term."

Veronica tucked her wood carving and blade into her pocket and folded her hands in her lap demurely. The glint of her onyx eyes told Callan she had no intention of following Professor Cane's direction when he wasn't in eyesight.

"So, this is just group therapy," Callan said, glancing at the others to see if this revelation made them as uncomfortable as it made her. Veronica stared into her lap, Fray was watching icicles form on the tin roof outside the window, Roth's knee was bouncing and he had his chin cupped in his hands.

"This isn't therapy at all," Cane replied. "Therapy has the goal of making you good, functioning members of society. My goal isn't to make you good. My goal is to make you honest; to make your art true." That one small word was weighty on his tongue. It hung in shapes in the spaces between each of them. Callan wrung her hands under the table.

"How about we start somewhere easy? Let's go around and tell each other where we're from, our art medium, and a fun fact. Maybe a little about why you're here if you're feeling brave."

Fray clicked his tongue, shaking his head.

"Something to say, Mr. Fray?" Fray rolled his eyes at the window. Professor Cane hitched his ankle over his knee as he reclined back in his chair. "Why don't you get us started."

Without turning away from the window, Fray said, "Mum's from France, dad's from all over. Grew up between Paris and New York. The city, not the state. I work in all mediums because I'm not a fucking pansy." He paused, scratching at his large bicep as his gaze flickered over the others. Then, more rushed, he added, "And my fun fact is I once set a record for

New York high school track and field. The one-hundred meter."

"Thank you," Professor Cane said, nodding slowly as he continued scrawling in his notebook. Fray watched Professor Cane write like he already had ten different plans to steal the notebook and find out what was written inside. Professor Cane didn't look up before adding, "Lark, your turn."

It wasn't lost on Callan that he hadn't said "Ms. Lark," the way he'd said "Mr. Fray." It was just Lark. For some reason, this made warmth spread across her cheeks and behind her sternum.

"Right." She pointed at her chest. "Callan." *They know your name already, idiot,* she chided internally. Her cheeks were stinging. "I'm from Manhattan. Not Carrie Bradshaw's Manhattan. Manhattan, Kansas. Um. I mostly paint." Her hands were aching from squeezing them together so hard. "And my fun fact is that my best friend is eighty-seven years old."

"Am I really *that* old," Roth said, elbowing her lightly in the ribs and flashing a smile.

"Thank you for sharing," Professor Cane said mechanically. Now it was Callan's turn to watch him scrawl in the notebook and wonder what he'd gleaned about her already. "Ms. Fang," he said without looking up.

"Singapore. All mediums, but I prefer graffiti and woodwork. I once saw a person jump from a fortieth-floor balcony."

"Christ," Roth blurted, his face scrunching. "They didn't—I mean—did they live?"

Veronica touched her tongue to the corner of her mouth, fixing Roth with an impenetrable look. "Well, I never inquired about what they did with the sludge they scraped off the sidewalks. Maybe they're good as new. Modern medicine is something to behold."

"I thought these were supposed to be fun facts," Fray cut in. "If we're going for morbid, I want to go again."

Professor Cane wasn't paying attention to them. He was still writing. Callan had the urge to steal the notebook and run to her room with it. Better yet, maybe she would just light the thing on fire. If he was as good at psychoanalysis as he was at selling up-and-coming artist's art, then Callan could not, under any circumstances, let the others read the journal before she saw inside. The others seemed to have the same idea, all watching Professor Cane's notebook like dogs watching their master finish a meal.

"Mr. Heller?"

"Yes, Professor? Oh. Right. Uh." He jutted his thumb at his chest, miming Callan, though not mockingly. "Roth Heller. Sioux Falls, South Dakota. My fun fact is that I used to be a choir boy. Had the little white outfit and everything. I'm sure I still know at least three verses of 'Nearer My God to Thee.' Then my balls dropped and I found sculpting." He shrugged, eyes sliding to Professor Cane's notebook and holding. "You know, Dr. Cane, that journal of yours is a little off-putting."

Professor Cane's brow rose but he didn't look up until he'd finished scrawling out his thoughts. He sighed as he clasped the journal's binding together and set it on the kitchen island behind him.

"Why is that, I wonder?" Professor Cane said. If he was expecting an answer, he didn't get one. "Could it be that the four of you are used to being observers in your own lives? Artists always are. Perhaps it is a bit uncomfortable to be the subject of that degree of observation."

"Perhaps," Roth said, smacking his lips.

"Well, my medium of expression is the written word. I hope you won't mind me observing you in the same way you observe, let's say, the stream of light through a window at the golden hour." His gaze was a physical touch to Callan's shoulder.

"Fair enough," Roth said, though he was still watching the journal with an uneasy hesitance like it might grow legs and chase after him.

The conversation remained strained and stilted for the next hour, with Professor Cane acting more like a dentist extracting teeth than a psychotherapist. He was cold, detached, uninterested. He seemed bored with them; maybe even disappointed. When they finally broke for their morning journaling sessions, Callan's temples and jaw were throbbing with a tension headache. She stared at the blank page of her journal, stared through the window above the desk in her room, repeated this process until the grandfather clock chimed. There were only three words on the page when she closed it and returned to the living room: "Why am I."

"This is a fucking drag," Fray hissed under his breath, scrubbing his hands over his tightly cropped hair. There were large pillows arranged on the floor before the roaring fireplace, and Professor Cane was sitting on the stone ledge of the fireplace with his back to the fire. He sat cross-legged and barefoot, his eyes closed, his hands draped serenely in his lap.

"I hope I won't have to wash your mouth out with soap, Mr. Fray," Professor Cane said without opening an eye.

"Come near my mouth and you'll find out why my mother stopped that fun, little practice," Fray retorted. Then, seeming to realize himself, added, "Professor, sir."

Professor Cane's lips curled up as he finally opened his eyes. "How did everyone's journaling session go?" No one answered. "It's okay if it's hard at first to find something to say. It takes practice. We'll get more into the mechanics later on but I wanted you to all have a baseline to start."

Callan tugged her arms up into the sleeves of her sweater, retreating. At least if that was her baseline, she really could only get better. She wondered, not for the first time, if grades would be assigned for this course, and if so, how. She'd never failed at anything in her life, but this term seemed like an apt opportunity.

"Now we'll transition to some meditation before our first individual sessions. Meditation is a pivotal element of this course and intrinsic to the success of past attendees. I hope you'll take these sessions seriously. But that doesn't mean you should take yourself too seriously during the act of meditation. It's a balance. One you'll be seeking until you die."

"Lovely," Veronica deadpanned, drooping onto her pillow in a dark gray puddle of baggy trousers and oversized, layered sweaters. It seemed Callan wasn't the only one struggling to keep off the persistent cold.

Roth sat beside Callan, doing his valiant best to contort his legs into the same position Professor Cane was maintaining, his tongue pinned between his top and bottom teeth with the effort. Even Callan struggled to pretzel her legs, and Roth could have used an extra knee joint for all the extra leg he had on Callan and the others.

When everyone was settled, Professor Cane said, "The goal of this meditation is the same as the goal of this term: to strip ourselves bare." This time Fray didn't make a single snide remark, not even a snicker. They were all watching Professor Cane with a bit of wonder, a bit of awe. Maybe it was just that the day had been so dull, they had nothing better to do than listen. Maybe they were all too tired from the first uneasy night to say anything. Or maybe it was the way the flames at Professor Cane's back framed his broad shoulders, his stark face, like a depiction of a saint in a stained-glass window.

Professor Cane continued, his depthless navy eyes devouring each of them in turn. "We are never closer to the animal that lives beneath this fine, fragile human skin than when we are deep in meditation. In meditation, there is no ego, no self. There is only perception. And that perception lives only in the present. Now, and now, and now, and now." Professor Cane tapped his hand against his chest to the rhythm of his heartbeat. "In meditation, we are only a heartbeat, a pair of lungs, and five senses. Those are the only tools you need to grapple with what is eating you."

At the beginning, he guided them. It was gentle suggestions. *Close your eyes* and *follow your breath*. Just like at the lake, Callan couldn't help but follow where his voice led. Deeper and deeper, into the labyrinth of her mind. A winding staircase lined with doors, each one different, and sealed with its own unique key. They weren't trying to open the doors this time. They were just observing them, the same way Callan was observing the stinging itch at the edge of her nose, and the dull throb at the base of her spine. It was easy; watching.

Somewhere along the way, Professor Cane's suggestions fizzled out. It was like the candelabras lining the circular walls of the staircase in her mind were snuffed out, one by one, and she was left descending in darkness, tripping over her own feet. She looked up, and the world she'd left was only a pinprick of light. The space around her began to cave in. Thoughts returned. Imaginary arguments with professors at Melrose, a grocery list for when she returned, a gaggle of art projects she'd committed to finally putting to canvas during the term. Then there were the dangerous thoughts. They weren't thoughts, exactly. Just impressions. The curl of Professor Cane's wet eyelashes, the flex of his arms around her back as he lifted her, the tilt of his smile when he smiled, *really* smiled.

She couldn't say exactly what about the impressions felt dangerous. Maybe it was that they were addictive. They made her breaths feel hot and weighty in her chest. Made her see Ladon Cane as a male; as a body, a rush of blood, a collection of hormones and firing synapses, rather than the professor holding her future in his hands like wet clay.

Peeking through her lashes did nothing to usher in this cold reality. Because even with his face swathed in shadows, she could see that Professor Cane was watching her. From the way embers smoldered in the depths of his blue-black eyes, he was seeing everything, and he didn't mind what he saw. Callan recognized that look well. She'd seen him wear it on the plane, seen him wear it in the car. Then, she was sure she'd misunderstood. But there was no misunderstanding now. It was hunger. Wanting. Her toes curled within her fuzzy slipper socks. Professor Cane's gaze followed the movement.

Callan screwed her eyes closed and tried to find the

spaciousness she'd achieved before, but her mind was hot and claustrophobic and itched like a too-tight wool sweater. Her breathing was all over the place, and trying to slow it only caused a pain to start up beneath her sternum.

"Find your way back to your body now," Professor Cane said, his voice raspy. Callan's eyes fluttered open again. He still had her fixed with that look; his irises gobbling up every inch of her at once. "Good work," he continued, finally breaking eye contact to look at the others. "We'll have our individual sessions for the remainder of the afternoon. Feel free to use your time alone to exercise, walk outside, read, or journal. We'll regroup this evening for dinner and some fun."

"Sorry, uh, Professor," Roth said, blocking Professor Cane's swift exit. "I didn't hear you mention anything about art. Can we use this time to head to the studio? I saw it when I was rummaging around and I'd love to dig in."

"No," Professor Cane said, cutting him off with a sharp shake of his head. Then, to the full group, he added, "the art will come, don't worry. But we have a lot of work to do before you're ready. If you want to speed up the process, start volunteering information at our group sessions. The more progress we make early on, the faster you'll be back in the studio."

"But—" Veronica cut in.

"My methods are successful for a reason. If you'd like to find out why, I suggest you let me be the one to ask the questions," Professor Cane said, voice dipping an octave. He seemed to grow an extra foot when he spoke like that. Or maybe it was just Callan melting into the floor.

She took the opportunity and darted to her room, where she stripped off two of her three layers and cracked open her fogged-over window. Suddenly, the unshakable cold had been replaced by a restless heat that swelled beneath her skin. She shook out her hands and paced in circles.

A knock came. She froze, her chest still heaving. Her hands flexed, relaxed, flexed. "Yeah?" She called.

"You're up first," Professor Cane said from the other side.

Callan bit the inside of her cheek so hard she tasted metal. *Shit. Double shit.* She couldn't be alone with him like this. Not right now. Not yet.

"Coming," she said, or maybe she'd yelled it. She heard his footsteps trail off down the hall. She stalked into the ensuite bathroom and tossed some cold water on her flushed face, slapping at her cheeks a couple of times for good measure. "Get your shit together," she said, pointing a judging finger at her reflection.

She gave herself a calculated once over. Her skin felt too tight for her body, but it looked normal, even if it was a bit flushed, with raspberries dotting her cheeks. Her light brown hair had grown long enough to tuck behind her ears. It even held some of the waves she remembered from when she was a kid and her mother made her keep her hair waist length and matted into a rat's nest. Just the thought made her want to find a razor and shave it all off again.

By the time she snuck down the hall toward Cane's office, Callan was in a perfect mood for vomiting up her deepest secrets to the subject of her growing infatuation. Absolutely perfect.

"Come in," came Professor Cane's voice from the other side of the door before Callan had even lifted her hand to knock. The room was the last in the long hallway on the main floor; a small room made mostly of windows that looked out on the granite boulders and small, shaggy Ponderosas behind the cabin. Callan had expected the room to be dark and filled with comfortable furniture. Instead, it was modern, with gleaming wood floors and modular furniture set low to the ground. Professor Cane was sitting in the corner, framed by the ceiling-height windows on one side and a wall of books on the other. This left the large sectional sofa facing the fireplace for her.

She lowered herself slowly, her gaze drawn immediately to the green moleskin journal in Professor Cane's lap. She brushed her hair behind her ear. When it didn't stick, she used both hands to paste it back against her skull. It didn't stay. She huffed irritably.

"You seem upset, Callan," Professor Cane said without looking up from his notes. He wore navy-rimmed glasses now, with an ankle hitched over the opposite knee, his shirt sleeves pulled up past his elbows, and the top button of his shirt undone. It felt a little unfair to Callan. Like he was now purposefully trying to act out her fantasies of him, and refusing to acknowledge that he knew exactly what he was doing.

"I'm not upset," Callan answered, her voice tinny and full of hot breath. Professor Cane's gaze flicked up, assessing her. His eyes sparkled in myriad blue hues.

"Agitated then," he continued, back to his notes. "How did the meditation go this morning? I noticed you didn't seem to have trouble staying awake." His lips formed a thin, amused line that curled up at the edges.

"Are you toying with me, or is this all part of your methods?" Callan asked, the heat in her stomach flaring.

Professor Cane held his head up with two fingers to the temple, eyes tracking a line from her toes to her scalp. "Toying with you? I don't know what you mean."

"The—" Callan threw up her hands impatiently. "You know, the name-calling. Those looks you give me when no one is watching."

"I've called you names?" The harsh lines of his face sharpened into a question.

"You call me Callan when we're alone and Lark in front of the others," she said, her voice trailing off. Her heart thundered in her chest but she lifted her chin defiantly. "And you don't use any pronouns for me. Do I look like a boy to you?"

Professor Cane blinked slowly. "Do you want to look like a boy to me, Lark? What pronouns would you like me to use?"

A frustrated sound crawled up the back of Callan's throat before she could kill it. Fucking therapists.

Professor Cane's eyes only continued to twinkle. There was a devilish taunt hidden in the kaleidoscope of blues. Eventually, he peeled off his glasses so those eyes could thoroughly pin her in place.

"I'm sorry if I've given you the wrong impression, Lark. My use of last names during the term is an effort to establish boundaries and maintain professionalism while we're all stuck in such tight quarters up here. I should have begun that practice during our first meeting. I didn't realize just how confusing it would be to slip between the two. And as soon as you let me know what pronouns you'd like me to use, I will absolutely do so. The others already have." His words were clinical, cold. His eyes were anything but. Callan got the distinct feeling that she was in the midst of playing a game that she didn't know the rules for. "Are you attracted to me, Lark? Is that what this is really about?" He asked, tipping his head to the side as his brows pinched.

"No," she sputtered. The twinkle of his eyes and the heat on her skin called her a liar in unison. "Not at all," she added.

"It's okay if you are. It would give us a place to start. Remember what I said before. There's no place for shame or embarrassment here. Your only goal should be to improve yourself, to improve your art."

She gawked at him for a moment, finding only bald sincerity on his face. "Fine," Callan huffed. She pulled her sticky, itching wool sweater away from her neck. "You're attractive. Are you happy? Is that what you wanted to hear?"

A flash of teeth. "Why do you ask that? 'Am I happy'. Do you feel that I've backed you into a corner with my questions? Do you not like discussing things as basely chemical as physical attraction, Lark?"

Callan's eyebrows had climbed halfway up her head. "I *feel* that you are goading me," she said slowly, hands making tight, unconscious fists in her lap. "I *feel* that you know exactly what effect you have and you're using it to mess with me. I just don't know why. It doesn't seem very professional. This isn't like any therapy I've received in the past."

"That's good," Professor Cane said, shrugging. "I would hate to mimic those who have failed before me," he continued slowly, precisely. Those words hit Callan like a backhanded slap. "If you hoped for another wind-up-doll therapist working from memorized flashcards and diluted, step-by-step protocols, I'm sorry to disappoint you. I find tiptoeing around the truth to be tedious and unhelpful. I'd rather get into the meat and bones of it upfront so we can start wading through the mess together. From what I've gleaned so far, you have a phobia of intimacy. You self-isolate and hide in your art. You find it difficult to relate to your peers. Am I wrong?"

Callan made a choked sound.

"And when you look at me, you feel like running. But you haven't decided if you want to make it to the next county over or for me to catch you and fuck you in the dirt like an animal. Yes or no?"

Callan swallowed to keep from choking on her fury. Professor Cane seemed to be enjoying this. A pleased smile was etched into the corners of his eyes, his mouth. He might as well have been asking her what her favorite color was, or the status of the weather outside. Slowly, languorously, he leaned forward, bracing his bare elbows on his knees and looking into the depths of her with the kind of cold, clinical disinterest that only he could achieve.

"You think I want to crack you open?" He asked, his voice the serrated edge of a knife. "You aren't wrong. But it isn't to hurt you, Lark. I want to crack you open because I know there's something vital waiting to be released in your art. You're holding yourself back. I know you're frightened. I know you're ashamed. But you don't have to be. Not with me."

He sat back and stared at her for a moment. She only knew his eyes were on her from the prickly texture of his gaze. She kept her eyes firmly on the grains of the wood floor beneath her. She'd never been so thoroughly peeled apart and dissected. She needed a hot bath and six layers of clothing just to feel adequately covered again.

The long column of Professor Cane's throat bobbed in her periphery. He glanced at his watch. "Let's call it a day, Lark," he said, his voice cool and distant as a gathering storm, all the heat from before gone. "Please enjoy your afternoon and let Mr. Heller know to find me here at the top of the hour."

Callan's brows pinched as she glanced at her watch. "It's only been ten minutes."

Professor Cane dropped his journal on a nearby table and massaged the back of his neck. "I've been doing this long enough to know when I've hit a wall of granite. This is as far as you're willing to go today. That's fine. We'll pick things up tomorrow. Please use the afternoon to continue chipping away at the wall. I expect you to use your words tomorrow."

Callan knew then that she was excused. She watched Professor Cane shuffle some papers on his table before reclining with his pen and journal, where he was undoubtedly documenting all the disturbing abnormalities of Callan's mind. She had never felt quite so small, quite so brittle, as she did making the walk from the sectional to Professor Cane's door. She seemed to shrink with each step until she wasn't sure she could even reach the handle when she got to it. She felt the moment he looked up from his journal; felt his eyes pouring over her every move, seeing right through her translucent skin, eviscerating her completely.

"And Lark?" He said as her fingertips brushed the brass doorknob. "I think it's best to acknowledge up front that you and I *can never* and *will never* happen. It's perfectly normal to have daydreams about your professor. But I want to make it clear, I need you to understand, that those thoughts are only that. It will never happen. Understood?"

Callan's shoulders were brushing her burning ears. She had a sudden, violent impulse to turn around and let all the venom swirling in her mind loose on him. She didn't know what she would say, but she knew she'd make it cut, make it sting. Surely, there was some combination of words that would knock that smug smile off his too-perfect face, even if he was little more than a hunk of cold marble. But she knew if she let that violence out, there would be no lassoing it back in. Even Professor Cane wouldn't know what to do with her monster. So, with shaking fingers, she silently opened the door, slipped through, and let it fall silently closed behind her.

Reflections

Callan's vision was pulsing red and fuzzy around the edges by the time she hit the front porch. There was steam between her ears, steam leaving her nostrils, steam slowly boiling every one of her organs from the inside out. Embarrassed wasn't a good enough word for what Cane had made her feel. She didn't think an adequate word existed. Even if one did, she wouldn't be able to find it. Every time she tried to order her thoughts into a coherent line they exploded behind her eyelids like tiny fireworks. The only words that made their way through that red haze were Professor Cane's, and every time they echoed through her skull it was like being cut open for the first time again.

"Inappropriate asshole," she hissed to herself. She swatted at branches as she fought her way into the bramble of tightly arranged trees adjacent to the cabin. They fought back, tangling in her hair, sending clouds of crystalline snow down her collar, biting into her exposed and already stinging cheeks. This only made her whack at them harder, loosening that barely restrained violence that had been prodding at the undersides of her skin. It felt good to fight, to be hurt by that fighting. The steam inside her hissed through the cracks that the violence opened. Finally, when she had deflated completely, she paused, her chest heaving as she took in the dark lace of barren branches and pine surrounding her. They were the only witness to the first tracks of tears down her cheeks. "Fucking shrink asshole," she gritted out, but the curses had far less bite when her bottom lip wobbled like a little kid's.

She stood there, listening to the sound of her breath sawing in and out of her as her skin cooled and the chill set in deep. The forest watched her with the same cold, still indifference as Professor Cane. That was fine. The forest couldn't use what it saw against her the way he did. Suddenly, those branches that had felt like clawing fingers were only caresses urging her deeper, shrouding her, protecting her. She let the forest embrace her, let it pull her in and wrap itself around her shoulders. She followed its urgings until the dark web opened on a clearing, the branches at her back leading her right to the lip of Pitch Lake. The bare trees towering above her creaked and groaned as they leaned in to watch her approach the dark edge. It was still disorienting to see nothing in the lake's surface; not the trees looming above, not her own flushed and tear-streaked face, not the blaze of light above where the winter sun was trying to cut through a thin gray haze. It was dark, and empty, and still. Until it wasn't.

A slight ripple in the surface of the lake drew Callan's attention to the nearby shore.

"Roth?" Roth was seated at the lip of the lake, leaning over the surface. He had a finger poised just above the surface. "Roth," she called again, making her way to him through the lattice of branches edging the lake like eyelashes. He didn't move a muscle.

When she was behind him, she placed a hand tentatively on his back. That hand ran up the solid plane of his back as she came to stand beside him at the lake's edge. From this angle, she could see his reflection in the water clearly. Strange that it was the only reflection the water allowed. The image held beautiful symmetry, with the two shapes, Roth's and the reflection's, meeting at the pale point of their fingertips.

"Roth, hey." Callan shook his shoulder, but he was frozen in a trance. She bent down on her haunches, peering more closely at the reflection.

The reflection squirmed.

Callan gasped, falling back on her butt. Roth's face remained downcast, staring at the water. But his reflection was gazing up at Callan, a raw, animalistic expression turning his kind features sinister. Slowly, the reflection turned back to Roth. Skeletal fingers snaked up from below the surface to grasp Roth's wrist. Then they tugged.

It happened fast. One second, Roth was there. The next, he was completely beneath the surface, not even his scalp visible in the pitch-dark water. Callan was screaming, cursing, but the others wouldn't hear her from so far away. It only took a second for Callan to know what she needed to do. She stripped off her outer layer and dove into the water.

The sting was familiar now, but that didn't lessen its effect. It hit her like grass shrapnel. It was so cold it felt fiery hot. Her muscles cramped immediately. Roth was sinking like he had stones in his pockets. Like he was being dragged downward, because he was. Callan had to kick hard to even reach his fingertips. Then there was the problem of dragging him up. He was dead weight that kept slipping from Callan's grip. Her lungs screamed as she hefted him up, only for him to be dragged down again by a force far hungrier than her.

Lights were bursting behind her eyelids when she finally let go; kicking her way towards the grimy green light that marked the surface. She'd get some air and go back down. There was no way she was leaving Roth to die in this godforsaken lake. Her head breached in a cloud of steam that almost obstructed the hand reaching out for her.

"Grab on!" Roth yelled from the shore. Callan's head bobbed below the surface, earning her a mouthful of the brackish water. Her lungs were pruned in her chest, each breath painfully tight. She hefted her arm out of the water, her fingers so cramped she couldn't even grip Roth's hand. In one swift motion, he yanked her out of the water, falling back on his butt in the process. The icy shore was a relief from the water. But the fog that had descended over the forest made Callan question if she'd really escaped, or if she'd just died along with Roth and now they were both in a strange, frigid purgatory.

"What the hell were you thinking?" Roth demanded, gripping her sopping head on both sides until she looked up at him. "Are you trying to kill yourself?"

Callan's brain moved slowly as her eyes traced over Roth's dry hat and coat, his rosy cheeks and the mittened hands rubbing circles into her drenched shirt to get her warm. Her eyes dragged a line back to the lake; its calm, reflectionless surface.

"Christ, we need to get you inside," Roth said. "I'm not strong enough to carry you like a baby. Potato sack will have to do."

"I can walk," Callan found her mouth saying. Her teeth were chattering, her lips numb, but her legs wanted nothing more than to get her as far away from the lake as possible. She gripped Roth's arm with what strength she had left and let him drag her in the direction of the house, never once taking her eyes off the lake while it was still in view.

Icicles had formed around strands of Callan's hair and set up residence in her nostrils by the time they reached the cabin's clearing. Callan kept her eyes on her feet, willing each one to shuffle her a bit closer to the warmth the cabin promised. Up ahead, she heard the echoing crack of the front door slamming closed, and someone sprinting through the crunchy snow.

"What happened?" Professor Cane demanded. Suddenly, he was everywhere. His hands patting down her tingling arms, prying at her blue lips, gripping her nape. "How did you fall in the lake again?" This time the question was only directed at her. She looked over at Roth who was watching her with the same concerned horror. They thought she did it on purpose. They thought she was trying to hurt herself.

"There was something in the lake," she mumbled, words

tripping over her useless bottom lip. "There was—I thought—I thought I saw. Something."

"Okay," Professor Cane said, cutting in. "It's okay. Let's get you warm first." He tugged his coat off and pulled it tight around her shoulders, guiding her toward the house. Roth trailed behind them, lingering in the living room where the others had been watching from the window. Callan could hear them whispering about her, even after Professor Cane kicked her bedroom door shut behind them. He went directly to her bathroom as she shivered by the door.

"You need to get out of those wet clothes," he ordered as the squeak and groan of the pipes announced that the hot water had been turned on. She stared at the ring of water forming on the floor around her, her toes curling into the carpet. "Why are you still dressed?" He asked, coming back into the bedroom.

"I'm not getting naked in front of you," she said, though the bite of her words was lost in the chattering of her teeth.

The Professor's face tightened, but his eyes remained fixed. "I'm not leaving you alone until I feel certain you won't try harming yourself again, Lark. It's my duty to keep you safe while you are in my care."

A choked, incredulous sound barked out of her. *Again*, he'd said. "I didn't try to—you think that was a suicide attempt?" She searched his face, finding her answer immediately. "Right. The damaged, orphaned artist must be looking to self-destruct. If I can't screw my teacher, I might as well drown myself in the lake like Ophelia. Is that it?"

Professor Cane's throat worked on a swallow. His eyes were glittering swimming pools.

She smiled at him. It wasn't her usual smile, nor her real smile. This one was thin and sharp, dripping venom. In one smooth motion, her sopping shirt was over her head and she was bare from the waist up. She could feel her skin tightening with the rush of warm air.

"Is this what you want?" She asked, taking a step toward him.

"You didn't quite get your fill of humiliating me earlier. Do you get off on it?" At some point, her shame would catch up to her. But for now, that buzzing violence was back, itching at every inch of her skin, keeping her embarrassment just out of reach. The way he swallowed, the bob of his throat, made her feel powerful in a way she'd never felt before. She liked the idea of him suffering because of her.

Professor Cane's gaze flicked down to the simple cross that draped over her clavicle lingering there for only a second before darting away. Callan knew his jaw must be aching from how hard he was clenching his teeth. His hands were tight fists pressed to his sides. She pulled off her pants next, not missing the strain in Cane's neck. Then she was standing bare before him as he made a performance of looking away. She took another step forward, which he matched with an uneven step backward.

"Shower," he gritted out, pointing a finger feebly toward her bathroom. She continued forward until Professor Cane backed into her closed door.

"What's the matter, Professor? You aren't having inappropriate thoughts about a student, are you? I guess it's only normal, right? There's nothing to be ashamed of," she said, lips curling tauntingly around the words as she placed a single finger on his chest. Professor Cane's eyes blazed. Before she could blink, he had her spun around and pressed against the wall beside the door, his body a cage around her own, her wrists pinned above her head with just two of his fingers. That was the only place he touched her and god, did it burn.

"Be careful who you choose to play games with, Lark," he whispered hoarsely. "I don't play fair. And I don't play nice. Now, get in the fucking shower and warm yourself up. You're freezing."

Just as quickly as he'd pinned her, she was released; the heat of him gone. Her door opened and shut a second later. She braced her head against it, going dizzy on the scent of him clinging to her skin, the searing, cold burn of his fingers sinking deeper and deeper into her blood.

Visitors

For a full week, the snow did not let up. For a full week, Callan drowned in the Professor's silence. The others didn't question why she was excused from solo therapy sessions, or why Professor Cane seemed to skip over her in their lectures and group discussions like she was invisible. Frankly, they seemed happy to have her out of the running for whatever prize came at the end of the term. At least, Fray and Veronica did. Roth tiptoed around her carefully, his eyes searching her skin for fissure lines.

She used her time alone to haunt the lesser-used parts of the cabin, Schrödinger clinging to her ankles. She felt adrift without the ability to throw all the chaos in her mind onto a canvas. So, she began making her way through Cane's extensive bibliography and the reading list he'd assigned for the term. When she tired of theory, she'd wander the halls in search of backdoors into the locked studios. She'd counted at least four of them in addition to the kiln, the drying room and the red room. But there were no backdoors. No hidden oasis that she could slip away to. Just cold, empty rooms and locked doors.

The isolation also gave Callan's memories from the lake time to fester. What started as a confused and embarrassed kind of paralysis became a restless clarity. There was something in the lake. There had been something in the lake the first day they visited, and the same thing lurked there now. Whatever it was, it felt too similar to the thing that had stalked her nights at Melrose. She didn't bother trying to understand what it was. All she knew was that it wanted her in the water. If it had meant to kill her, it had ample opportunity. But it hadn't. Both times, she'd been dragged out without so much as a scratch. The one noticeably absent emotion was fear.

She took to sketching the scenes she remembered in her journaling notebook, even if sketching was technically prohibited. Fuck Professor Cane's rules. He didn't ever come close enough to notice what she was putting in the notebook. A part of her hoped he might, so she could scratch at the itch he'd planted deep in her mind. The itch to argue with him, test him, rake her fingernails over his skin. Just the sight of him turned the air in her nostrils hot. Even the indifferent tilt of his lips, sketched furiously on a piece of lined paper with a mechanical pencil, was enough to do her in.

A light tap came at her door, pulling her from the third sketch she'd made that day. As with all the others, she crumpled it into a tight ball and wedged it between the box spring and mattress beneath her.

"Come in," she said, smoothing back the unruly strands of her short ponytail. Not that it mattered what she looked like when the whole house saw her as the mad woman being kept in the attic.

Of all the people she expected to slip through her door at close to midnight, Veronica was the last. Yet, there she was; staring around Callan's neatly arranged refuge like the floor might shatter if she took a wrong step.

"What do you want?" Callan asked.

Veronica finally looked at her. She held up something small and white between her fingers. A joint rolled with the kind of precision Callan had come to expect only from Veronica.

"Thought the cabin pariah could use a little fresh air," she said, nodding at the door. "Everyone's in their rooms already." When Callan hesitated, she added, "Come on, I know a place." The loneliness must have been driving Callan a little mad because she followed.

In all her wandering, Callan had missed the stairwell behind the kitchen. It was impossibly steep and narrow. After climbing what felt like five stories in a house made only of three, they hit a door. Cold air breathed through it, the surface dappled white with hoarfrost.

Veronica propped the door open with a brick and led her onto the roof. An ancient camp chair and rusted cooler were positioned at the base of one of the towering stone chimneys.

"Found this the first night," Veronica said, brushing the snow off the chair before sitting in it on her knees.

Callan sat cross-legged on the cooler. The warmth of the stone, heated by the fire burning deep within the house kept the frigid night air at bay. "It's a little comforting to know we aren't the first bunch that needs a reprieve from all this," Veronica continued, waving the joint in her hand, indicating the whole of Pitch Lake. She struck a match, sucked in a long inhale, and offered it to Callan.

"Why did you actually invite me out here?" She asked, accepting the joint. She'd never smoked before, but she wasn't about to admit that. She sucked in just enough for the end of the joint to sizzle and held the smoke in her mouth. Veronica took it back, inhaling once, twice, a third time, before finally exhaling with a long sigh. Her gaze flicked to Callan and away, to the banks of snow below.

"What did you know about this term before you came?" She asked. It felt like a trick question.

"Probably the same as you," Callan said. "We all got the same unhelpful packet. Everything online is just as vague and cryptic."

Veronica nodded thoughtfully, rolling her lips between her teeth. She opened her mouth. Closed it. "I know the girl from Brighton that attended two years ago," she finally offered. She pulled one of her arms up into her heavy coat, snaking it around her torso. "Knew," she corrected.

That one word cut colder than the wind swirling ice crystals around them.

"What happened to her?"

Veronica shrugged, taking another long drag before offering it to Callan. This time Callan inhaled. "Not a clue. One day, she was the happiest I'd ever seen her. Literally unbearable. Going on and on about Dr. Ladon Cane and his group of perfect, brilliant artists. A couple weeks later it was like June Parker never existed. Her apartment was gutted and she was officially unregistered from Brighton. That's why I enrolled in that stuffy arts and crafts penitentiary to begin with. I need to know what happened to her."

"What about her parents? They must be looking for her."

Veronica smiled coldly. "You need to start paying closer attention, Lark," she said. "What do we all have in common except absent families and abysmal social lives?"

Callan wasn't sure if it was the weed or the conversation making it feel like a hand was slowly fisting around her throat.

"We're just artists," she offered weakly. "That's pretty normal for our crowd."

"Sure, artists. Artists with unusually gruesome pasts," Veronica said. She lifted a brow. "Am I wrong?"

Callan didn't answer. She didn't need to. A cat-got-the-canary smile spread Veronica's lips, then fell as she looked Callan over.

"I tried to kill myself once," Veronica said. It felt like an offering. One Callan wasn't sure how to accept, let alone hold in the still, silent night. "Actually, it was more than once. A few times. Nothing outrageous. Drugs, of course. I'm not brave enough for guns or hanging. I always wanted someone to be able to save me." Now, even Veronica's stare felt like a question.

"I didn't," Callan said eventually. Her voice broke. "I didn't try to kill myself. There was—There was something in the lake. It grabbed me. I swear to god, I'm not crazy. I wouldn't. I wouldn't do it." These last words rushed out of her in a gust of hot breath.

"I know you wouldn't. And I know you didn't. But I also know that look on your face means the thought has crossed your mind a time or two before." Veronica's tongue prodded the corner of her lips. Her eyes were sharp, assessing. "It's something about this place. It's twisting what's already there, inside us. I feel like the rage is carving its way out of me with a box cutter. That shifty bastard, Cane acts like he's our professor, yet he prohibits the craft he's supposed to be helping us hone. He acts like he's our therapist, yet he taunts and pokes at us like he'd rather watch us suffer. I don't know what he's up to yet, but I'm going to find out. And I know whatever it is, it's tied back to June."

"I saw Agnes Greer at Melrose last spring after she came back," Callan said, each word coming out carefully. She was trying to convince herself of the story even more than Veronica. "She was practically glowing. She'd just sold her third six-figure piece and she hadn't even graduated yet. She was buying an apartment in New York and already had a studio locked down." Laced through those words was something Callan had been avoiding as much, if not more, than Professor Cane himself over the past week. The appalling truth that she had been dodging in all her restless wandering around the cabin. Callan had decided right after Professor Cane walked out of her room, her body still bare and wired, her hair still sopping from being dragged into the water by god-knows-what, that she wouldn't leave the program under any circumstances. She couldn't leave. Not if it meant there was a chance she could create without the incessant buzzing of the real world always at her ear. If that was the prize, she would win. At any cost.

Veronica sucked on what remained of the joint like it was a lollipop. "I'm not saying the program isn't effective. I'm sure at least one of us will find ourselves in a heap of glory if history is any indication. I'm just saying... if it comes with a side of human or animal sacrifice or some other weird ritual, I'm running for the hills and reporting his ass. Or, at least, selling it to TMZ." Her head fell back against the stone and she blew a cloudy breath into the air. She didn't seem all that concerned from where Callan sat. If she really thought Dr. Ladon Cane was capable of murdering a student or being an active participant in her death, she probably wouldn't be getting stoned in his house, right? Veronica offered the sooty remains of the joint to Callan who waived her off, already feeling woozy and a bit panicked by the lack of control. At this, Veronica flicked the joint off the roof. Callan's stomach swooped.

"Jesus, Fang, watch it," she said, springing up and rushing to the edge to make sure the butt had landed in a snowbank and not on the highly flammable, log house.

"Easy. We're surrounded by ice," Veronica drawled, coming up behind her. She halted abruptly. "What the fuck is that?" She whispered, grabbing Callan's hood. Callan glanced back at her, then followed her stare. She blinked. She blinked again. Then she began to back away slowly until she bumped into Veronica, every cell in her body vibrating.

Standing in a line in front of the house were four people. They were close enough for Callan to see that they were naked, but their bodies were too shadowed to make out much else. Callan swallowed around shards of glass.

"Get inside," she hissed, tugging Veronica after her as she ran for the door. She could feel them watching, their silent, too-still stares at her shoulders. Once they were on the other side of the door, she rounded on Veronica. "You saw them, right? You saw them?"

Veronica nodded frantically, her eyes saucers. "What the—what the fuck—what the fuck was that—what—"

"Come on," Callan said, tugging her down the stairs. On the fifth stair from the bottom, she caught her ankle wrong, and blinding white pain zinged up her leg like a lightning bolt. She bared her teeth in a wince but didn't stop. She was sure the figures would be gone by the time they reached the living room. She was wrong.

They were closer. Or maybe that was just Callan's frayed nerves. The outside lights were off, but their bodies were darkly silhouetted against the snow.

"Get Cane," Callan whispered, not daring to take her eyes off them. Veronica was whimpering. She hadn't let go of Callan's hand. "Run," Callan insisted, leveling her with a stern look.

Veronica swatted at every light switch between the living room and Professor Cane's door to no avail. The electricity was out, the generator too, apparently. Callan could hear the imprint of her hysterics and the low drone of Professor Cane's tired voice as she roused him. Then there were two sets of footsteps pounding back toward the living room. Something like pride swelled in Callan's chest when the figures remained for Professor Cane to see.

"What is it?" He demanded. All he wore were his glasses and a pair of gray sweatpants that sat low on his hips. Veronica was blubbering. Callan pointed a shaking finger at the window. Professor Cane squinted, his face scrunching up. Callan watched him closely; for what, she wasn't totally sure. A tell; a sign that he knew what he was seeing. A rough exhale brushed past his sleep-swollen lips.

"Damn Andersons," he muttered. He was already stalking toward the door, throwing on the coat hanging beside it. Callan ran after him.

"What? Who is Anderson? What's happening?"

He turned on her so quickly she bumped into his warm chest. He braced his hands on her arms to steady her.

"It's just the Anderson family from down the road," he said, annoyance clear in the clip of each word. "They're pagan. Or their ancestors were. It doesn't matter. I'm sure this is just one of their stunts. Stay here."

The door slammed behind him. Veronica and Callan crowded the window, watching him tromp through the knee-high snow to where the Anderson family stood. Callan still couldn't make out their faces or anything else about them. But she knew they were very much naked, and must be on the brink of hypothermia and frostbite. She hoped they were at least wearing shoes.

Professor Cane marched right up to the one in the middle, his chest puffed up, his posture angrier than she'd ever seen him. It only took a couple of big hand gestures from Professor Cane before the two at the periphery started walking down the road. The two in the center lingered longer. Callan almost opened the door to listen in on what was being said between the three of them. But the rigid hold of Professor Cane's shoulders, the tightness of his fists at his sides, kept her feet planted indoors. A few moments later, the last of the Anderson clan was walking down the snow-covered road, metaphorical tails tucked between their frozen, exposed butt cheeks.

"What a weird night," Callan muttered, rubbing the back of her neck. Whether it was the weed or the adrenaline fizzling out of her bloodstream, she was exhausted. Her ankle was in bad shape and her head felt like a loose bowling ball on her shoulders.

"I seriously thought this was about to turn into a slasher film," Veronica said, still wiping snot from under her nose. "Maybe there was a reason Cane prohibited any mind-altering substances up here."

Callan hummed in acquiescence just as Professor Cane thundered through the door. He knocked his boots against the door jamb to get the snow off.

"Fucking morons," he said, growling when he struggled to get his bootlaces undone.

"I'm gonna—" Veronica jabbed a thumb toward the stairs, wrapping her coat tighter around her as she crept away.

"I'm sorry that they scared you," Professor Cane said, back down to just his sweatpants, but now with a fresh sheen of sweat on his chest that made Callan aware of every inch of her overly warm skin. "You can go back to bed. They won't be coming around anymore, I promise."

It was more words than he'd said to her in the whole week combined. She gnawed on the inside of her cheek, testing her sore ankle in her boot and wondering if she could slip by him without limping. "I think I'll stay up for a bit longer. I'm wired now." She didn't say that she was wired for reasons that had nothing to do with the Andersons.

Professor Cane scraped his fingers through his hair. "Yeah, me too. You want a drink?"

A few minutes later they were seated on the couch before the fireplace, the embers popping and fizzing. Callan was wedged into one corner of the couch, Professor Cane's legs were sprawled over what remained of it, one knee hitched up so he was half facing her. The bourbon Professor Cane had offered her tasted like caramel and cherries. It was warming her from the stomach out.

"I can't stand your silence," she found herself whispering when there was no more bourbon left to distract her mouth. Professor Cane glanced briefly at her before returning his attention to the winking embers. Callan was uncoiling her legs from beneath her, ready to return to her room and more of that roaring silence, when his hand shot out to grip her leg just above her injured ankle. He pulled the ankle into his lap carefully, lifting up her pant leg to get a better look. Callan could already see the shadow of a bruise forming.

"That's rich coming from the master of suffering in silence," he said, the corner of his mouth lifting as he pressed a thumb into the joint, earning a hissed wince from Callan.

"It's just twisted," she said through her teeth as he continued to massage.

"It's already bruising," Professor Cane replied. "I'm surprised you could even walk on it. Probably not the brightest idea to run around a dark, unfamiliar cabin when you're high," he said, his voice tightening over the admonishment as he eyed her knowingly. He continued to massage the area around the sprain. The pain relented with each knead of his thumb and forefinger. She relaxed, muscle by muscle into the plush couch cushions, her eyes fluttering closed. "I'm only giving you space, Callan," Cane said after a while. "I told you what I expected of you, what you needed to do to succeed here. The next move is yours."

Callan eyed the side of his face as he continued to work on her ankle, his fingers splaying down to the top of her foot and up to her calf muscle. "I feel like you don't want me here," she said quietly. "I feel—I feel like I don't really deserve to be here."

His hands stilled. His head ducked into his chest. When he leveled his eyes on her again, they were burning.

"Do I strike you as the type of man to make mistakes often?" He asked. Callan felt like the couch was swallowing her. She shook her head. If she was being honest, he seemed like the type of man who got exactly what he wanted and didn't even have to ask for it. "You deserve your place here just as much as the others, and every artist who has come before your class. But talent will only get you so far. Plenty of artists overflowing with talent have self-destructed before they saw the spoils of their work. Being an artist is ninety percent self-care and the rest is the actual making of the art. What I'm showing you here is how to tend your mind. How to live so you can continue this pursuit of yours. Nature has gifted you all this creative fertilizer. But it'll be up to you whether you use it to grow, or to blow yourself up."

"I've been to plenty of therapists before," she mumbled. "It never worked. It never did anything." Art was the only thing that had ever helped her move *through* her problems. Therapy had only ever forced her to sit in a room surrounded by them with her fists in her lap. Remembering didn't help. Talking didn't help. It only made her feel stuck, useless, helpless.

"Fortunately for both of us, I'm not your therapist." The shadows stole all the light from his eyes, giving them the same gravitational pull as the lake. Callan's gaze drifted to the sculpted lines of his chest; a grave mistake. Professor Cane rocked forward until Callan had no choice but to meet his eyes. "I'm not here because I need to be. I don't collect a paycheck for this work, or even a tax deduction. I do this because I want to. Because I think it's important. The art you make—the art you will make—it's important, Callan. Art is the only thing that makes all this suffering worth it."

"I just don't understand what you want from me," she whispered.

He gripped her chin between thumb and forefinger, tipping it up gently. "I want your pain," he said.

"You've been playing hide and seek with it for so long I think you've forgotten it's there. It's haunting you. But you won't be able to access it until you acknowledge it. If you want to know the crux of this retreat, the secret of my method, that is it. It's quite simple. Confront yourself."

Callan wet her lips. Her skin fizzed beneath his touch. "If I told you who I was, if I gave you what you asked for, you wouldn't look at me like that. You wouldn't even be able to touch me."

A laugh rumbled deep in Professor Cane's chest. "You think you could scare me away?" He cocked his head, his gaze dipping to her lips, the hold on her chin tightening imperceptibly. "Unfortunately for you, I quite like monsters."

Small Truths

The next morning's lecture was scheduled in a room on the second floor; a room previously locked according to Callan's extensive inventory. It was a cavernous, wood-paneled, mock classroom, with the same rickety, mahogany desks and attached swivel chairs as the tiered lecture rooms at Melrose. Light filtered in from small, rectangular windows just below the vaulted ceiling. There was a large hourglass sitting on the lectern at the front of the room.

By habit, Callan sat at eye level with the lectern, sipping on the tea she'd barely had time to grab from the kitchen. The events of the night prior were tangled up with the vivid nightmares that had consumed her sleep. She wasn't sure where the line between dream and reality lay.

The others filed in looking just as tired as she felt; orbiting her like moons. Veronica took the far back corner where the light couldn't reach her. Fray took the front center, his body melting around the desk. Roth arrived last and took the seat beside Callan with a tentative smile. They sat in silence for so long, Callan's tailbone began to ache from the unforgiving chair. Then slow, methodical footsteps were clipping up the stairs, down the hall.

Callan's breaths ran hollow, her heart drummed a staccato rhythm around each footfall.

His glasses were being used to push his still damp hair away from his eyes. He wore a hunter green sport coat that hugged his shoulders and matched the moleskin journal at the top of his stack of books which supported a tottering mug of coffee. It wasn't possible for someone as strait-laced as Professor Cane to appear flustered, but this morning he'd come close. There were dark smudges under his eyes and his fingers kept tracing over the same lines on the book splayed open before him on the lectern. If she closed her eyes, Callan could still feel his touch linger over her jaw.

"Good morning," he said, his voice gravelly. He continued organizing his things on the lectern. Was he... nervous? The thought made a ripple of triumph flutter through Callan's stomach. "I know the schedule says we'll be discussing the impressionists this morning, but let's save the academics for when the caffeine has fully hit our bloodstreams. Given the late night a few of us had, I've decided we're going to try again with show and tell. You're all exceptionally gifted students who no doubt contribute meaningfully to every classroom you enter. Let this one be no different. I expect effort today. And if you feel like sitting in silence instead, well—" he tipped the hourglass. "We'll have exactly three hours of it. Who wants to start?"

For the first time since he'd entered the room, he looked directly at Callan. His face, his icy cold eyes spoke in full sentences that required no translation. A single eyebrow hitched up. She could feel her heart thumping in her shoulders, her teeth.

"I'll go," she said anyway. Her hands snaked up into her sweater as every eye in the room fell on her. All triumph and confidence flew through the window. "Sorry, um, what should I say exactly?"

Professor Cane tipped his head. "Whatever comes to mind," he said. "Whatever feels right." He left his notebook on the stack of books and leaned against the front of the lectern, crossing his arms. Callan cleared her throat.

"Right." Blackness crept in at the edges of her vision. She really needed to try breathing. If that didn't work, she could also just drop dead. She stared down at the whirling wood grain of the desk. "My parents died when I was fifteen," she blurted. She thought she felt the room take a collective inhale, herself included. It almost felt good to spit the words out; like a piece of gristle chewed on too long. "My dad was a pastor and we lived above the church. It was a candle that started the fire, they think. It happened fast. I don't remember much. I'd just had a lesson in school about staying close to the ground in a fire because smoke rises. I think that's how I made it out and no one else did, but I can't remember that either. I don't have many memories for months after that. But that's how I found painting." Callan took a breath, "I was stuck on my front from all the burns. They set me up with a massage table and art supplies underneath so I could paint and sketch. It kept me from screaming. Sometimes."

By the time she stopped speaking, Callan's shoulders were scrunched up to her ears.

"Thank you for opening up to the group, Lark," Professor Cane said when it was clear she wasn't going to carry on. "Let's take it a step further and practice what we discussed a few days ago. Describing the experience through the lens of emotion. What did you feel? And if you can't remember, what does it make you feel now?"

"Numb," Callan said instantly. Her cheeks flamed. She wiped her sleeve over her face nervously. "It doesn't even feel like it's my story. I don't mean to be evasive. but I don't really feel anything about it."

"No," Veronica said from the dark corner. All Callan could see of her was the slash of silver hair and her grimace catching the light. Callan got the sense Veronica hadn't meant to say the word out loud. When she spoke again, her voice was back to its cool monotone. "It's normal not to remember things from a traumatic childhood. Trauma amnesia, right?"

"Let's keep these discussions in first person," Professor Cane said, failing to hide his annoyance. "Please, continue." He waved her on as he took his coffee to the desk closest to the door. He sat, kicking his feet up on the next over. Veronica held her hands up like there was a gun pointed at her.

"No thanks," she said.

"I remember everything," Roth murmured. He had to sit sideways because the desk was too small for his long legs. His knee bounced as he studied a scar on the desk's surface, tracing it with his fingernail.

"What do you remember, Mr. Heller?" Professor Cane prompted.

Roth tapped his freckled fingers against the desk and shrugged. "I remember the smell in the kitchen when my mom used to make breakfast on the weekends. She worked a lot, but on the weekends, she always cooked. There was music too. You could tell her mood by what was playing. There's not—" his voice broke and Callan's stomach dropped with it. "She doesn't play music anymore."

"How does that make you feel?" Professor Cane asked. Roth inhaled sharply. He shrugged.

"Bad," he answered.

"Okay," Professor Cane said. He watched Roth for a moment, deciding whether to say more. "Okay." His attention pivoted to Fray. "What about you, Mr. Fray?"

"I don't have a sob story, if that's what you're asking," Fray grumbled. He looked like he was halfway to dying of boredom with his head balanced between his fists.

"I suppose congratulations are in order then," Professor Cane said. "Though I imagine you've still got some memories banging around in that head of yours." He cocked his head. "Or did they pull you from a cryogenic freeze the morning before you came here?"

Professor Cane's lips quirked as Fray glared at him.

"My dad's an asshole," he finally said.

"What else?"

Fray shifted in his chair, sucking in a long inhale. "My dad's a *huge* asshole."

"Your dad's Aemon Fray," Veronica said.

"No shit," Fray retorted. "Didn't realize show and tell was so interactive," he said through his teeth, tossing a glance at Professor Cane.

Veronica lifted a single brow. "Touchy. You seemed keen on cramming it down our fucking throats when we first got here."

Professor Cane studied the tense hold of Fray's shoulders. His attention swiveled to Veronica. "Let's allow everyone to speak their turn. If questions are invited, feel free to contribute." Turning back to Fray he added, "Why don't you tell us something about him?"

"Seriously?" Fray gave him a look that somehow achieved both boredom and incredulity. "Should I run through his biography for you? What could I tell you that you don't already know?"

Professor Cane was unflinching. "Tell us something he wouldn't want us to know."

Fray scoffed. He glanced at Callan, his gaze sharpening as it shifted over Roth.

"He's jealous," he said, his voice unusually quiet as he slumped down into his seat. "He gets jealous of other artists. Dead greats. Fucking no-names. It doesn't matter. No one's allowed to take the spotlight from him."

"Not even his son?" Professor Cane asked.

A hollow laugh pushed through Fray's lips. "He can't decide if I'm an extension of him or his competition. Maybe I'm both. Either way, I think he'd prefer to stuff me in a box."

"That must make you feel very claustrophobic," Professor Cane said. "To always have your creative works compared to another's."

Fray tipped his chin to the side. Even from behind him, Callan could see the way his neck strained, the way the muscle in his jaw jumped.

He straightened out the sleeve of his gray wool coat. "Yeah," he conceded. "Yeah, it is."

Callan worried the silence might choke her, but luckily, Veronica ended it.

"My dad was an asshole too," she said. "He had this palatial house in Singapore and every single wall was white. He called it a spa but it felt more like a psych ward. The rich bastard hated art; hated anything he couldn't understand or control. Getting a little reputation for graffitiing private property was my parting gift."

The gears in Callan's head were churning slowly from the lack of sleep, but eventually, things clicked into place. "Wait. You're not—are you YellowFang?"

Veronica's slow, thin smile glowed from the shadows. YellowFang was known for tagging state buildings and politicians' private residences. Their art—Veronica's art—was so valuable, one benefactor chose to deconstruct their house so they could take an entire wall—a YellowFang mural—with them when they moved. Callan hadn't been on social media in weeks, maybe months, but the last she'd seen, YellowFang had well over a million followers. There was no reason someone like her would even be wasting her time with a retreat like Professor Cane's. The conversation she'd had with Veronica the night prior took on a much different shape, now.

"No fucking way," Fray breathed. "*You* broke into Beaumont Prison?"

Veronica shrugged. "Twice, technically. But a condition of enrollment at Brighton was not to commit any more *alleged* misdemeanors." She made air quotes with her fingers. "At least until I graduate."

"There's no way you'd get reported at this point," Roth said. "Those murals are way too valuable."

Veronica hummed skeptically. "Yeah, well, they aren't everyone's cup of tea."

An understatement. Callan had seen her fair share of YellowFang's works. They were violent and grotesque. So grotesque they were difficult to look at. The piece in Beaumont had depicted seven men hanging from the gallows, their bodies left to the crows and the elements. And that was among her tamer works.

"We're getting off topic." Professor Cane interjected. "Let's bring it back to father figures."

Several hours later, Callan and Roth were sneaking sketches of each other into their journaling notebooks from the far side of Callan's bed, their toes to the radiator beneath the window. Outside, the snow was blowing parallel to the ground, carried by a banshee wind that sounded like it was taking off strips of the log siding.

Callan laughed at the third snap of Roth's mechanical pencil. "You really hate drawing, don't you?"

Roth sighed as he clicked a new tip into place. "My hands are too big and my attention span is way too small."

"I'm sure your attention span does just fine with a brick of clay," she said.

"Yeah, well, let me know if you find some," Roth replied, his frustration creating deep gouges that made the sketched version of Callan look more demonic than human. "What kind of art retreat doesn't allow art?"

Callan chewed at the inside of her cheek. "I don't know what I expected, but it definitely wasn't this."

"Yeah," Roth said. "My life's not that interesting. I hope shitty parents aren't a prerequisite for whatever we're getting here. I might have to start lying." His eyes flew to Callan's face. "Sorry—shit. I didn't mean to sound like an obnoxious prick."

"It's okay," Callan said. "My parents weren't shitty, they just died."

Roth winced. "That makes it even worse."

"Sounds like we both left out some key details in our catch-up," Callan said, peeking up at him through her eyelashes before returning to her sketch.

Roth abandoned his notepad and pulled his knees to his chest.

"Frankie died," he said. Callan's head shot up.

"What?" She couldn't possibly have heard him right. But she had. The vacant look on Roth's face confirmed it. She pressed her fingers to her lips to keep any other exclamations from pouring out. When the ache in her sternum subsided, she said, "I'm so sorry. I can't even imagine. God, Roth, I don't know what to say."

Roth lifted a shoulder. "Not much to say. It happened years ago. The winter before I was supposed to go off to college. That's why I delayed. We were ice fishing on one of the lakes around the farm and he just went through. He was fourteen and a good swimmer. But his clothes were heavy in the freezing water and I didn't get to him in time." The casual horror of it flashed in Callan's mind in vivid detail every time she blinked.

She realized in that moment, how easily platitudes came to the tongue. It was almost impulsive, the need to comfort someone with those hollow words. She was often on the receiving end of them. The thoughts and prayers, the instructions to look for grace or comfort somewhere none would be found. Instead, she grabbed his hand. His fingers were cold, as if the memory had brought him back to that day on the ice.

Roth offered a brittle smile when he spoke. "I'm really fine. I promise. It was forever ago."

Callan nodded, even if she didn't believe him. She knew first-hand how little distance and time meant to monsters like grief. But holding grief didn't make her an expert on it.

"Does Dr. Cane know?"

Roth scratched at the threadbare corduroy covering his knee. "Yeah, that's what my essay was about. It's practically all he wants to talk about in our solo sessions."

Callan's brow crumpled. "Your essay?"

Roth gave her a questioning look. "To get into the program," he said, cocking his head.

"Right," Callan said quickly, nodding her head like she'd simply forgotten. But she hadn't written an essay for the program. She hadn't even applied. She thought the others had simply been plucked from their respective schools; nominated by anonymous professors like she had been. How else had they been vetted? How had *she* been vetted?

An hour later, Callan was alone on her bed staring at the door and counting the minutes to her next solo session. Roth had excused himself for a nap before dinner, and the silent isolation had only helped her fears and anxieties to crowd her small bedroom.

Her heart did rhythmic gymnastics in her ribcage as she considered how best to confront Professor Cane. She could try being direct like she had the night before. But it was a gamble with Professor Cane's mercurial moods. At this point, she wasn't sure she could trust his answers. The only option was to try catching him in a lie, but that option seemed futile. Callan wasn't arrogant enough to believe that she could manipulate Professor Cane's mind. If anything, she'd only find herself further tangled in his web.

She wasn't sure whether to be annoyed or grateful when she heard crashing and cursing coming from the living room just seconds before she'd planned to head to his office. The voices got louder as footsteps pounded down the stairs overhead. Callan went to her door and peeked through to see Roth grabbing for something in Professor Cane's hand. Professor Cane used an elbow to hold him off as Roth went bright pink in the face, using curse words she'd never once heard or expected to hear come out of his mouth. Callan hid behind her door as they passed. A knock came seconds later and Callan opened it to find Veronica on the other side.

"What's going on?" Callan whispered. She ushered Veronica into her room. The commotion frayed at her already hypersensitive nerves.

"I don't know who told him, but Cane got tipped off about drugs in Roth's room."

"Drugs?" Callan exclaimed, too loud. She slapped a hand over her mouth. "Roth doesn't do drugs," she hissed.

Veronica grimaced. "Well, he does, actually. There were a ton of them in his room from what I saw."

"What the hell," Callan murmured, mostly to herself. Maybe she didn't know Roth as well as she thought she did. It seemed to be a recurring theme for the day. She could still hear him yelling from rooms down, and the guttural, raw tenor of it set her arm hairs on edge.

"He took my weed too," Veronica said, gnawing at her thumbnail. "Now I definitely won't be sleeping." Callan felt a pang of guilt. If she hadn't lingered with Professor Cane on the couch the night before, maybe he wouldn't have gotten the idea to go searching for prohibited substances in the first place. She didn't understand what harm a little weed could possibly do in a house full of adults. Especially a house full of artists.

"Do you think he'll get kicked out?" Callan asked.

"No way," Veronica said with a sharp shake of her head. "Even if Cane wanted us out, we're stuck here until the temperatures rise above freezing again. I couldn't get the front door open earlier with all the snow. There isn't even a road to drive down at this point."

Almost immediately, Callan's relief was replaced with an urge to run to the front door and try it herself. She needed fresh air and lots of space. She knew they would be snowed in eventually, but in all the times she'd imagined it before, it had seemed cozy and quaint, magical almost. Now, it just felt claustrophobic. Outside, dark had descended and the snow and wind began to blend with the sounds of Roth and Professor Cane arguing.

She didn't really know what her plan was, but she found herself marching down the hall, her hands flexing into fists. She found Fray standing outside the door, his ear pressed to it. From the self-satisfied lift of his lips, she knew exactly who had tattled on Roth. She shouldered past him and into the dimly lit room.

Dark

"What the hell is going on?" Callan said from the doorway of Professor Cane's study. Roth's vision pulsed an uglier shade of desperation. He couldn't let them see him like this. Especially not Callan. He lunged for the pill bottles in Cane's hand, which was now poised over the blazing fire. The Professor sidestepped him.

"Lark, go back to your room," he said calmly. "This is between me and Mr. Heller."

"I'm not going anywhere," Callan said, crossing her arms. Veronica stepped into the room behind her. Cane sighed, and Roth took his opportunity.

"Please, please don't," he begged, his voice dropping and cracking all at once. Yelling had gotten him nowhere. But he wasn't above begging. "Just— just let me explain, okay? Just let me explain. You can't throw them out. I need them."

"Professor," Callan insisted from the doorway, her gaze darting between Roth and Cane. There was an edge to her voice that made Roth's eyes narrow on her like he was seeing her for the first time. "If he says he needs them, maybe don't roast them when we're stuck up here for god-knows-how-long."

"I don't doubt that Mr. Heller believes he needs these," Cane said, nodding at the unlabeled bottles. From the way he turned the bottles over, inspecting them carefully, he knew just as well as Roth that no licensed doctor had prescribed them. Returning his attention to Roth, he added, "But I know these counterfeit pills are doing more harm than good for you." There was nothing patronizing about the earnest look on his face, but Roth still had a violent urge to rip that look off him.

"How the hell do you know what's good for me?" Roth seethed. "All you do is point out how fucked up I am. You don't want to make me better. You just want to see me squirm."

Professor Cane's gaze darted to the three others crowding the doorway.

"We don't have to do this with an audience, Mr. Heller. Why don't you and I take a walk outside? I won't throw these away if you can explain how they are more effective than the treatment protocol we've discussed at length in our private sessions."

"Because these let me fucking sleep," Roth screamed. The withdrawal hadn't even begun, and already he could feel those familiar beasts clawing their way up from his stomach, peeling apart his skull. There was nowhere safe when they were free. "If you throw these away, it's as good as killing me. I'll lose my fucking mind."

Professor Cane took a step toward him, slipping the pills behind his back and pitching his voice low so the others couldn't hear him. "You won't lose anything, Heller. Trust me. All that shit that sneaks up on you when these wear off? It's still there, festering. You need to confront it. You need to feel it. There's no better time than now."

Roth's stomach continued to twist and churn, but some of the tension went out of his shoulders.

"I can't," he whimpered. "This is the only thing that works." The corners of his eyes pricked and he swiped at his nose before snot could start running out of it. Professor Cane dipped his head to catch Roth's eyes.

"Is it? Working?" Roth's chest heaved with each breath. He

opened his mouth, but couldn't bring himself to say the words. "I'm going to put these in the fire," Cane said slowly, making sure to keep hold of Roth's eyes. "Tomorrow morning, we can discuss alternatives with clinically proven efficacy." Roth became acutely aware of the other eyes in the room pouring over every pathetic inch of him. He wanted to scream, but that would only prove Cane's point.

When Professor Cane tipped the contents of the bottles into the flames, Roth lowered his shoulder, ducked his head and marched through the door. He was vaguely aware of the *oomph* sound Fray made as he pinned him to the wall outside Cane's office.

"I fucking hate you," Roth growled into Fray's ear. He was close enough to smell his expensive cologne. It showed remarkable self-preservation skills on Fray's part that he didn't make any snide comments in reply. When Roth pulled back, all he saw was a dumbfounded, if not a little frightened, look in Fray's amber eyes. The shape of them remained embedded in his mind as he hauled himself to the side door and shouldered his way into the whistling cold of the night.

The first fifteen degrees of heat left his body immediately, like a scarf carried away in the wind. The next seeped away slowly, with each trudging step. His nose was the first to go numb, then his ears and his fingertips. He clutched his skull to keep the contents of his mind from sloshing out.

He didn't stop walking until his boots hit the tar-black earth that edged the water. Steam rose from the cursed sinkhole as snowflakes obliterated themselves on the surface. He watched and wondered if his body might do the same upon contact. The longer he stood still, the more aware he became of the stinging pain of the cold, the snow. He had snow caked up to his thighs and the wind tore through his sweater at his frigid skin. Maybe the water would be pleasant by comparison. It looked warm, inviting. There was something relieving about the thought of melting into it, becoming it.

He stooped down to test it with his finger. His hand hovered an inch above the surface when an equally pale, bony set of fingers emerged from the lake's dark depths. They weren't wet as they breached the surface. Roth's brain was tied up in too many knots for him to freak out. Instead, he curiously waited to see what else might emerge. He watched as the hand felt for the lip of the lake, grasping at the rocks and soil. Then it was pulling itself out, its veins bulging and skin tightening. First a freckled forearm, an elbow, the pale curve of a youthful neck. Roth knew the constellation of freckles just below its collarbone even before its head was dragged from the depths, dark blonde hair mixed up with deep green algae and dead leaves. Hair fell over its eyes but stopped just above a freckled nose and pronounced Cupid's bow lips.

The breath Roth had been holding punched out of his screaming ribs. "Frankie?"

The head swiveled slowly on its shoulders.

Roth pitched forward, grabbing for Frankie's hand. It was cold and slimy and slipped from his grasp like river rocks. Frankie's lips peeled back on a silty, gray smile.

"You never were fast enough, were you? Is that why you just watched when your little friend fell in? I almost kept her for myself." His voice wasn't right. It turned all the sound in Roth's head to static; made his breath catch painfully in his throat. He was perched precariously at the lake's edge and realized too late that whatever bobbed in the water ahead of him wasn't his dead little brother.

"What are you?" He cried, scooting back frantically until a sapling hit him between the shoulder blades. The thing continued to smile with Frankie's face.

"Fish food and fertilizer, thanks to you. That's what you wanted, right? You hated me. You were jealous of me. When I went in the water, what was the first thing you thought?" The thing paused, cocking its head. It didn't even need to move its arms to stay perfectly suspended in the water. Through the curtain of algae and hair, Roth caught the eerie blue glow of its eyes. He felt those eyes in every corner of his mind, turning over notebooks and rifling through old boxes. "Why was it that you didn't make it to me? You were so close." This time its voice matched its appearance perfectly; pitched deep and as slimy and cold as the tar that made up the lake.

Roth did the only thing he was ever capable of doing in his miserable life. He gathered his lanky legs and he ran.

Not What You Think

Veronica's ears were still ringing long after Roth fled Cane's office. Cane had followed after him, and the rest of them stood around in various caricatures of unease. She didn't like when people yelled, didn't like the guttural pitch of a man's voice when he was both angry and desperate. It reminded her of the ever-present echo in her childhood home. The festering hate that lived in the sanitarium white walls like mold. The only thing that had ever been predictable about her father was the yelling. It made her insides crawl with the need to be louder, meaner; to strike first so she wasn't caught on the back foot.

When she was sure Cane was out of the way, she bolted up the stairs to her room. As expected, the gallon freezer bag full of weed she'd stuffed behind the toilet was gone. Confiscated. She peeled the porcelain lid from the water tank and peered inside to find the other freezer bag was right where she left it. She pulled the gun from the tank and peeled it from the bag, checking to see that it was still fully loaded and dry. If her fingers trembled a little, she blamed it on the all-knowing look in Cane's eyes as he'd lectured them. She knew he was coming for her next. She wouldn't be caught vulnerable like June. She would fight back.

With the gun in the inside pocket of her baggy parka, she

crept through the living room and up the narrow stairwell that led to the roof. The door was nearly jammed shut by the mix of snow and ice, but eventually, she wrenched it open.

Peering over the edge of the roof she saw nothing but twinkling snow and the still line of the forest. She hid herself by the chimney, reclining into its warmth and staring up at the night sky. It glowed a greenish gray thanks to the blanket of white covering the earth. The sky was unmoving, unchanging. Thick as stew and occasionally spitting out a snowflake here and there that might have just been the air particles freezing in place. She sat there long enough that she thought she might turn into a statue herself.

Jagged breaths puncturing the still night air tugged her out of her trance. She glanced over the edge of the roof in time to see Roth running into the glow of the cabin lights, his head twisted around on his shoulders like something was hunting him. Veronica could see perfectly well that there wasn't. That didn't stop the fine hairs on her nape from rising. She palmed the cool metal of the gun in her pocket for comfort.

Professor Cane materialized at the bottom of the steps, catching Roth by the shoulders. Roth was sobbing unintelligibly, grasping at the lapels of Cane's coat like he might fall to his knees otherwise.

"You've had quite the scare, haven't you," Cane said.

Veronica swore there was a hint of amusement in his voice as he held Roth. Veronica crept closer to the ledge so she could hear better, keeping her feet light like she'd taught herself to do while tagging.

"It's alright," Cane was saying. "It's alright, they won't come here. They stick to the woods and the lake."

Roth pushed away from Cane, wearing the same pinched look of confusion that had slipped over Veronica's face. "What?" He choked out. "You—you know what that thing was? You've seen him? You've seen Frankie?"

Cane grasped Roth by the nape, pulling him into a forced,

awkward embrace, their foreheads nearly touching. Roth looked strangely childlike, even standing a few inches taller than the Professor.

"It's not what you think," he said, his voice dipping low. "You have nothing to fear, do you understand me? It won't harm you, or the others. But I must ask you to keep this to yourself until tomorrow night. I'll explain everything then, I promise."

Roth was casting frantic glances over his shoulder at the path he'd taken from the woods. The path that led to the lake.

"Here," Cane said, pulling something from his coat pocket. It was a single white pill the size of an aspirin. "This will help you rest tonight while the drugs start to clear from your system. I've had Hilde draw a hot bath and fix you some tea. I promise, Roth. Nothing bad will happen while you're with me."

Roth nodded, wiping the snot from his nose before accepting Cane's offering. Cane placed a hand on his quivering shoulder and guided him up the porch steps.

"What the fuck," Veronica breathed into the night air. What had Roth seen? What was Cane planning to tell them? She couldn't tear her eyes away from the forest, watching the textured shadows for a monster without a name. The prickle on her arms, her neck, told her something was watching her back.

"You know, this door has been known to freeze shut," Professor Cane drawled. Veronica spun, losing all the air in her lungs in the process. "You could die of hypothermia within an hour." He took a step closer, craning his neck as if to look over the lip of the roof behind her. "Or fall to your death trying to escape the cold."

"What did Roth see in the lake?" Veronica demanded, her fist tightening around the gun in her pocket. There seemed no point in tiptoeing around the truth. Cane shoved his hands into his jacket, eyes twinkling with an unreadable look.

"It doesn't really matter what Roth saw," he said.

A gust of air escaped Veronica's lips. She dared a glance over her shoulder, at the shadows edging the forest. She felt Cane take another step toward her, and she matched him with a step back. She froze at the sound of ice cascading to the ground behind her.

"I think the real question is: what will you see when you find the courage to look?" His gaze had teeth. "Care to tell me what you have in your pocket, Ms. Fang?"

Veronica's mouth twitched, and she resisted the need to tell him by biting at the edge of her lips. It was an obvious tell. Her father would hate it.

A thin smile sharpened Cane's cheekbones and the shadows beneath them. Veronica's eyes narrowed on him, her nostrils flaring.

"Are you going to kill me, Veronica? Is that what this is all about?" His curiosity held no fear.

"I haven't decided yet," she said, letting the gun fall free of her pocket. "What did you do to June?"

Cane sighed, long and deep. "I don't know how many times I can tell you. June left this retreat perfectly safe. What she chose to do after is none of my business."

"That's horseshit and you know it," Veronica spit, raising the gun at him with a shaking hand. "She had a life, a job. She had—she had people. If she was alive, she would have come back. People don't just walk away from their life."

Professor Cane took a step forward, disregarding the weapon. He raised a single brow as he said, "Maybe it didn't feel like a life to her anymore." Another step forward. "Maybe she was running from something. Or someone."

Veronica shook her head, adding her other hand to her grip on the gun to bolster her courage. "She came here and she never left. Just tell me what happened to her. Is she alive?"

"Oh, she's alive," Cane said. "She just doesn't want to see you. How does that make you feel? Does it make you want to lash out? Maybe hurt someone?" His eyes drifted to the gun.

"Fuck you," she spat. Cane lunged forward. Veronica's finger flexed. The night froze in place around the empty click of the trigger and Veronica stumbled backward. *It was loaded, it was loaded, it was loaded*, the thudding of her heart protested. Her gaze collided with Cane's just as he tore the gun from her hands. There was murder written on his face. It was all the proof Veronica needed that he was capable of hurting someone; capable of hurting June.

Veronica watched her last form of defense disappear into Professor Cane's back pocket. Slowly, that murderous look on his face morphed into amusement. "I can't wait to see what your shadows have in store for you. I wonder if they'll share your penchant for violence."

He turned to leave. She lurched. "Wait."

Cane paused but didn't turn back around. He wasn't afraid of her at all, even after what she'd done. Her fingers flexed around the emptiness in her pockets.

"Will they hurt us?" She asked. She didn't know what she was trying to shape from her fear. Her mind was a sickening kaleidoscope of fleshy red, bone white, and the murky unnamable colors of the lake. When her focus landed back on Cane's face, it was waiting with a question.

"What makes you ask that?"

Veronica laughed, not because anything was particularly funny, but because her guts were twisted in a way that demanded it. The question only spurred another roiling, squirming sensation through her stomach. She ground her teeth together, fearing that if she let the hysterical sound go on too long, she might never stop. Cane extended his arm like he meant to touch her. When she flinched, his hand withered to his side.

"Nothing, myself included, will hurt you here," he insisted, and dammit if his glacial eyes didn't compel her belief. "Nothing except, possibly, you."

"Then why won't you tell me what Roth saw? What happened to June?"

"I can't tell you what Heller saw," Cane said. "Because I don't know. I don't know what he saw. I don't know what June saw when she was here either. None of us will ever truly know what any of the others see in the woods surrounding Pitch Lake. That is the legacy of this place. It found him, as I suspect it has found Lark. Soon, it will find you, too. I've been trying to prepare you, but truthfully, I don't know if anything can."

"I don't want to see it," Veronica said, jaw set so hard her molars groaned. "I don't want to know. I don't want to see. I didn't ask for this."

"The more you resist, the more frightening it will be when it appears. It feeds on what you give it, Ms. Fang. And if you give it fear, gods help you."

"You said it wouldn't hurt me," she said. The cold of the night was sharp in her lungs.

"It can't hurt you. It can't even touch you. But that doesn't mean it can't scare you."

"But—but Callan—it dragged her into the lake."

Cane cut his chin to the side sharply, stopping her. "That wasn't the same." He paused. "What happened to Callan was concerning for other reasons."

"Such as..."

"I'll explain more tomorrow night at the solstice celebration. Usually, the shadows are most active in the longest, darkest, nights of winter. That's why I chose this period for the retreat each year. I promise you that this process is tried and tested." He gave her an imploring look. "I know your trust is hard to come by. More so than any of the others, and rightfully so. But I am determined to earn it, Fang. I will have it. Now, let's get you inside and warmed up. It's fucking freezing out here."

Three hours later, Veronica's eyeballs ached from staring so long at her bedroom door. The door was locked with the dresser pushed in front of it and the bed pinned in front of that. There wasn't much she could do about the window, but she was grateful she'd at least been assigned a room on the second floor. She shuddered at the sound of wind rattling the house, imagining long curved claws hooking around each plank as something faceless and menacing hoisted up toward the opening. She had the urge to check below the window for signs of an intruder, an observer. But the fear sat so heavily on her chest she didn't know if she'd be able to scream for help if something did come for her.

Cane insisted whatever waited in the woods wouldn't harm her. But the voice of something slithering in the darkest recesses of her mind told her that her shadow would be different. It whispered that her rage, her hate, her *everything*, might create a monster capable of eating all the others.

It told her that her shadow would still be picking their bones from its teeth when it came for her.

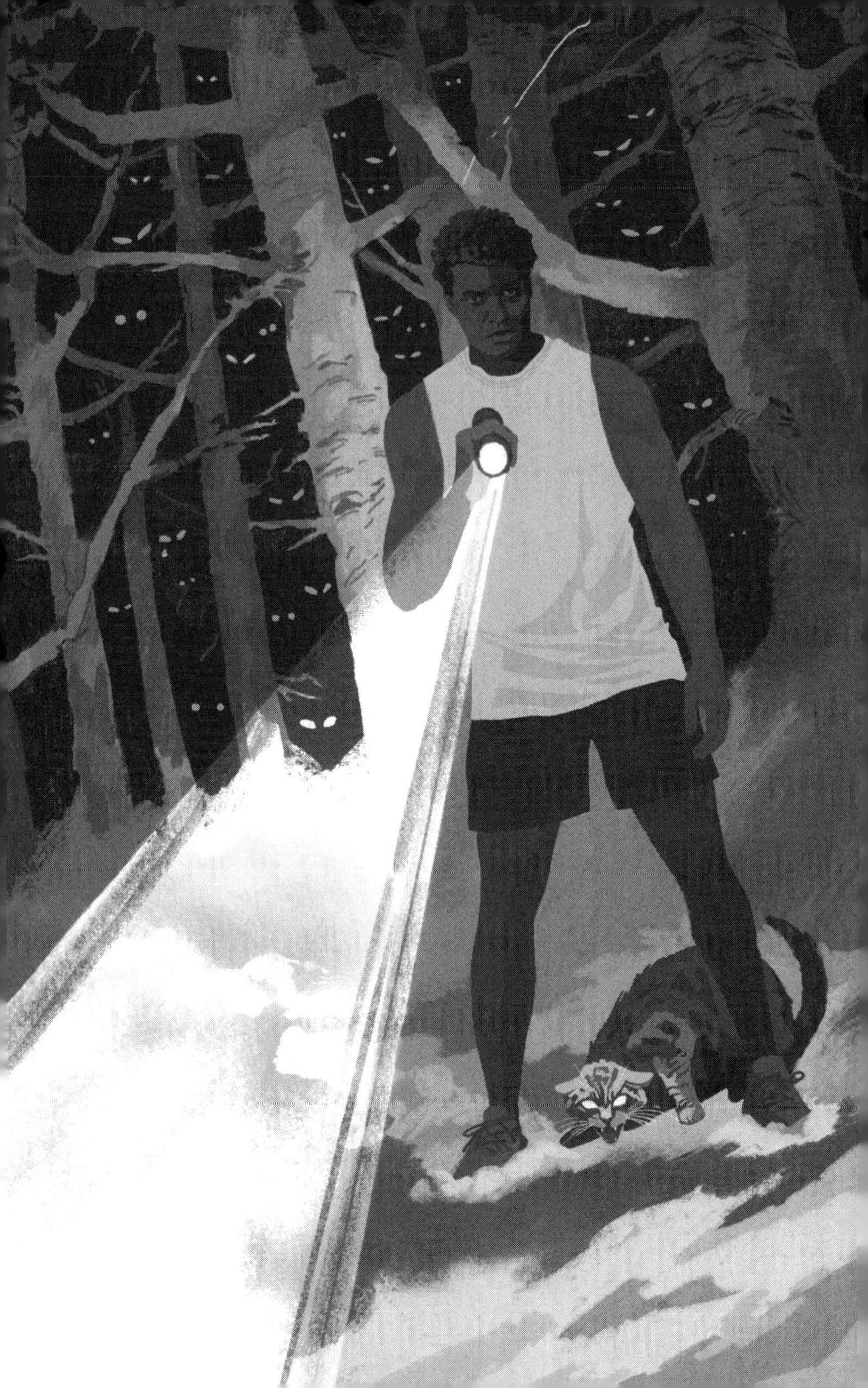

Run

Fray couldn't sleep either. He'd grown used to his restless, useless mind; his thoughts were trapped in a labyrinth. Sometimes they ran into the walls, other times they chased the same dead end, round and round and round. That wasn't alarming in its own right. What was alarming was the particular dead end they kept chasing. Roth Heller. Great Lakes Neanderthal. Unfriendly Giant.

Fray would cut his tongue out before he admitted the substance of these thoughts. The flush of Roth's pale cheeks, the raging heat in his usually dull, gray eyes, the surprising strength in his wiry arms as he pinned Fray to the wall. That dragged Fray deeper into the spiraling delirium. He wondered how those lean, freckled arms would look bracing against the bed as Fray pressed with equal force behind him. He wondered what that flush in Roth's cheeks would look like spread down his throat, his chest, further. He wondered what his gray eyes might look like through heavy lids as Fray dropped to his knees before him.

If he kept wondering, he would need to do something about the situation escalating in his shorts. And that was a line he refused to cross. He hated feeling guilty. But even he knew he deserved it this time.

He shouldn't have said a goddamn thing to Dr. Cane. He was a fucking coward for it. He shouldn't have been snooping through Roth's room to begin with.

He'd thought that maybe, if he directed Professor Cane's attention to the party drugs in Roth's sock drawer, the stash behind Veronica's toilet, it might buy him some time to figure out how to hide a little longer. There was only so long he could insert his father into conversation before everyone realized that he was nothing but a cardboard cut-out of the man. A prop that could walk and talk and even hold a brush like Aemon Fray, but who could contribute nothing original of his own to the world of art.

The thoughts had him sweating all over his sheets. He kicked his legs free of the covers and sulked to the wall separating his room from Roth's. He pressed his ear to the plaster. A soft whimpering came from the other side. He stepped back. His fingers drummed at his bare thigh.

Don't you fucking dare, he told himself. He paced back to his bed, but just looking at the wrinkled, damp sheets made his skin crawl. Before he knew it, he was back at the wall listening to Roth writhe around in his bed.

He cussed in a creative mix of English and his mother's native French as he pulled on shorts. He didn't make a sound leaving his room. He held his breath as he crept past Roth's door, but couldn't keep himself from trailing his fingers lightly over the door for a brief moment.

The gym was on the first floor near the garage. The lights flicked on as he walked in, the smell of rubber and sweat hitting him immediately. He was fairly certain he was the only one other than Professor Cane to use the gym. That had turned the space into a kind of solace for him. He went to the treadmill, cranked up the volume on his earbuds and then the speed. Soon he was sprinting, the music blaring in his ears.

There was no room for thoughts in a brain deprived of oxygen and vibrating to haptic beats. It took longer than he hoped to run himself ragged, to make his muscles cramp up and his stomach seize. He was making his way to the pull-up bar when a whisper of movement passed by his calf. He yelped, tearing out his earbud.

Callan's orange menace of a cat, Schrödinger, pressed himself against Fray's calf again, seeming not to mind that Fray was dripping with sweat.

"Fucking cat," Fray said, but he didn't shoo the furball away. He squatted down and patted Schrödinger on the head, noticing then that he was sopping wet. No wonder he hadn't minded the sweat. "Where have you been, Dingleberry?" He asked the cat, who crackled in response, his golden eyes mischievous. He'd tracked paw prints into the gym which Fray followed into the hall. Schrödinger trotted ahead, tossing occasional glances over his shoulder like he hoped he would be followed, his shaggy orange tail swishing.

The cold hit Fray's sweaty skin before they'd turned the corner. The wind whistled, sending crystalline snowflakes into the living room where a small bank had formed on the welcome mat.

The cat darted through the dark, open mouth of the front door and disappeared into the night.

"Hey, wait you little shit," Fray called. If he was smart, he would have turned around and returned to his room as if he hadn't seen a thing. If the cat disappeared while Fray was up and about that night, he would surely be blamed. He didn't need to place himself at the center of any more drama. But he was already at the base of the cabin steps and he could vaguely make out the occasional glint of the cat's eyes about halfway between the house and the forest.

"Get back here, you idiot," he said. When that didn't work, he proceeded to make the clicking, kissing sounds he'd heard Callan use, patting his leg impatiently.

Schrödinger continued to stare at him, eyes occasionally flashing with the reflection of the cabin's porch light. It took several more paces for Fray to realize there was something at the cat's feet.

"What's that you've got there?" He asked, taking a tentative half step. The closer Fray got, the less sure he was that he even wanted to know the answer. The chill began to sink into his bones as he stooped down. Schrödinger nudged Fray's knee proudly just as the last of his dinner threatened to reappear.

It was a baby rabbit. Snow white and small enough to fit in one of Fray's palms. It wasn't white anymore though. Its flesh had been torn and shredded as if Schrödinger hoped to rival Jackson Pollock with the gory masterpiece. It took a moment for him to make sense of the dismembered parts.

Fray cursed colorfully as he backed away from the scene, eyeing the cat with disgust. The torrent of expletives was the only thing keeping him from vomiting. Between the exertion of his run and all that blood, he wasn't sure his stomach would ever stop churning. Something so small had no right to produce so much blood. The cat watched Fray with what could only be described as amusement.

"Get in the house, you monster," Fray said, shooing him toward the cabin. Schrödinger danced around his legs and then trotted further from the cabin.

Fray realized as he stared after the troublesome cat that the tiny rabbit wasn't the only conquest of the night. There was a goddamned trail of them, dotting the snow all the way to the forest's edge.

"Nope. No. Absolutely fucking not," Fray said weakly, shivering as he tucked his hands into his armpits. He turned and jogged back toward the cabin. A sharp wind tittered across his shoulders, sounding eerily like a desperate, human cry. Fray spun to face the wall of trees behind him. In the path of carnage, the cat had left, where before there had only been the occasional dead forest critter, stood a figure.

"Professor Cane?" Fray called. The figure twitched but didn't answer. "Who are you?" He tried again. Nothing. He squinted, but the harder he looked, the tighter the shadows seemed to wrap themselves around the man's shoulders. Surely, it had to be a man standing at that height. Fray's eyes caught on something dangling from his hand. Not a gun or a knife, not even a baseball bat. Fray's gut knew what it was before his mind did. Long and jointed with a cloven hoof. A deer leg.

The porch light flickered. Died. That was fine. Fray didn't need to see any more. He backed away slowly at first, then scrambled when the stranger jolted forward. Fray nearly tripped over himself, his arms wheeling. His desperate cry was punctured by the crack of the door slamming closed behind him. Fray fumbled with the door lock and spun around before he realized he wasn't alone inside either.

Professor Cane struck an emergency match, revealing Veronica at the base of the stairs in a defensive position, and Callan wiping sleep from her eyes.

"Everything alright, Mr. Fray? What were you doing outside?" Cane asked, lighting a hurricane lantern and heading for the stairs.

"Where are you going?" Fray demanded breathlessly. "He's out there."

Professor Cane paused. "Heller is outside?"

"Heller? What are you talking about? There's a man outside killing bunnies." Fray's frenzied gaze jumped between Professor Cane and the door he expected the intruder to barge through any moment. Professor Cane pinched the bridge of his nose.

"Heller's having a night terror," Cane said. As if on cue, a brittle scream tore through the walls. Fray ran without thinking, spurred on by the pulsing image of the intruder holding Roth's severed leg.

"Don't wake him," Professor Cane said calmly from behind him. "You'll only make it worse."

Roth's screams were animalistic and raw. Fray nearly ripped the door off its hinges as he rushed inside the bedroom, but Professor Cane was right. Roth was asleep. The bed covers were twisted around his mostly nude body, barely covering him. Fray turned back to the doorway, giving Roth the privacy he'd stolen a moment before.

"What do we do?" Fray asked.

Professor Cane watched Roth, his eyes unreadable. "We just make sure he doesn't hurt himself," he answered eventually.

Fray nodded. His hands felt useless at his sides. He crept over to the bed, out of Roth's thrashing reach.

"There's someone outside," Fray said quietly, his nerves zinging back to life with just the thought of the man. "He killed a deer. Fucking mutilated the thing. He was watching me."

Professor Cane turned that twinkling, unreadable look on Fray. "What did he look like?" Cane asked.

Fray shifted uncomfortably, "He didn't look like anything. I could hardly see him."

"I'm sure it was just one of the neighbors. They do a lot of hunting and trapping. It's barbaric but technically legal on private property. Nothing to worry about."

The prickling sensation at the base of his skull told him Cane was lying. "It seemed like something I should worry about," Fray said, his voice rising. Who hunts in the dead of night? And what hunter would leave a trail of dead animals to rot in the ice and heavy snow? "He followed me back to the cabin."

Cane considered him for a moment before walking to the window and peering through the blinds. He jutted a finger at the window as he turned back to Fray.

"I'll go talk to him," Cane said. The calmness of his voice all but forced the tense muscles of Fray's shoulders to release. "You stay with Roth and make sure he doesn't harm himself. If he doesn't start thrashing again in the next fifteen minutes, then I think you're safe to return to bed. If he starts convulsing or anything of the sort, call down immediately."

It was the least Fray could do after exposing Roth's dirty secret to the entire house.

Fray kept watch long past the fifteen-minute mark. There was something meditative about watching the rise and fall of Roth's chest, the sighed breaths leaving his lips. Fray could look at him without being caught, without having some snide, deprecating reason for his careful perusal of each of Roth's stark features.

He was still in Roth's room when the dawn light broke through the window. In the greenish gray of morning, the guilt from the night before had slipped deeper into the pit of his stomach. He glanced over his shoulder to check for any sign that Roth might stir. Matching bruises had settled into the crooks of his eyes in the night. Somehow, he looked more tired after all that sleep.

Fray rose silently, the knot in his neck casting sharp accusations. His gaze drifted over the small, cluttered space to make sure there were no signs of his presence that Roth might discover when he woke. While there was nothing physical to mark his intrusion, something lingered in the air nonetheless. He could feel the space on the ground where he'd sat, could feel the long-gone indent on the foot of Roth's bed, could feel the weight of his own eyes over every exposed inch of Roth's cream skin. There was a sick dread to that weight, a sick thrill as well. It ached. He thought he might never have hated Roth Heller more.

Solstice

Callan woke to heat. The kind of heat with hands. It pressed its scalding fists into her and made everything heavy and tight and swollen. Her lips were tacked to her teeth, stinging and ready to crack. Her eyes were crusted and nearly swollen shut too, but she peeled them open just enough to see the liturgical banners hanging between the rafters crinkling like candy wrappers in a bonfire. Fire. *Fire.*

She rolled onto her front just as one of the banners drifted down beside her, sending embers skittering across the pine floor. Then one of the rafters broke free. Callan rolled under the nearest pew and stared up at wads of gum and carved initials, her heart crashing against her ribs. Around her, the church moaned and shrieked. As the stained-glass windows lining the room began to shatter, Callan made a cage around her head with her arms, pressing her face into the soot-covered floor.

A whisper of cold passed over her exposed arm. She was sure it was death coming to claim her. Callan cringed away from the relief of it. She didn't want to die. She didn't want to die, and if she did have to die, she refused to let it be in this church that felt like a coffin. Her elbows stung as she dragged herself along the ground beneath the pews, over colorful shards of glass. Her hands were already cut and burnt to shreds; entirely useless.

The cold was back at her ankle, dragging her out of her shelter and into the blazing, blistering aisle of the church. She saw his brown shoes first. The leather was branded with a dark, intricate lattice of flowers and leaves that shined in the firelight. She followed his pristine navy suit up, and up, and up to a pair of curious navy eyes.

"Why are you hiding in your own mind?" The man asked. His voice was as familiar as the whisper of the wind outside Callan's bedroom window in the dead of night.

I'm not hiding. I'm running, she thought, because there was no way words would make it past her heat-swollen lips. The man's eyes narrowed like he heard her perfectly well and didn't like or believe her response.

"That's enough," he said, and the flames fell away, though they remained in his crystalline blue eyes. There was a swooping sensation in Callan's guts as her awareness shifted to the soft chair beneath her. The blazing church was replaced with the cold light of morning filtering through the windows of Professor Cane's office. Cane was watching her in that careful, quiet way of his. Callan wondered how he could maintain such a rigid, still posture for so long. He reminded her of a stalking panther with his pen poised over the journal on his knee.

"That was a good start," he finally said, scratching out a series of notes on the page. "You should think of hypnosis as just another skill that your mind can be trained in. We'll continue working up to deeper and longer sessions throughout the term."

"You were there," Callan said, her voice hoarse. She could still smell the smoke, could still feel the sensation of her arm hairs singeing in the blistering heat. Professor Cane didn't look up from his notes.

"Of course. I was guiding you through the hypnosis, offering suggestions for reflection. You should have continued hearing my voice even when you relaxed into the exercise."

That wasn't what she had meant at all. The truth of it was almost as heavy as the heat in the burning church. He had been there, in the memory. Not just his voice, all of him. She remembered him. When Callan didn't respond he finally set the pen down and glanced up. "Is something troubling you, Lark?"

She shook her head like that might knock him free of the memory. But now that bits and pieces were floating back to her, she couldn't smudge away the dark image of him framed by roaring flames.

"You were there," she said again. She cleared her throat and it tasted like wet, scorched wood. "I knew you before."

A smile ghosted Professor Cane's lips. "That's just a side effect of hypnosis. Because I led you into the memory, your mind has rationalized the event by placing me within it. It will pass with time as more of the repressed memories come back to you to fill in the gaps."

She stretched out her cramping arms. "Is it always this draining?" She asked. It felt like she'd been in a wrestling match for the past hour rather than slumped in a wingback chair. Her skin, even her teeth, ached.

"It can be," he said with a nod. He considered her for a moment. "You were fighting it for quite a while. Practicing our meditation techniques will help with that. Try to come into future sessions with an intention for the process. I can tell that doesn't come naturally."

At this, Callan laughed. "I imagine most people are pretty resistant to manipulation of their memories. Everyone has parts of themselves they don't want to share."

Cane's head tipped from side to side as he weighed her response. "Most of the people who come to me want to understand what's troubling them. They want to access repressed memories so they can link their past together and better know themselves..." He trailed off with a rise of one winged eyebrow.

"I know myself," Callan said.

"Do you? Or have you just been looking past the chaos and

blank spaces inside your mind until it all resembles something you can live with?"

Callan paused to consider his words. "Is there a difference? I think we're all just doing the best we can with what we're given. Is it so wrong to want to endure, even if it means leaving behind parts of yourself along the way?"

He didn't answer her question aloud, but the cold flames smoldering in his eyes said that it was.

"I think you're still burning in that church," he said instead. "I think for some reason you believe you deserved to be there. I think you're afraid of yourself. I think you feel safer pretending all the ugly, unknowable parts of yourself burned in that fire with your mother and father. You've been carrying on like a ghost ever since. You haven't had any significant relationships, you don't have any deep friendships. The more detached you are, the safer.

You can't be detached from reality as an artist. Attachment is the crux of art. Love, attention, *obsession*—all the hallmarks of great art are rooted in attachment. So, are you going to float along in grayscale, feeling and seeing nothing real? Or are you going to make something of that chaos that's been consuming you in brilliant color?"

His face remained still and impassive as he waited for her answer.

"Why didn't I have to write an essay for this retreat, Professor?"

She only knew he heard her by the slight flex of his jaw.

"I didn't apply like the others," she continued, watching him in the careful way he watched her. "You told me I was nominated. Who nominated me? Or was that a lie too?"

He looked at her like his answer was written on her skin. "It wasn't a lie. A professor did nominate you."

"You. The professor was you, wasn't it?"

"Your file was intriguing," he said, reclining in his chair and propping his head up on his fingertips.

Callan's eyes narrowed. "If you're not going to tell me the

truth, I have no reason to give you the same courtesy," she said, getting up from the couch.

"Sit," Cane commanded. She didn't listen. The spark it ignited in Cane's dark eyes sent a thrill through her. "You're asking the wrong questions."

"How could you have known me if I didn't take any of your classes?" Cane's tongue tracked a slow line along the backside of his bottom lip. "Who gave you my file?"

"I took it," he said sharply. "I'm on the board of trustees at every major art school in the country. Those schools are begging me to give their students the opportunity I handed you. And you didn't even apply—" Something in his voice told her this had hurt his pride. She lowered herself to the couch slowly.

"Why would you want *me*?" She demanded.

At this, Cane laughed. He took his glasses off and pinched the bridge of his nose. "I think the better question is, why were you so certain you didn't deserve a spot in the retreat to begin with? Why didn't you try?"

"I was a little busy last semester," she said, fists tightening. "I didn't exactly have the time or the resources to bet everything on an asshole professor."

"I'm sure you were busy," Professor Cane said with a scoff. "With all the wrong things. You've been holding the reins so tight. The classes, the extra credit. It's useless. Nobody will pay you for the A+ you got in Advanced Figures. Nobody is going to hold your hand and show you the way in this world." Frustration was carved into the pucker of his lips, his brows. "If you want a life of art, Callan, you need to start taking it for yourself. Not hoping it will fall into your lap. You're lucky I wanted to give you a chance because not many will. I like your art. I like your story. Now, show me I was right about you."

The ensuing silence inflated inside Callan, filling her with enough hot air to pop herself on. "My father was insane," she said. "Was that in my file?"

A line formed between Professor Cane's eyebrows as he

peeled open the manilla folder beneath his journal. "Paranoid schizophrenia, obsessive compulsive disorder, alcoholism." He adjusted his glasses. "He wasn't insane. He was very sick."

"He hurt people. Children. After he died all sorts of stories came out. Is any of that in my file?"

Professor Cane shook his head slowly, blinking. His lips rolled like he wasn't sure which question to ask. "Did he hurt you?"

A broken laugh wedged its way up Callan's throat. There were tears at the corners of her eyes and she blinked rapidly to clear them before Cane could see. "Not like them, no."

Cane gave Callan his full attention, elbows braced on his knees, his journal abandoned to the side table. Callan thought it was the first time she'd seen him look genuinely interested, all smugness and superiority gone from the lines of his face.

"How did he hurt you?"

If he moved any more, their knees would be touching, a thought that shouldn't have even crossed Callan's mind in the moment but did with a hair-raising thrill.

"There was a cellar in the church. It didn't have any windows or lights. He locked me in there as punishment. If I screamed or made a sound, the time doubled or he brought out the belt. Sometimes both. I learned to be very quiet. He forgot me down there a lot."

"What was he punishing you for?"

Callan lifted a shoulder. "Anything at all."

The ticking of the clock above the door came into focus as Callan watched the rise and fall of Professor Cane's broad shoulders. He eventually tented his fingers in his lap. Callan knew she was only imagining the slight tremor to his fingers, the stiff, mechanical way he moved.

"It must have been a relief when he was gone," he said. Callan's eyebrows inched up her forehead.

"You mean when he burned alive inside his own church, along with my mother?" Callan asked. Her lips formed a halfhearted smirk. "I was a little too distressed to have any sense of relief."

"Did you start the fire?" Professor Cane murmured. His eyes were tracing over her's like he was committing every facet of green, gray and yellow to memory.

Callan blinked. "What?"

"You heard me," he said, shrugging. "Since reading your file the first time, I've been curious. The fire marshal didn't even conduct an investigation. It was summarily ruled an accident and the case was closed. Was it really that simple?"

"Are—" Callan's voice broke and she had half a mind to let it stay that way. There was no accusation in Professor Cane's expression, but that didn't minimize what he was implying. "Are you asking if I committed arson, Professor?"

Another shrug. There was mischief in his expression. "Personally, I think the idea of staring down a monster and making him burn is quite cathartic, poetic even. I'm not here to cast judgment, Callan."

"You mean that theoretically, right? Academically?"

"Sure," he said around a smile. He looked away from her then, and she realized the full effect that his eyes had on her. It was like another kind of hypnosis; a far more dangerous one.

She passed the remainder of the day in an electrified state of procrastination. There were assigned readings for their group discussions she could have been working on, journaling entries that remained unwritten, meditations she had yet to log. But she kept drifting back to her conversation with Professor Cane. She was embarrassed by how much she'd shared, sure, but she was also eager for more. She wanted to see how much she could say, how much of herself she could pour out before him before that carefully constructed mask on his face cracked. The thought of it made every breath hot in her nostrils, made her blood feel effervescent. The thought of being truly seen, truly witnessed, for every dark and awful thing inside herself. It was as intoxicating as it was terrifying.

After the incident with Roth the night before, the house held a current of unease that seemed to be growing like mold in the walls. Every hallway, every room, seemed a little darker, a little smaller, a little colder and damper.

But all that gloom fell away upon entering the kitchen. Hilde had outdone herself, which was saying something considering the never-ending assortment of meals Callan had come to expect from her. This space was piled with enough food to keep them all occupied through the holiday three times over. There were meats, soups, vegetables, and other dishes covering every inch of counter space along with mulled wine and spiced, buttered whiskey. Fairy lights, tea candles, and candelabras were dotted among them, twined with sprigs of balsam, holly, and orange garland. A cedar fire crackled in the adjacent dining room, completing the cozy atmosphere.

"Where's everyone else?" Callan asked. Hilde hummed distractedly, turning to face her from the pecan pie she was working over. She scrubbed at a dusting of cinnamon dotting the bridge of her nose like freckles.

"Oh, I think Roth has been sleeping most of the day. The other two I haven't seen at all," she said, her brow crumpling slightly. She dusted off her hands over the sink before wiping them against her apron. She sighed. "And Ladon, well, I suppose he's still outside getting everything ready for the solstice."

"Outside?" Callan drifted to the window behind the table and peered through the curtain. Snow was falling in fine crystals over the deepening blues of the meadow. The snow was the lightest it had been all day, but it was still falling fast enough to form a thick layer over the porch railing. "We're going out there tonight?"

"Oh, yes, of course," Hilde said, back to her pie. "The bonfire will keep you warm, dear, don't worry. Everyone always has a great time at the solstice party. It's Ladon's favorite tradition."

From Callan's vantage, she couldn't glimpse the fire, but she did catch the occasional shadow being thrown by its light into the shaggy blues of dusk. There was just enough light remaining to illuminate just how frigid it was out there. Icicles dotted the stoop, ice crusted the surface of the snow in the meadow beyond the road. Even the trees looked frigid, painted navy blue against the glowing white caps covering each of their limbs.

"Hey," someone said from the doorway. Callan turned and blinked at the hunched, rough-edged figure. Roth came into the glow of the candles, but it didn't do him any favors. His usually bright eyes were deeply set and swollen, with dark swathes at the inside corners. His white hair was pulled into a messy bun at his nape. His hands were like fluttering birds, never lingering anywhere too long. They messed with his bun, rubbed at his face, swiped over the back of his neck. Callan could almost see the kinetic energy pulsing beneath the pale, freckled skin of his forearms. He crossed the kitchen without making eye contact and slumped into his chair at the dining room table. He put on his hood and pulled his hands into the sleeves of his sweatshirt before using them to create a pillow between his head and the table.

Callan lowered herself into the seat beside him. "Roth," she whispered. Her fingertips skittered over the tablecloth in his direction. He didn't look up, but he flinched away from her advance. "Roth, what happened yesterday?"

One gray eye peeked through the stray hairs that had fallen loose from his bun. His lips wriggled, calling Callan's attention to the dark, fleshy marks on them where it looked like Roth had bitten down hard enough to draw blood. The skin around the marks was chapped and swollen.

"You can tell me, Roth. I can help," she continued. Her hand came forward again, earning her another flinch. She turned away from Roth, placing her palms down on the table. "Sorry," she said.

"We need to get out of here," Roth whispered, his voice like worn-out tires over gravel. Callan kept her gaze forward, watching the darkening meadow for signs of Professor Cane. Behind them, Hilde continued to hum, but Callan got the sense she was observing them.

"Okay," she murmured. Callan didn't want to give Roth any reason to stop talking, so she didn't ask why. "How?" She asked instead, because from where she sat, the world outside looked deadly cold and vastly barren. Even a four-wheel-drive vehicle with chains wouldn't get them out with the road in its current condition.

"I noticed a large shed when we arrived, maybe about a half-mile down the road. It could have a plow truck or a snowmobile. We have to try to get out. If we go soon, we might miss them," he said. He used his shirtsleeve to wipe at his raw nose.

"Miss who?" Callan asked. Roth sat up and turned to her. In the candlelight, the bruises at the corners of his eyes, and the paleness of his skin, made him look all the more ghostly than he normally did.

"When you fell in the water the second time, what did you see before you went in? Was it your parents?"

Callan's face scrunched up. Just the thought of seeing her dead parents in the lake made a swell of anxiety rise from the depths of her stomach.

"No," she said. "No, it was you that I saw." Roth's gaze flicked back and forth over the lace pattern on the tablecloth as the divot between his brows deepened.

"It changes depending on who it sees," Roth muttered to himself. His hands were fluttering restlessly again, tangling fitfully in his hair and clothing. "I wonder how far from the lake it can go. Maybe he's one of them. We would never know. He could be lying about it being able to hurt us. If we run, it could stop us. It's already dark and—"

"Roth. Roth, what are you talking about?" Roth's stormy gray eyes collided with hers.

"That thing out there is coming for us tonight," he whispered, nodding toward the window. Night had all but claimed the day, its jagged fingers creeping out from the shadowy wall of the forest and blanketing the white world in glittering black. The longest night of the year was officially upon them.

Don't Touch

The shadows were restless. The lake churned like a dark sheet over a body in the throes of a night terror. Pale limbs occasionally kicked through the tarry surface in a tangle that thrashed like salmon spawns in overcrowded rivers. This was the normal order of things, this was how it was supposed to be. No more unscheduled visits with the students, no more tricks and taunts in the dead of night. For some reason, this particular batch of students brought out the curiosity in his shadows, and they were eager to play. This brought a smile to his face that didn't feel so falsely human. He tucked it away immediately. He wasn't looking to feel at home in this costume. It itched and bunched at the seams like an untailored suit.

He sent a flicker of magic skittering over the surface of the lake in a glittering cloud of black. The shadows stilled. All those limbs and spines were reduced to four bodies. The crowns of their heads rose until glowing eyes breached the pitchy surface.

"You'll wait for my cue," he said in the language they shared, his mouth curving delicately around the wad of vowels and sharp consonants. "Not a second sooner. No more tricks. There will be order, understood?"

The lake churned in acquiescence. Ladon shoved his hands in his pockets and marched away. The wind was at his front for the trek back to the cabin. It bit at his ears, at the fine point of his nose. He meant to circle the cabin and begin building the bonfire, but the light from one particular window drew him in like a moth. He stepped carefully through the snowdrifts to peek through the opening in Callan's blinds and immediately regretted it. Callan was lying on the bed, wearing long, fuzzy socks, and a baggy sweatshirt that stopped just at the swell of lean thighs.

Every one of the students held their own unnerving, asymmetrical beauty, and Callan was no different. But Callan's pain was prettier than the others. He wanted to be the maestro conducting that pain like the fragile thread of a violin. He wanted to know what Callan's fear tasted like when it was all for him. And that absolutely could not happen. It would not happen. He had a retreat to run, artists to help. He couldn't turn one of them into his plaything. Especially not this one.

His gaze zoomed in on the journal Callan was sketching in, the line of a jaw being shaded with rapturous attention. His breath fogged the glass in a surprised exhale. That was his jaw. Well, his human jaw. The realization sent a tingle of electricity from the base of his skull to the tip of his tailbone. Schrödinger, who was perched beside Callan, hopped onto the dresser to stare accusingly at Ladon through the window. He turned away abruptly and stalked for the shed. He freed a cigarette from his pants pocket and put it to his lips, mostly just for the distraction it provided his hands and mouth, which itched with incessant, near-painful wanting.

He took a long drag. Callan was drawing him. How long had that been going on? Were there other sketches? What did those depict? Another smile cracked his frozen veneer. His mind drifted to all the ways he could punish Callan for breaking his rules. He saw the swell of hips bent over his suit-clad knee as his palm came down to form a pink imprint of him. He took another drag on the cigarette to stave off the craving.

"Absolutely not," he warned himself, tossing the half-smoked cigarette in the snow. "Absolutely fucking not." He arranged the wood from the shed into a towering pyre for the solstice, all the while reminding himself of the many, many reasons why playing with a student was not just a bad idea, but cataclysmically forbidden. This human suit was convincing enough from a distance, but Ladon knew with perfect certainty that all the power coiled neatly under this skin's surface would tear its way free with one touch, one taste. And that was the real problem. He didn't just want to *taste* Callan Lark.

By the time Ladon had finished with preparations outside, showered, and dressed, he could sense the subtle shift in the air of the cabin. A porous fear had wound its way through the halls, the scent layered with the haze of confusion, and viscous, sappy dread. His artists were not so entirely clueless as he might have originally believed. He entered the kitchen with a smile on his face. From the way Fray ducked his head back to his food at the sight of him, Ladon should have checked this particular smile in the mirror. Perhaps it showed a little too much teeth. He tucked it away.

"Good evening," he said. Heller flinched. Callan's fork clattered. Ladon pretended not to notice. There was no room for distractions on a night like the solstice. He took a seat and feigned eating; an art long since acquired. There was a prickle of anticipation at the tips of his shoulders as the others resumed their eating. Unease knotted in his stomach. He made a mental note not to linger in his human form this long again. Human emotions were pesky devils that he had no use for. They only clouded his judgment.

Callan's spoon dropped into the morel mushroom sorbet for the second time.

"I feel strange," Callan said, pressing fingertips into their temples as they began pushing away from the table. "I think I'll go lay—"

"Sit," Ladon commanded. Callan froze under his compulsion.

Mechanically, Callan sat. The others stared at him. In the candlelight, the fear in their eyes was as deep as the lake. Their pupils were blown, reflecting the flicker of the candle flames on the table.

Fang inhaled sharply. "You drugged us," she said, her shoulders rising defensively. Her attention shot to the stairs as if she was calculating whether she could make a run for her room. It took physical effort to keep the smile from creeping over his face again. He hoped she wouldn't run. The thing coiling round and round inside his chest would like that a little too much.

"I gave you each a clinical dose of Psilocybin, as provided for in the waiver you signed," he said, his gaze traveling slowly around the table. "It's been used for millennia to help open the mind. That's exactly what we will be doing tonight."

"Mushrooms? These aren't mushrooms. You're so full of shit," Fray said, his hands fisted around his fork and knife. His gaze kept sliding to Heller down the table. Interesting.

"Clinical doses can be considerably higher than what most people use recreationally," Ladon continued unperturbed. "I have extensive experience with these types of therapies, and I will be monitoring you closely."

"I've never done drugs before," Callan whispered, that obstinate bottom lip quivering along with their voice. Tears pelted down their cheeks in unison and Ladon's chair groaned as he forced his hands under his thighs to keep from moving to catch and taste them. It took most of his inhuman effort to drag his attention back to the others.

"You all came here for a reason," Ladon said, a bit irritably. "My methods work. *These* are my methods."

"This is so fucked," Heller moaned, tugging his head down toward his lap with his hands fisted in the hair at the back of his head, his spine bowing.

This was not how the evening was supposed to begin. Ladon could feel the tug of the shadows, could hear their incessant whispering. He itched at the skin on his nape but found no relief.

"Tonight, you all will confront yourselves whether you feel ready or not," he said. "How we prepare for this trip will determine how that first encounter goes. Your tension, your fear, your anger, have no place here tonight. If you have concerns, we can take them up tomorrow morning. While the shadows are here, you need to use the tools we've been developing to find the stillness within yourselves and let it take over. If you don't..." *If you don't, your monsters might devour you,* his mind filled in helpfully. "You'll have a bad trip."

"I'm already having a bad trip," Fang snapped.

She had both hands braced on the table, her head bent to her chest so her long hair covered her face. Ladon had anticipated that Fang might encounter some bumps in the road. She'd been evasive in their individual sessions, opting instead to interrogate him about June Parker, and was arrogant enough to believe that her tactics were working. They weren't. He saw right through her to the scared little girl underneath her tattooed skin. She had a long way to go before she understood what that little girl needed to heal, and Ladon wasn't convinced she wanted to know. Though he couldn't read minds, he knew that no part of Fang was at the retreat to improve herself or her art.

"Let's move outside," Ladon suggested, rising from the table. "The ascent with mushrooms tends to be smoother when there are calming natural stimuli. Being inside can dampen the senses and cause the visual disturbances to become more pronounced."

Their collective distrust was a skunky, low-hanging perfume. But the psilocybin made their minds all the more open to suggestion, especially suggestions that felt innately aligned with what their bodies knew. Their bodies, like all humans, craved the natural world. That craving was only heightened by the psychedelic.

Outside, night hung heavy on every surface, the shadows deepened by the sparkling, firelit snow. The fire crackled invitingly at the center of the meadow and was surrounded by waterproof tarps piled with blankets and pillows. Ladon sat and the students followed his lead, their attention dragged here and there to the stars winking in the sky, the embers of the fire sizzling, the trees swaying gently with the breeze.

"I feel out of control," Callan said breathlessly, laying down in the blankets with their hands folded over their chest like a corpse.

"Good," Ladon murmured, watching the rhythmic pulsing of the vein in their throat. Callan was safe, even if they were incapable of understanding that fact. "You are."

"Is that supposed to be comforting?" Fang asked from the opposite side of the bonfire, shivering at the edge of the light.

"No," Ladon answered. He pulled another cigarette from his pocket and lit it. Staring at Callan's pulse was beginning to make his fingers tremble. The swell of energy among the shadows did nothing to quell his cravings. "The only comfort you'll find tonight is what you can create for yourself within your own mind. I imagine the same will be true for every night for the rest of this term. Try to relax."

Veronica's laugh was pure acid, but Ladon's attention was pulled to Heller.

"They're coming, aren't they?" He whispered, so quietly it might have been only to himself. He sat with his back to the fire and his knees to his chest, rocking rhythmically. His eyes scanned the line where the snowy field met the black wall of the forest.

"Yes," Ladon answered. The students froze, drugged eyes swimming to him through the haze of whatever they were seeing before. He wondered what he looked like to them now, with so many of the tricks of light peeled away. He looked to Callan expecting horror, terror, disgust. He saw curiosity. Wonder. He inhaled sharply on the cigarette before chucking the remains into the fire.

"They've been waiting in the shadows taunting and teasing you. But when they come now, they will be different. It may be overwhelming at first. But remember: they can't touch you, they can't physically harm you, and you are safe."

"What happens if they do touch us?" Fray asked. He rose to his feet, assuming a defensive posture as he scanned the darkness. His human eyes weren't sensitive enough to mark the deepening of the shadows, the tightening of them. The night was gathering at their backs. A chill worked down Fang's spine and she scooted closer to the fire.

If they touch you, you're already dead, he answered mentally. "They won't," he said out loud. He wouldn't allow it, and his shadows would never try it. He might not have had the power to eradicate the shadows completely, but he could make their existence extremely unpleasant if they fell out of line. He kept them well fed, they kept politely to the lake unless invited in.

A jagged gasp cut the quiet night in two. First Callan, and then the others, stumbled to their feet.

"They're here," Ladon said calmly.

At the place where the fire met the night, a sentry stood. What Ladon saw was not what any of the students would be seeing. He saw the shadows for what they truly were, which was not as terrifying as what they could pretend to be. What they were was the leftover stuff of souls long since returned to the earth, the pieces that could not be taken from this world. Everything ugly, everything evil, everything wrong. It tugged at those very qualities in each of his students like a frenzied, inelegant puppeteer.

"Who are all these people?" Roth demanded, kicking himself closer to the fire.

"I don't know, Mr. Heller. Who are they?" Ladon asked. It sounded like a taunt, but it wasn't. Ladon couldn't see Roth's shadows any more than Roth could see what Ladon saw around the fire. Roth squinted into the dark, all the while backing away from it. Ladon's attention dragged to Callan who was frozen in place, mouth forming a small "o" shape. Callan was the only one of the students who had crept forward, staring into the dark curiously, a finger coming up as if to touch the shadow before them.

"Don't touch," Ladon said. Callan's hand fell away, head swiveling to look at Ladon. Though Callan's face was mostly shadow, he saw roaring flames dancing in their eyes. The hair framing Callan's face lifted outward, as if by a static charge. Then, with a violent tug, Callan was being dragged across the snowy field.

What Comes By Night

The fire multiplied in geometric patterns the longer Callan kept her eyes open. The flames pulsed green, purple, and pink, vining in every direction. When she blinked, they went back to normal. She let herself stare until her eyes were dry and burning. The patterns the light made, the way everything seemed built out of complex, geometric configurations, it all made perfect sense in Callan's mental state. Everything felt right. Including the man at her side, who was far less man than he had been inside.

Callan stared at him with the same rapt attention she had given the flames. He was looking out over the dark field while the flames danced playfully, catching every unnatural angle of him. Even the glittering, bouncing air particles seemed to avoid the outline of him, which was heavy with a dark aura that Callan couldn't believe she hadn't noticed before. And his eyes—when he turned back to face her, she swore they were lit from within. The blue was too bright, too cold, consuming her.

"They're here," he said. Callan registered the change immediately, the way the air was charged with their presence. She turned and faced a single figure at the edge of the fire's light where the deep shadows pressed inward. She blinked and it was closer, though she knew it hadn't really moved.

Skeletal fingers peeked out from the sleeve of the creature standing before her. Those fingers mirrored the movement of her hand as she lifted it to push back the hood hiding the thing's face. For some reason, it felt important to know what it looked like behind the charred, violet liturgical vestment it wore.

"Don't touch," Professor Cane said from beside her, and she froze. His voice was so much more in this mind state. It crawled beneath her skin, demanding every cell of her attention. She turned to him, taking in first the glowing, icy blue of his eyes, and then the aura that surrounded him, as dark as the space between stars. *This* was Ladon Cane. Not the professor, not the therapist. This. She ached to touch him to be sure he was real. He looked far from it. But she didn't get her chance. In a split second, those preternaturally glowing eyes of Cane's widened then narrowed. His hand lurched toward her. Then all the lights in the world blinked out, the lights of his eyes last.

There was no saying how long the absence of everything lasted. It seemed to stretch and multiply in her mind the way an old, unfamiliar house doubles in size with the descent of night. The first thing she registered in the darkness was the murmur of wind through high grass. She blinked and the darkness gave way. She was back at the church; her father's church. She sat on the warm clay earth so her eyes were just barely above the golden puffs at the top of every blade of grass. They swayed gently, creating a sea of movement that frothed in mustard and marigold tones with accents of burgundy and rust. From there, she could see the church's stark white façade, the streaks of black char running up from gouged-out windows along with the tarry flames occasionally licking outward from the openings. It was too quiet for such a violent burning. There wasn't even the distant howl of sirens yet. The dirt road leading toward town was a flat, gray snake twisting through the autumn-kissed fields with not a single car in sight.

Rising, Callan realized she wasn't alone. The cloaked figure that had met her in the high alpine field was lying on its front on the ground before her, barely moving. With the sun high above, she realized that the thing's cloak was riddled with holes where embers had singed through. It reached a hand forward with agonized slowness and Callan could make out the stark white bone and fleshy tendons revealed by its burns.

Her attention snagged on the church again; the wide-open door with thick, black smoke pouring through. It looked like the spewing maw of a dragon. And this *thing* lying before her had been spit out by it. Instantly, she knew who it was; why he was determined to reach her, even burned to the bones.

She backed away on shaking legs, flinching every time it moved to lift its head or extend its charred hand. No part of her wanted to see its face now. When she was a safe distance back, she turned and ran. The field surrounding her childhood home had always felt like a vast, golden ocean. Now, it became one. The brackish water was to her shins by the time she stopped. It kept rising around her, overtaking the grasses. She watched the rust-colored water pass her knees, her thighs. Turning, she tried to run back toward the church, but the grass underfoot had formed a web around her ankles that only tightened and tugged when she struggled.

Relax, a voice said. Callan could feel the word spoken against the shell of her ear. It sent a cascade of goosebumps down the side of her neck. She jolted around to find the source. But the marshy world around her was as still and barren as it had always been. Her thighs burned as she kicked her way through the rising water.

You have to give in to it, Callan, let it take you, that same voice said again, somewhere within her mind, harsher now. She recognized it, even if she didn't have a name for it. A whimper passed her lips as the water overtook her shoulders. It felt like a vice around her chest, squeezing the life from her. Cold. It was the coldest thing she'd ever felt. Already, her legs were only working in fits and spurts, the muscles cramping. She was only able to keep her head above for a couple of seconds at a time before she got a mouth full of silty water and grass seeds. The water made a tomb around her body. It forced her arms to her sides and locked her legs in place. *Give in,* that voice whispered again. Something gripped her throat. Her mouth popped open. The water rushed in.

Then with a swift pounding between her shoulder blades, the water rushed out in a violent retch. Her swimming vision came into focus on the sopping-wet rug beneath her cheek. She rolled onto all fours in time for more water to come up, dredging up the last of dinner from the depths of her stomach. The hand beating at her back stilled when her retching subsided to gasping breaths. A trail of spit clung to her bottom lip as frigid water dripped from the tips of her hair.

Hands snaked under her stomach and pulled her up against a body so warm it made every frozen, waterlogged cell in her body tingle. She wanted to protest the way it made her rattled brain swim again, but all that came out was a moan.

"I've got you," Cane said, cradling her gingerly. Alarm zinged through Callan's skull and down her spine. Her body tensed all at once. Professor Cane set her down on the lip of a large jacuzzi tub. Her head swiveled slowly, taking in with muted awareness the soft browns and deep grays of his bathroom, lit only by the candles edging the tub and the warm fire glow coming from the open doorway leading to his bedroom. He helped her out of her sopping boots and her toes curled in the rug as he checked the temperature of the bath water. He lowered to his haunches so his eyes could meet hers. "Clothes on or off?" He asked. Callan's thoughts tried and failed to swim through the syrupy stuff that made up her mind. His hand wrapped around her knee, sending a pulse of warmth through her. "Your lips are blue, Cal. We need to get you warmed up. I won't look if you want to get out of these," he said pinching the material of her drenched pants.

Her head bobbed. Professor Cane's gaze scanned over her features before he too nodded. He sighed as he rose. His clothes were dripping the same as Callan's. If he was uncomfortable or cold, he didn't show it. He walked out of the bathroom but left the door to the bedroom open.

The cold in Callan's hands made them tight and useless. It took four tries to release the clasp of her pants. She was panting, her muscles cramping, by the time she shimmied the wet pants to her knees.

"If you need help, I'm here," Cane said hesitantly from around the corner. But Callan had just gotten the pants over her heels and peeled off her shirt. She lowered herself into the hot water, and with every inch, the fog lifted.

Professor Cane came back into the bathroom in a fresh pair of sweats, his chest bare. Without a word, he moved her sopping clothes to the bin in the corner and then sat on the mat beside the tub, pulling his knees to his chest to mime Callan's position. His eyes burned into hers. They flicked down to the cross on her chest and back.

"Where are the others?" She asked in a hoarse whisper. Professor Cane's face was so close she could see the colors of his eyes shifting like the lake she'd just been drowning in. Surely, it was just the comedown from the mushrooms making them churn like that.

"In their rooms, resting," he said. His throat worked as his eyes continued to burn. "You were in the water for a while."

"The water?" Cane's eyes pinched at the corners. So, it hadn't just been a nightmare produced by her bad trip. She had been in the lake again. Maybe there was a death wish written into her DNA. "How long is a while?" She asked, tightening her hold around her knees. The unease itching at the underside of her skin told her she might not want to know. Cane's shimmering eyes told the same story. His jaw flexed; the movement caught in deep shadows by the candlelight.

"The lake is a trap door," he said. He picked up the shampoo bottle perched beside the faucet, poured an oversized dollop into his palm, and looked up at her with a question etched in the tight set of his eyes. She ducked her head to give him better access and he began massaging her scalp, starting at the space just above her nape where a tension headache had started to brew. "It can let things out, like the things you saw tonight, and the others that have been haunting the woods since you all arrived. But it's rarely in the business of taking living things in. You seem to be an exception."

"Why didn't I drown?" She asked. Cane turned on the faucet and rinsed the shampoo from her scalp before proceeding to lather in conditioner. The muscle in his jaw ticked.

When she looked up at him expectantly, he shook his head, his eyes far off. "I don't know," he answered.

"Why hasn't it touched the others?"

He cleared his throat. "I don't know," he repeated, quieter this time. He didn't meet her eyes but applied pressure to her head so he could wash out the conditioner in the stream of water.

"What do you know?" She demanded. He had dragged them there for some kind of experiment that even he didn't seem able to understand or control. He had drugged them and left them vulnerable to these creatures without knowing what they were capable of or what they wanted. He looked just as frightened as she felt.

He hesitated before he answered her. "I know that they will be back," he said finally. "I know that they want you desperately, and they want far more than what they got tonight. I know that their desires, their motivations, are simple, animal. And I know that you cannot stay here another night."

Those last words fizzled in the space behind her sternum where the heat had been. Though her knees were already to her chest, she folded further around herself. Didn't she want to leave? Wasn't she relieved at the prospect of avoiding another night of torment from whatever monsters haunted the lake? The answer in the pit of her stomach didn't feel like a yes. She felt the warmth of Cane's hand at the back of her head before the sting and pressure of him gently pulling her back by the hair. His eyes bore down into hers.

"You want me to leave," she said.

"I *need* you to leave," he corrected, his voice straining. "I can't focus, I can't do what I need to do here when it's you they're after. I won't let them have you. I need to know that you are safe."

"But you would let those monsters in the lake have the others?" She asked, gaping at him. At this, Cane froze, his brows knitting as his eyes solved the riddles tangled in her own.

"I suppose that makes me your monster," he said, the hold on her hair tightening infinitesimally. "How lucky for you that I'm so much worse than all the others."

"What if I don't want to leave?" She asked, her lips a hairsbreadth from his. His answering laugh was a harsh whisper of breath over them.

"You've been tormented by monsters capable of transforming themselves into your worst nightmares, you've nearly drowned three times, and yet you want to stay and see more? It's too dangerous. I can't protect you and keep the others safe."

"I have nowhere to go," she said. The words ached in her throat. "I have nothing to do. No one to be with. You were right about me before. I always thought painting was my therapy but since being here I've realized it's a way for me to hide. Nothing in my art has been honest. It's all mimicry and self-indulgence. I want to know what this version of me can do. I'm not frightened of the things in that lake, I'm frightened of what might happen if I have to go back to the life I left. That skin doesn't fit me anymore, and I've yet to find a new one..." By the time she trailed off, she was barely whispering. Tears were prickling her eyes and running from her nose, but she held Professor Cane's gaze.

His throat worked, but he didn't speak. He held up an oversized towel for her to step into. She did so, still held captive by the searching look in his eyes. His hands traveled slowly over the outside of the towel, drying her off while sending small electrical currents along the paths of her nerves. His hands slowed as he reached the bottom edge of the towel, but picked up their pace again as he swiveled her to dry off her back. Callan hadn't realized how jagged her breathing had become. Suddenly, Cane's hands froze. His slow, rhythmic breathing faltered. Fingertips feathered over her back in a pattern she knew well. She turned abruptly.

"What happened to you?" He demanded.

"I told you before," Callan said, tugging the towel tight around her and still feeling woefully exposed. "I was burned in the church fire." Cane grasped her arm and made to spin her around again, but she stood firm, returning the hard set of his features.

"Those aren't just burns, Callan," he said, softly, his voice taut as a bowstring. It set the small hairs on her body on edge. "Who?" That one word held so much weight.

"You know who," she said, averting her eyes. He grabbed her chin and tilted it up so his eyes could drown her again. That shadowy aura was back, peeking over his shoulders in smoky tendrils. When Callan's attention went to it, it disappeared. Cane tugged the towel tighter around her and led her into the bedroom. When she steered toward the door, he made a low, disapproving sound. It almost sounded like a growl.

"Not a chance. You're not leaving my sight." His arm formed a cage at her back as he steered her toward the bed where her pajamas were already waiting. Once she was deposited, he stepped away and sat on the other side of the bed.

She gawked at him. "What about those boundaries you were so insistent on, Professor?" His gaze slid her way, but he didn't defend himself. "And what makes you think I feel safer in here with you than out there with the others?"

Some of the glow slipped back into his irises creating a stark contrast with his pupils. "I don't really care if you feel safer. You *are* safer in here, so you'll stay in here. The others weren't dragged by their hair through the woods and tossed in a lake that should have killed them."

A fair point. One she still was having trouble wrapping her head around. She crossed her arms. "What did happen to the others?"

Cane sighed as he gave her his back again. She dropped the towel and changed. "They stayed near the fire. They interacted with the shadows for a short period of time and then the shadows retreated to the lake. They had the exact experience each of them needed to have."

"Do you control them? The shadows?" She asked. Now that the shock was peeling away, all the questions began bombarding her at once. She could tell from the tightness in Professor Cane's face that she wouldn't get all the answers she wanted, but it wouldn't be for lack of trying. If the look on his face was meant to deter her, he wasn't succeeding.

"No," he grumbled. Callan settled back against her pillow, facing him. He leaned over her and blew out the candle on her bedside table. "They act on impulse. I can destroy them, but new shadows will always form to take their place."

"But they can't travel far from the lake?"

"Right," he said. "Their influence wanes with distance and daylight. As does mine." Callan was suddenly reminded of Cane's strange behavior on their flight to Montana; the way he fell into unconsciousness the second the plane had lifted from the tarmac.

"Are there other lakes like that one?"

"Many," Cane answered, blowing out his candle. With the candles out, and the fire reduced to winking embers, darkness covered them in a staticky blanket. The dark made Callan aware of her skin, of her breathing.

"Did we lose electricity?" She asked, just to get rid of the static growing louder and louder between them. She knew the prickling, warm flood of anticipation it was making her feel was entirely one-sided.

"Yes. The shadows absorb a lot of energy on nights like these."

As the silence stretched, the inches of distance between their bodies felt charged. Heat bloomed beneath Callan's skin, uncomfortable enough to make her toss and turn, seeking a position where Cane's nearness wasn't so glaringly apparent. She should have known it would be impossible. And the friction of her skin against the sheets, the tangling of them between her legs, only made matters worse. She kicked her legs into the cold, untouched swathes of sheets at the foot of the bed, only for that incessant prickle to resume moments later. After what might have been an hour of restless tossing, Callan made up her mind to return to her room. Cane hadn't moved an inch in the time they'd been laying there, and she could hear the deep, rhythmic hush of his breathing. She moved to sit. A hand shot out and grabbed her forearm. She yelped.

"I wouldn't run if I were you," Cane said. His voice was tight, betraying that he hadn't been sleeping in the time they'd been lying there either. "I've practiced more restraint than I possess tonight where you're concerned. If you run, I will chase you. And I will catch you."

His words sent a thrill through her, but she relaxed into his touch. "I wasn't running," she said. "I can't sleep here, next to you." His hand disappeared from her arm. The absence burned.

"You're afraid of me," he said flatly. Callan turned to face him, though his face was veiled in shadow.

"I should be," she said. Whatever he was, it wasn't human. She lifted a shoulder, her loose sweater falling free of it. "And yet, I've been laying here wondering how your skin tastes, how it would feel against mine." Her fingers covered her lips to keep anything else from spilling free. She made to leave the bed again.

A low, frustrated sound rumbled in Cane's throat. The shadows in the room gobbled up the last light from the fire as Cane captured her from the edge of the bed. His arms caged her torso, tucking her flush against so much hot, bare skin she was dizzy on it.

"What are you doing to me?" He murmured against her temple. His nose made a trail from her temple to the nape of her neck as he inhaled slowly, his chest swelling into her back. He groaned and the sound vibrated in Callan's chest. She whimpered as his hand trailed down her hip, roughly tugging her back from the edge of the bed so every part of her was aligned with him. There was nothing soft about the press of his body to hers.

"You don't need to do this for my benefit. I won't fall apart without your attention." Her voice was so small it was eaten up by the roaring gallop of her heart.

The hand still at her hip seared her skin through the thick sweats she wore. It tightened as Cane tugged her closer. He rocked against her and she gasped. "Does this feel like pity?" He asked, repeating the motion. His hand slipped up to her chin, tugging it to the side so she was forced to look at him. His features were equal parts beautiful and terrifying in the dark, the pinpricks of glowing blue in the depths of his eyes the only light left in the room. "If I was acting selflessly, you'd be alone in this bed and I'd be guarding the door from the outside. I am not a selfless man, Callan. Apparently, I'm not a strong one either."

Despite the heat pooling in her stomach and Cane's tight grip on her chin, she shook her head. "You're toying with me," she rasped. He didn't crave her the way she craved him. This was just part of the game he'd been playing with her since the very beginning. It was a cruel game; one she couldn't play when her nerves were so frayed. She made to pull away from him again. Every inch of her was strung taut. If she didn't run now, he'd really see the effect he had on her, and there would be no coming back from that embarrassment. Already, she could feel that betrayal of her own body in the warmth between her legs. She pressed them together tightly.

Cane chuckled, a sound that vibrated low in his chest. "Toying with *you*? No. It's you that is the torment." His fingers wound through her hair and tugged, forcing her fluttering eyelids to open. She had to bite the inside of her lip to keep a sound from scraping out. He swiftly freed her lip from the hold of her teeth with the pinch of his thumb and forefinger. "I can taste you from across a room. Every emotion, every impulse. I didn't think there was anything sweeter than your fear. But this?" He ground against her again, groaning into the skin between her neck and shoulder. "I want to eat you alive."

Callan strained against him, baring her neck. A soft cry broke her lips, a fissure line in a dam. His mouth came down on her, hot and demanding. His fingers dug into the skin at the top of her thighs, her hips. His teeth dragged across her bottom lip followed by his tongue. He explored her with deliberate, near-painful restraint, seeming completely unbothered. Only the hard press at her back gave him away.

Eventually, he pulled away, but her heart continued crashing against her ribs, tearing at the seams that held her together.

"Not yet," he said, his fingers fluttering over her lips. Callan's heart tripped, sputtered, began beating in reverse. She tipped her chin into her chest and did everything she could to slow her erratic breathing. Cane's fingers gripped her cheeks. "You can't hide from me," he said. "I know what you want, Callan. I also know what you need. And tonight, you need sleep. Someday soon, I'll show you what I need."

The promise sank deep into the dark waters within her, dragging her along with it. Sleep poured into the hollow places he'd made within her, leaving her heavy and weightless at once. She drifted off with his lips at her nape and his taste still stuck on her tongue.

Phantom Threads

Veronica did not like drugs. She needed the weed to function, to keep her head on straight, to leave the house in the morning. It kept her level and her mind quiet. It didn't even give her a buzz anymore. But magic mushrooms were another story. The ascent was like being strapped to a rocket ship, the g-forces convincing her head that it could not, under any circumstances, move from the pillow. Even if every cell in her body wanted her to run.

"They're here," Professor Cane said. Veronica tightened her grip on the blankets beneath her, bracing herself for impact. Nearby, she heard Roth moan into a pillow. Her eyes popped open and the night sky above her was vast and deep, with dusty clouds of pale pink and green and purple tucked among the pulsing stars. Like the entirety of the cosmos belonged to one synchronized set of lungs, and it tugged her along with each inhale. Veronica felt tears leaking from the corners of her eyes, cooling before they dripped into her ears.

Couldn't all that vast space make room for her? Would she finally find a place she fit out there? Beneath the enormity of the worlds outside of her, Veronica became more aware of the world within her, the world that held her. Something tugged incessantly. It began inside her chest, pulling at one of the many stray wires that had long since been severed from the person on the opposite end. It tugged and tugged, even when she reminded it that there was nothing on the other end to be tugged toward. Her heart was full of phantom threads that needed constant reminding.

Commotion on the other side of the fire stirred Veronica's attention. She dragged herself upright, stars spinning in her vision as the universe pressed with near-equal force against her chest. As she blinked the pulsing colors, she made out the shape of two figures disappearing into the dark hold of the forest edging the clearing. A guttural roar hung on the night air long after it should have died away. Her head pivoted, eyes colliding with Roth's.

"The Professor's gone," he whispered. "The shadows took Callan."

Veronica's stomach somersaulted. That wasn't possible. Cane had said the shadows couldn't touch them, couldn't hurt them. Veronica stared into Roth's face, seeing the same fear reflected there. Slowly, Roth's gaze slid to something beyond Veronica's shoulder, his face draining of color.

"What is it?" She hissed. Roth shook his head, slowly at first and then so fast his brain must have been sloshing around in his skull. His chin fell to his chest and he covered his eyes with quivering fingers.

"No," he moaned. "No, no, no, no, no."

The pain in his voice flicked a switch inside Veronica. Bits and pieces of herself came back to her. She scooted toward Roth, rubbing a hand over his arm.

"It isn't real," she told him. "None of this is real. It can't hurt you." Even if it was a lie, it was worth believing. Roth dared a glance through his fingers and cried out.

"Don't," Veronica said. "Just watch the flames. They'll get bored eventually." She continued to rub a hand over his arm, ignoring the twinge in her heart as that thread tugged and tugged. "It isn't real," she said again, this time to herself.

Beside them, Fray's feet kicked as he backed toward the fire, blurting a string of curses.

"Don't look at them," Veronica yelled. Fray's face contorted as he shut his eyes tightly. "If we don't give them what they want, they'll go away eventually," she said. "Think of a good memory. Anything. Pretend we're somewhere else."

The daydream came to Veronica easily. It was late summer in New York; she was eating green tea mochi in the park. June was there because June was in all the good memories.

"What if Cane doesn't come back?" Roth asked from beside her, cutting off the memory.

"We should get back inside," Fray said. His spine and shoulders were rounded defensively as if he expected the shadows to grab him any second.

"I don't think we should leave the firelight," Veronica countered.

"We have to eventually," Roth said.

The persistent warning in Veronica's gut told her to wait until the sun rose.

Minutes crept by slowly as they each kept their attention on the embers in the fire. The shadows were clever, using the wind to toy with a stray lock of hair, or tugging at the blankets they sat on. But they never touched, just as Cane promised.

"Maybe they physically can't come in the light," Fray mused. "What if we made a lantern of one of the branches from the fire and ran for the side door?"

Veronica glanced toward the door. It was so close. But the swaths of snow between the fire and that door accordioned in the dark. A shadow stepped into her eyeline. Her heart turned over and over like the engine of an old, frozen car. She couldn't make out its face, but that thread in her chest was pulled so taut it threatened to drag her heart out through her throat.

At that moment, a screech peeled through the forest. It continued to rise in volume for several agonizing seconds before cutting off with an abrupt gurgle. The sound should have set every creature in the forest running, but Veronica knew nothing with half-decent survival instincts would ever stray this close to Pitch Lake to begin with. They were the only ones foolish enough to linger with these monsters, Dr. Ladon Cane the worst among them.

From beside her, Veronica heard Roth murmur, "They're leaving. She followed his gaze to the twinkling snowdrifts in the clearing beyond. He was right. The shadows were slinking back to the forest, back to Pitch Lake. Either Cane had been successful in saving Callan from them, or they were having a feast. The shadows' movements were disjointed, almost mechanical. Their forms seemed to change as they progressed, their bodies hunching forward and eventually falling to all fours. By the time they reached the tree line, there was nothing remotely humanoid about them. They were little more than moving pools of shadow.

"Let's get inside," Fray said, pushing to his feet. He ushered them toward the house, his eyes never leaving the tree line as they shuffled to the side door. They were midway there when Roth gripped her upper arm and she screamed.

"Sorry," he whispered, dropping his hand. The dark woods seemed to grow denser with the sound of her scream. Veronica rushed through the side door and slammed it shut behind her.

Hours later, there was still no sign of Cane or Callan. Veronica, Fray, and Roth had barricaded themselves in Roth's room, which had the fewest and least accessible windows. They passed around a very expensive-looking bottle of bourbon pilfered from the very back of the supply closet. The floor was littered with candles they'd stolen from nearby rooms, chasing off every last shadow.

"I can keep watch if you want to sleep," Fray said, though he seemed to be only speaking to Roth. Roth didn't respond; he just shook his head and took another long drag of the bourbon. Veronica wobbled to her feet.

"I'm going to grab the blankets from my room," she said.

She didn't give them a chance to disagree. Her room was two

doors down. She took the opportunity to use the bathroom and slapped some cool water over her face. A banging sound came from the old water pipes, but when she walked back into her bedroom, it grew louder. She walked to her door, but the hallway was empty, silent. She turned, staring at her covered window.

Don't look, she told herself. It would be her undoing and she knew it. But the banging continued as she gathered up her blankets. She was just about to walk back to Roth's room when the urge overpowered her. She lifted the dark curtain away from the window and peered through.

There was a man in the snow below. He looked up, a snarl curling his lips. He saw her and his face instantly became another.

It was June. She was here, just as Veronica knew she would be. She wasn't dead, or missing, or gone. She hadn't run from Veronica, or been taken from her. She was, impossibly, right here. Veronica's fingers shook as she worked the clasp on the window. It gave with a sharp crack as pieces of paint came off the window pane.

She leaned over the edge, feeling the heat from the house collide with the cold night. "June?" She whispered loudly.

June's face was all pink cheeks and crinkly eyes as she smiled up. "V," she called back, waving both mittened hands. "Come down here, there's something I want to show you."

Veronica's stomach knotted. "Have you been here this whole time? Why didn't you come back to school?"

"Of course, I've been here," she answered, her smile going lopsided. "This place. It's worth it. You have to see it to believe it, V. It's worth giving in."

"What do you mean?"

June cartwheeled her arms in a move that insisted she would have to come down to find out. Veronica glanced around the surrounding woods for signs of the shadows that had hunted them before. But it was only June.

"What about those... things?" She asked. June stilled.

"What things?"

Veronica didn't hear Roth enter the room behind her. He put a hand on her shoulder and she yelped, ducking back inside.

"Thank god, you're alright. We got worried," Roth said. Fray lingered at the door with his arms crossed, his eyes scanning the room for a reason to bolt.

"June is here," she blurted, hitching a thumb at the window. "The girl that came here from Brighton two years ago. My friend. She never came home. But she's safe. She's right outside." Roth leaned out the window while Veronica went to her closet to put on thicker layers so she could go out to June.

"Jesus H. Roosevelt Christ, Fang," he said, banging his head on the window in his rush back inside. He rubbed at his forehead.

"What?" She asked, turning with a scarf and gloves in hand.

"*Not* June," Roth said, his eyes wide as he pointed at the window. Veronica dashed to look out. June waved and beckoned her to come down.

"Yes, it is," she said. "She's right there."

Roth's eyebrows shot up. "Right there? Like, right by that pine tree?" He pointed. Fray came to get a look as well. A sharp exhale punched out of him before he turned around and marched from the bedroom, muttering curses the whole way. "I don't see June, Veronica. I see a boy with marsh weeds stuck in his wet hair and blue, drowned skin. That," he said, jabbing a finger at the window. "That is a shadow."

"No," Veronica said, shaking her head. She looked down at June again. It was *June*. All four feet and eleven inches of her. The shadows were meant to scare her, to dredge up all her worst fears. But June was everything good. June was her whole reason for living.

Roth sighed, his gaze flicking out the window and back. His eyes were sunken and the grays had become flat and still. "I promise you, it isn't her. Now, please, come back to my room. It's safer if we stick together."

Veronica cast one last, long glance out the window. Her friend looked cold in the snow, but the hope on her face lit her up from the inside out. Veronica pressed her hands to the glass.

"She's trying to get you to come outside, right? She's pretty desperate, too," Roth said at her shoulder. "If she was here, if she was real, she'd come inside, wouldn't she?"

"Come inside, June," Veronica called down. "You've got to be freezing. Come to the door and I'll let you in." The smile on June's face wobbled as she stepped backward, deeper into the hold of the night.

"See?" Roth said. "It's just an illusion."

Veronica swallowed thickly before turning away. She heard Roth force the window closed behind her and draw the curtains. A chill worked through her at the thought of leaving June in the snow. It wasn't right. She belonged wherever June was, even if that meant dying of hypothermia in a haunted, snow-hushed forest. Even if it meant drowning in the lake.

"If it's really her, she'll come back in the morning," Roth said, winding an arm around her shoulders and guiding her down the hall to his room.

"The boy you saw down there, with the weeds in his hair… is he dead?" She asked. She was desperate to know.

"Yes, he's gone. He's been gone for a long time."

Veronica's throat ached. "Do you think they're all dead, the things the shadows show us?" They'd reached Roth's room where Fray was pacing in slow, wide circles.

"No," Fray said, shaking his head at the floor. "Not everything they show us is dead."

"How do you know?" Veronica asked, crossing her arms tightly. He paced to the window to steal a glance outside. His shoulders stiffened before he dropped the blinds back into place. He wet his lips, his gaze pouring over Roth like he wasn't convinced he was real.

"I just do."

Keeping a Secret

Callan's fingers roamed through miles of cool sheets. Her eyes opened to her empty room. Light streamed through the blinds at an unfamiliar angle. Shame settled deep in her bones as the previous evening washed over her. She pushed herself up the headboard, clutching her aching head.

The cold floorboards creaked with disuse as she crept into her bathroom. Callan hardly recognized her reflection. Her short hair was poking up at all angles, the skin around her mouth pink and raw, lips swollen. But there was something else. There was a shine to the green of her irises and the smudges at the corners of her eyes were mysteriously gone.

She peeled back the edges of her sweater to see if there was any evidence of him on her skin. Of course, not. Cane was meticulous. He wouldn't leave a mark on her. He probably did this with a student every year. Maybe more than one.

Returning to her reflection in the cool fluorescent lighting, she could almost believe it had all been a hallucination. But when she turned her head, she smelled his lingering scent. It was faint but undeniable. By the time she'd pulled on a heavy sweatshirt and clipped back her unruly hair, she'd inhaled enough of him to be in a fabulously foul mood. She marched toward the kitchen, determined to drown all her senses in coffee, fat, and sugar.

The kitchen was empty except for Hilde, who was wiping down the countertops with a rag, humming along to old jazz Christmas music, and Schrödinger, who was cackling for any scraps she had to offer.

"Oh, you're up," Hilde said, sliding a mug Callan's direction. "Everyone else is already upstairs for the lecture."

Callan looked at the clock and blanched. "Shit." She bumped her hip trying to sidestep the island, managing to spill coffee down her front and scalding her fingers with it. "How long have they been up there?"

"Maybe twenty minutes," Hilde said with a shrug. "Ladon said to tell you to rest and that you're dismissed from the lectures this morning."

"Of course, he did," Callan grumbled. Professor Cane could dismiss her all he liked, but he couldn't send her home. The deep timbre of his voice in the hall sent a shiver of recognition down her spine. Every ounce of bravado she'd felt before vanished as she halted at an unfamiliar door. Before she could reach for it, it swung open on creaking hinges. Then Cane was looking at her. Well-rested, calm, and characteristically academic in his midnight blue blazer and charcoal chinos. Callan had the urge to punch him in the face for looking so unaffected by the events of last night.

"Good morning," he said. Callan tugged at her collar as she brushed past him. In her distraction, she hadn't realized that this wasn't their usual lecture room. It was the studio. It smelled oddly sterile, but that wasn't much of a surprise after weeks, possibly months of disuse. She made her way to an open workstation and sat, ignoring the urge to rearrange the supplies in front of her.

"Now, as I was saying, there's absolutely nothing that I can tell you about form and technique that you haven't already learned from artists far more skilled than me," he said. His practiced, appraising gaze shifted to each of them in turn. "I'm not here to teach you. I'm not here to tell you how or what to paint. I'm—"

"I'm not painting a fucking thing until you tell us what the hell happened last night and why," Fray said through his teeth. His fingertips were blanched white from how tightly he gripped his desk.

"I'd be happy to address any questions after class, Mr. Fray," Cane replied coolly as if Fray was simply asking about an answer on an exam.

"What are you?" Veronica demanded, the question more of an accusation. "And what do those things want? I saw—"

"You took my meds and then drugged us," Roth said, rising to his feet. Callan hunched over her mug of coffee as the lecture descended rapidly into a shouting match. She flinched under the volume at this hour.

In all the times Callan had read the course packet before arriving, the seemingly innocuous liability release about Dr. Cane prescribing and administering medications had always conjured images of flu medications or antihistamines. Not psychedelics. "It was in the contract," she said hesitantly into her hands.

"Yeah, sure it was in the contract," Veronica retorted. "I just thought that meant the good doctor might slip us the occasional Valium for a panic attack. Not drug us and feed us to his fucking monster children." Callan couldn't argue there.

Professor Cane watched the four of them like he was watching paint dry. After waiting for any more outbursts, he asked, "Are you done?"

Roth had his fists planted on his desk, his shoulders hunched around his ears, breathing heavily.

"No," he said. "What happened to her? Where did you take her?"

Every eye swiveled to Callan. She choked on the coffee already in her mouth. "What happened to you?" Roth turned the question on her, now. The usually placid silver of his irises was a violent, churning storm of grays. She wondered if he'd slept at all.

Callan's gaze dragged to the Professor. His face gave nothing away. A single eyebrow arched.

So much for Cane's story about them resting the night before. She let go of her coffee, snaking her arms into the sleeves of her sweater. "One of them dragged me to the lake. And Professor Cane got rid of it."

"He got rid of it," Fray repeated. He turned back to Cane. "Then why the hell don't you get rid of the rest of them?"

"Because I believe there is symbiosis in structured interactions with them," Cane said. He tore his glasses off, massaging the bridge of his nose. "And because I can't." Without looking up, he gestured toward the windowless wall. "Those shadows will continue to exist and regenerate no matter how many times I destroy them. Souls pass through this plane every second of the day, leaving behind what they cannot take with them for me to tend. The shadows present as whatever evokes the most visceral, emotional response. A familiar face could just as easily be the creak of a branch, a voice on the wind, the shadow of a predator. They feed on what they are. And what they are is fear, and anger, and pain, and guilt."

"So, we're just pigs roasting over a fire?" Callan hadn't been prepared to take the full brunt of Cane's look.

His head dipped. "That depends. Do you plan on giving them exactly what they want? Or do you want to learn to use what they show you for your art?"

"What are we supposed to learn from them trying to kill us?" Roth interjected. Cane's head swiveled slowly to Roth.

"They embody the darkest parts of your soul when you meet them, Mr. Heller. Perhaps the question you should be asking is: why do *you* want to kill you and what will it take to stop yourself?"

"I don't want to kill myself," Roth said, his voice suddenly hollow. The corner of Cane's mouth jumped.

Cane didn't say anything. He didn't need to. He pinned Roth with that smug, knowing look a second longer before turning it on the rest of them. "You've all been burning to know why you were chosen. Well, this year I wanted a challenge. I wanted to see what my little shadow friends would think of a collection of souls absolutely determined to snuff themselves out. You want them to stop terrorizing you, stop terrorizing yourselves."

None of them spoke. Callan wished she could hide under the weight of the silence. Did she want to die? The fact that an answer didn't immediately spring to mind only made her uneasy. She looked to the others for confirmation that at least one of them felt differently, but only saw the same guttered expression on each of their faces. So, they weren't here because they were brilliant, talented artists. They were here because Dr. Ladon Cane was bored.

"Now," Cane said. "If it's all right by all of you, I'd like to get into the art. This project will help when you confront your shadows again tonight." Roth sank back to his seat. "Let's talk about motion," Cane said, stripping off his jacket and rolling up his sleeves. He made a few hurried strokes on the chalkboard with a stub of chalk. "There are many techniques you can employ to convey motion in art."

Callan began to realize just how little she understood Ladon Cane. His hand flew over the board with the kind of efficiency and technique that spoke to decades and decades of practice. Even half-distracted, with his back to his blackboard canvas, he had more instinct, more style than nearly all the instructors she'd ever learned from. The drawing showed a runner in motion, conveyed through horizontal strokes and backward pull of the figure's touch points. As soon as that image was complete, he began with another.

"But there are more subtle ways of creating movement within the canvas," he continued, smudging away his hurried masterpieces like they were nothing impressive. "A decent, and incredibly famous example of this style is found in the Mona Lisa. Lark, can you tell us what that is?"

Callan recognized her name and blinked at him, "Sorry, what?"

"The Mona Lisa," he prompted. Her attention zeroed in on the chalk smudged on the side of his hand, the veins of his arm that disappeared beneath the cuff of his pushed-up shirtsleeve. "How does de Vinci convey movement when his subject is sitting still?"

Callan pulled the image to the front of her mind. The subtle smirk, the suggestion in her secretive look. "Her eyes," she said.

"Say more," he prompted.

"Well, there isn't any physical movement. But you can almost *see* what she's thinking. It's very seductive. She's keeping a secret."

"Good," Professor Cane murmured, jotting notes on the board. "Sometimes the most compelling movement is the movement you can only sense. The most bewitching pieces in history are unsettling for the very reason that the subjects in the pieces aren't settled. They have thoughts and feelings. They live and breathe. They give the sense that if you step away from the frame, something may change in your absence. There's a certain magic to it."

Cane stepped away from the board, revealing the small sketch he'd made in the time he'd been speaking. The blood in Callan's head drained into her cheeks. Even in black and white smudges, and rough lines, it was her. And she was keeping a secret too. The movement was held in the expectant gleam of her eyes and the gravitational pull of her mouth. Cane watched her closely as she took in what he'd made.

"Your assignment for today is to create a self-portrait that uses movement in this way. Tell a secret. Invite a conversation. Convey an intention."

Callan's hands craved movement. And although she didn't have the casually masterful technique that Cane possessed, the image came together far quicker than she expected.

Dominating the canvas were the eyes, her eyes. They pleaded with the observer. Begged. The only source of brightness came from the tiny crease of light that cut across the drawn Callan's facial features, illuminating the moisture in those eyes and making them appear backlit like a night-dwelling creature. In a sense, her younger self had been nocturnal, learning to occupy the dark, silent spaces she was cast into for so long that she began to seek them out for their safety instead. Who was she looking up at? What was she begging for? Even Callan didn't feel equipped to answer.

"You're trying too hard," Cane murmured over her shoulder, startling her. She stepped back from the canvas and directly into the wall of his chest. Her cheeks flamed and she ducked her head to hide it from him.

"I don't know what you mean," she said, stepping back up to the painting.

"You're tense here," Cane said, tracing the muscles that connected her shoulders to her neck. "And here." The fingertips dipped to the space between her shoulder blades. "You can't muscle your way through this practice. See what your hands show you when you stop operating them like they're heavy machinery."

Callan dropped her brush on the easel and rubbed out the pain in her finger joints. "This is my technique."

"I can see that," Cane said. "And I can also see that your technique is trying to force an expectation of what you've been taught art should be. Stop being a student, Lark. Start being an artist."

Grinding her teeth, Callan forced her feet to take another step away from the canvas. She stared at it for a moment, trying to see it through Cane's eyes.

His voice interrupted her again. "You can't become the artist you were born to be by pleasing me. Art shouldn't satisfy the observer. It should startle them. Give me something I can't replicate. Give me something I can't understand."

Without giving her a chance to respond, he moved on to the next workstation, where a small, clay figurine was coming to life beneath Roth's large hands. Callan watched for some sign that Cane was as displeased with Roth's creation as he was with Callan's. From the small smile that softened Roth's concentrated features, he wasn't.

She returned to the canvas, mixing more black into the deep blues she'd been using before. Every time her brain tried to direct her toward past lessons on color psychology and perspective, she summarily wiped it clean.

Callan's heart rate was slow, her limbs heavy and full of sand by the time Professor Cane called their attention back to the front of the studio. She had sunk so deep within herself that it took effort to kick her way back to the surface. The thing on the canvas before her looked nothing like it had a couple of hours before. In fact, there was almost nothing familiar about it at all. Even the desperation painted in her eyes was gone. In its place was a simmering delight edged in violence.

"Good work today," the Professor said. The pleased look on his face seemed genuine even when it turned Callan's direction. "There are still a couple of hours left until sundown. I recommend spending some time meditating and resting before nightfall. We'll pick this back up in the morning."

"They're going to come again?" Roth asked. Cane nodded. "And if we hide?"

"You can try," Cane answered. "But they'll find you. They'll find you every time."

"How do we stop them from coming for us?" This time it was Fray who spoke.

"You stop giving them what they want. You stop feeding them."

"What do they want?"

"I can't answer that. It will be different for each of you. That's why you need to get curious. Start asking questions, start paying attention to where and how they present to you."

Professor Cane waited until the others had shuffled out of the studio before leveling his gaze directly on Callan. The door shut without being touched, making her jump. Cane folded his arms. The tension in his shoulders remained, but his voice was soft when he spoke.

"I expected you to rest today. You needed it."

Callan desperately willed every drop of blood in her face to remain exactly where it was.

"I expected to be sent home today. I'm glad I wasn't."

Cane sat at the edge of his desk, his gaze tracing over her. "Luckily for you, there's not enough daylight left for me to correct that decision. It will be worse for you if they choose violence when your strength is exhausted."

"I'll be ready," Callan said. She meant it. At least, she thought she did. There wasn't much she could do if she was knocked unconscious again. And this time, presumably, she wouldn't be high on mushrooms.

Cane made a disbelieving sound in the back of his throat. He rose to his full height, towering over her.

"When the exercise is done, and the others have retired, go straight to my room, understood?" His eyes were unyielding. "You will wait for me there. You will not sleep until I come, you will not leave those four walls until the sun rises. Tell me you understand."

The sinking, sick feeling she'd experienced waking up alone that morning returned.

"Why?" She demanded, thankful for the way the anger warmed the coldness in her veins. "So you can toss me back in my own room once I'm no longer a liability to your little experiment? I'd rather fend for myself like the others. It's not like you want me there."

She shouldered past him for the door. He was already there, barring her exit. "Are you not frightened of me?"

Callan scowled. "Unlike those things in the woods offering highly ineffective swimming lessons, you actually seem to want me alive. So no, I'm not all that scared of you." She was far more concerned with what horrors her mind might be concocting for her in the night ahead. She made to bypass him again, but he stepped into her path.

"You're treading on thin ice, Cal," he said. Though he wasn't touching her anywhere, she swore she could feel the lines he traced over her with his eyes. "Last night, I was polite. I let you take what you needed and nothing more." He took a step into her, his lips going to her ear. "But I'm not feeling so generous today. I could make you very frightened. I'm sure it would taste divine. If you aren't careful, I'll show you exactly how I want you."

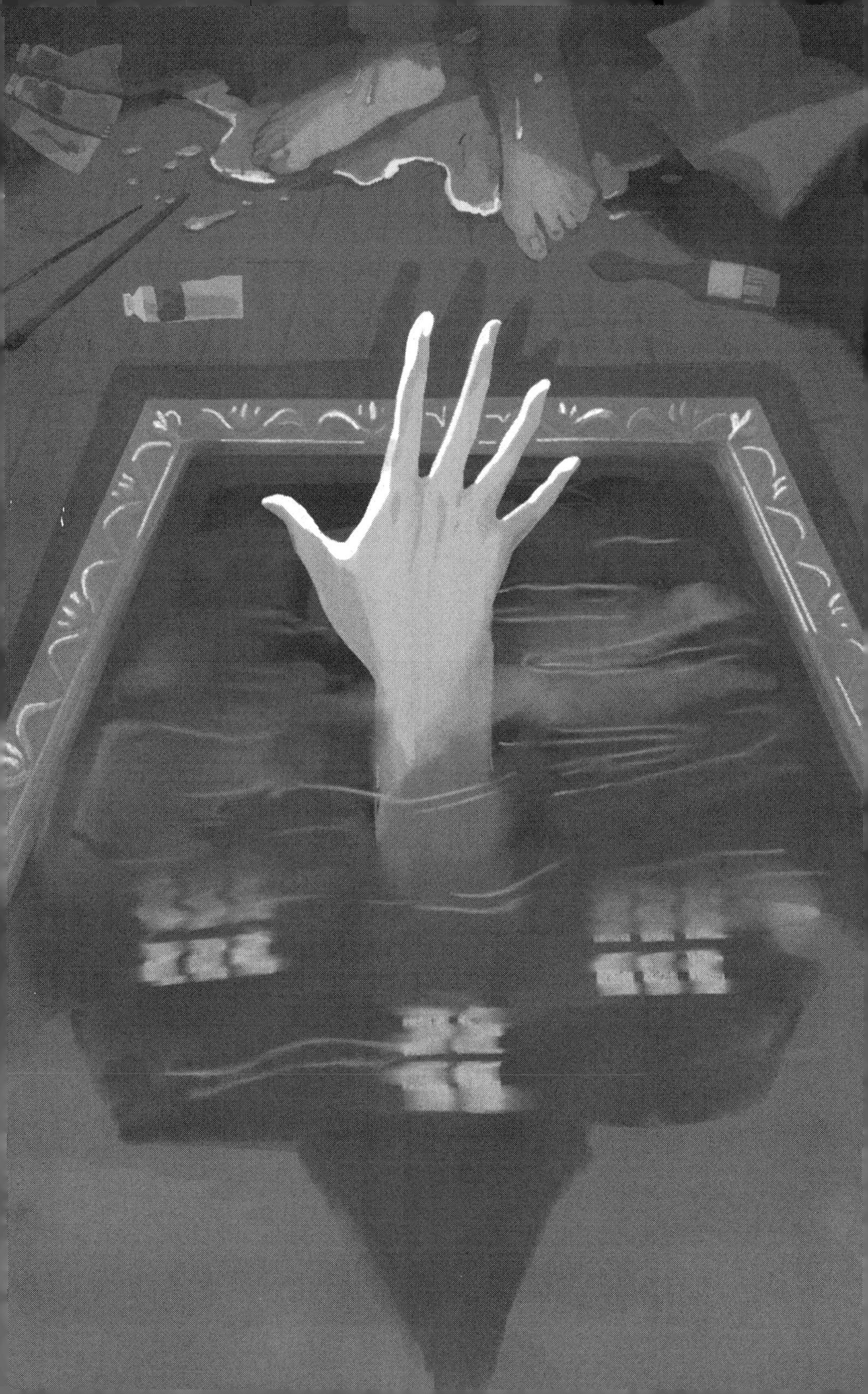

Drowned Things

The water was dark and silt-choked, a hazy green light barely making it through the inches of ice above Roth. He'd been suspended there, the top of his head bumping up against the ice, waiting for his lungs to give up.

He thought maybe he'd sink, maybe he'd float to an opening in the ice. Maybe fate would make its mind up for him. It never did. He just kept floating, drowning, waiting for something to happen. It might have been peaceful if it didn't hurt so goddamn much. Then he woke up.

He pressed his face into the mattress and sobbed until he gagged. This had been the order of things since Professor Cane confiscated his medications. He waded through the waking world, nauseous and foggy and barely able to remember his name. Then he dreamed of his death, vivid, sharp, and unending. Death was the only place he saw color these days.

A knock came at his door.

"Go away," he moaned. It was bad enough to sweat through his clothes and sheets in the middle of the day, he definitely didn't need anyone else witnessing it.

"You need to eat something before nightfall," Fray said from the doorway. "Sunset was four minutes ago."

"Get. Out." Roth gritted through clenched teeth. When Fray held his ground, crossing his arms, Roth threw a pillow. "Get the fuck out of my room."

"Why don't you make me, Heller? From here, it looks like a light breeze could knock you over. I'll be sure to hold my breath." Roth didn't think it was possible to hate someone else more than he hated himself, but Fray made the task easy.

"What, are you afraid to face your little monsters all by yourself?" Roth sneered. "Do they just stand in a circle telling you all the reasons you'll never be anything like your father? That must be so hard. Need someone to hold your hand?"

"I'm not afraid," Fray said, though he didn't comment further. Roth almost believed him. But he'd seen the way Fray nearly backed right into the flames to stay away from whatever form his shadow took. He hadn't said a word about it, not to anyone. Roth's dry, cracked lips lifted in his own attempt at a smirk.

"Sure. You're just hiding out with me because you love my company."

The longer Fray remained silent, the more exposed Roth felt.

"What do you really want? Why are you in here?" He demanded. Fray finally moved, reaching up to scrub a hand over his short hair.

"I heard you screaming."

Roth waited for the punchline. Fray watched him in a quiet, questioning way that almost felt like concern. But if he thought Roth was going to tell him anything about what he was going through, give him any more reason to make Roth's life difficult, he was out of his mind. Anyone could play at caring, especially someone with as many masks as Fray.

"Well, sorry to disappoint, but the shadows haven't killed me yet," he said. He rose from the bed. His head spun, but he covered the way he swayed by turning for the bathroom.

"I was trying to help," Fray said to his back, so quiet Roth thought he might have just been muttering to himself.

"Don't," he said and closed the bathroom door.

By the time Roth emerged from his room, he felt almost human. He hadn't eaten anything since the drugged meal they'd been served the night before, but then again, his encounter with the shadows hadn't left much room for an appetite. Just the thought of facing them again instantly quelled any hunger pangs.

The others were already seated around the table when he arrived in the kitchen. Callan's eyes searched his with questions and concerns etched into her tired features, but Roth wasn't ready to talk to her. He thought he might never be ready after the state she'd seen him in the night Cane had stolen his things. He didn't need to know what her face looked like when he told her everything. He preferred she remember him as the gangly, goofy kid from Christian art camp.

Everyone else seemed to trust the food Hilde had prepared. Roth didn't, but he made up a plate and sat down in front of it anyway.

Fray leaned over and whispered in his ear. "Apparently, we're going to the lake tonight," he said. Roth could feel Fray's gaze flicking over his tattered flannel shirt and worn-out jeans. "You're going to need better layers than that."

Roth hunched over his food. His teeth groaned around the urge to let out all the poisonous things he wanted to say. It felt like they were blistering his tongue.

"You really should eat something, Roth," Callan said, reaching across the table. "We don't know how long we'll be out there." Roth pulled away from her, dragging a hand through his messy, knotted hair.

"You don't know?" He asked, incredulous. "Really? Did Cane fail to mention what we'd be getting up to in this morning's pillow talk?" Callan's face twisted. Did she really think they were all that oblivious? Did she think they didn't see the glances and lingering looks, the smirks and innuendo? He hadn't pegged Callan as the hot-for-teacher type, but he supposed it made sense when the teacher looked like Cane.

"We aren't—" she began, shaking her head.

"Save it," Roth spit. He hated this version of himself, but that hatred only seemed to egg it on more. "Maybe next time you screw him, you can find out something that will actually be useful for all of us. I don't want to die here, do you?"

"We aren't going to die," Fray said, keeping his voice low and his eyes on the doorway where Cane might materialize at any moment.

"Oh yeah," Veronica chimed in, her spoon clattering against her full plate of food. "Says who? Because I'm pretty sure Cane never said we wouldn't."

"There's been a winter term here every year for the last decade," Callan said. "Not one of the past attendees has let slip a single word about this retreat being dangerous, let alone deadly, and I don't think our NDAs apply to murder. It's terrifying and uncomfortable, but Cane says no harm will come to us and I believe him. Aside from the mushrooms, which were discussed in our packets by the way, he hasn't done a single thing to harm us. From my perspective, it looks like he's trying to help us."

Veronica's brows shot up. "Did you come to that conclusion before or after you were dragged by your hair through the woods and drowned in the lake for the third time? Before or after he drugged us all and tossed us into the night like chum in dark, shark-infested waters? And do I really need to remind you of June? It's pretty hard to report your own murder, you know. Last I checked, people don't just vanish from thin air without a reason."

"He hasn't said we can't leave," Callan retorted. "The roads might be impassable, but I'm sure you could hike down and eventually find your way to town. You clearly don't need this retreat, *YellowFang*."

"You know exactly why I'm here," she seethed, her grip on her fork tightening until it looked more like a weapon. "I will kill that bastard before I let him do to me what he did to June," she said.

The table went quiet after that. Roth shoveled a few bites of potato into his mouth. They tasted like ash. Eating was supposed to make him feel better, but by the time Hilde came back to clear the table, his hands were shaking and his stomach was cramping. There was still no sign of Cane, so he pushed away from the table and made for his room. Cane might have said they couldn't hide from the shadows, but how could they reach him if he barricaded himself behind the door?

He was on the third step when he felt something brush his elbow. It wasn't a hand, but a shadow in the shape of one. Professor Cane was leaning against the doorframe to the living room, watching him with a masked expression.

"I hope you're just going to grab your jacket, Mr. Heller." Roth swallowed thickly. He nodded. The phantom hand at his elbow disappeared, and he jolted at the lack of support. The place where the shadow had been burned like black ice. "Good. I'll see you in the foyer in fifteen. We'll head over together."

Roth grabbed the banister for support as he made his way to his room. Every time his mind strayed to ideas of pushing every piece of furniture up against the door, he was reminded of the feel of Cane's shadow; the way it had felt solid and then ceased to exist in a split second. What else could he do? What could those *things* in the woods do?

He put on his heaviest barn jacket and a gray beanie, then sulked back downstairs, where the others were waiting for him.

Someone had packed down the snow along the trail to the lake. Someone or, Roth realized with a shiver, something. The prints in the snow were hard to make out in the glow of their headlamps. But there were many of them. Cane was at the front of the group, droning on about meditation techniques he'd learned from Tibetan monks, which they practiced even as they lay dying, and apparently, for several days after their bodily death.

Roth really, *really*, did not need any more reminders of death. Every time the light from someone's headlamp caught on the bleached, bare branches of an aspen, all he saw was gray, drowned skin sagging from the bone. At the bonfire, he'd been surrounded by drowned things. His brother, of course. But also his mother, his father, his youth pastor. Every single person he'd ever known was there, dripping wet, with gray lips and foggy eyes. They didn't speak, but when they opened their mouths only water full of leaf pulp and pine needles would pour out.

He kept his gaze down on the icy, packed snow beneath his feet as they shuffled forward. They stopped on the trail about a quarter-mile out of sight of the lake.

"There are only two rules for tonight," Cane said, his breath fogging around his face. "Do not run, and do not go into the lake. Those may seem fairly self-explanatory now, but believe me when I say that the shadows can be convincing. Keep your head on your shoulders. We stick together. We'll go through a couple exercises, and we'll go back to the cabin."

Cane seemed to be speaking only to Callan. To his credit, she did look terrified. It seemed her bravado from dinner had fizzled out with each step toward the lake.

Even the snow clinging to the branches didn't dare fall off. When they reached the lake shore, the silence became a static charge like the moments before an electrical storm.

Veronica hung back near the tree line as the others moved toward the tarp at the lake's edge. "If we're not supposed to go in the lake, why are we sitting here asking to be dragged in?"

"The shadows know better than to try touching any of you again," Cane said.

"Did you sit down with them over tea and remind them of their manners?" Veronica asked. "Are they planning to issue a written apology for tossing this one around like a rag doll last night?" She pointed at Callan.

Cane leveled Veronica with a look that could have peeled the paint off the side of a car. "No," he answered simply. "I unmade them. Their essence returned to the pits, which has allowed new shadows to take their place at the surface."

Roth had to tug at his nose to remind himself how to breathe. For all Cane's perfect features, his coifed hair and gleaming smile, it was becoming clear to Roth that he was the real monster among them.

But his fear of Professor Cane didn't have time to percolate. The headlamps flickered and fizzled out in quick succession. The water of the lake seemed to tighten, stretching to contain something inside. Then a single head breached the surface.

It was Frankie, because, of course, it was.

"Hello brother," he said. *It*. It said that because it wasn't his brother. Roth clamped his eyes closed and listened to the sound of his jagged breath.

"You should each be seeing only one figure," Cane said, as he paced behind them. "Fray, who do you see?"

"I'm not going first," he said, a slight quiver in his voice. "Ask Fang what she's seeing."

"I see Frankie," Roth said to the ground. If he got these exercises out of the way quickly, maybe they'd be allowed to return to the cabin sooner.

"Good," Professor Cane said. His boots crunched against the snow as he moved to stand behind Roth. "And is Frankie speaking to you?" Roth nodded. "What is he saying?"

Roth glanced at the others. They seemed absorbed in their own nightmares. He looked up at Cane and regretted it. His eyes were glowing the same iridescent blue as the night before.

"He's asking why I wanted him to die, why I killed him, why I don't kill myself. He doesn't sound like he used to. He doesn't act like he used to."

"That's because it isn't Frankie," Cane said, quieter now that he was sitting down beside Roth. He mimed Roth's hunched position with considerably more ease, pulling his long legs to his chest. "What you're seeing is only your mind, Mr. Heller. Right now, it's terrifying because so much of your mind is unconfronted. Your brother has lived in there for years, twisting every memory into a nightmare. I want you to look at him. Really look at him. Feel everything he makes you feel."

"I don't want to look at him," Roth said quietly, turning

pleading eyes on Cane. Out of the corner of his eye, he could just make out the figure in the lake. It didn't move, didn't bob the way something floating or treading water should move. It was still watching him, waiting.

"The more you avoid him, the uglier he'll become," Cane said. "The memory of him will continue to fester and spread over all the others. Don't let this rot you from within, Heller. You deserve peace, no matter what that shadow tells you. You walked away from that lake that he drowned in. You have to start acting like it."

The sob that rocked through Roth made his teeth rattle. His spine arched, his chin tipping down against his chest. Cane ran a gloved hand down his back before rising.

"Get curious," Cane said to the group. "Don't let your shadow do all the talking. Ask it questions. Look deeper. It can't help but show you things about yourself." He continued to pace behind them. Around Roth, the others didn't heed Cane's advice. If anything, their fear only grew louder.

"What feeds the lake is eating you," Cane said, his voice booming through the still woods. "Fear, pain, guilt, regret. Holding on to these monsters is like using a broken shard of glass as a weapon. You might get some cuts in on your opponent, but you'll do far more damage to yourself in the process."

Roth's gaze finally collided with Frankie's, who gave him a sinister smirk. He swallowed thickly, tears pricking his eyes. His grief was a serrated thing as it dragged its way up his throat.

"I didn't want you to die, Frank," he whispered. "I— I didn't know you were in trouble until it was too late. I thought you were playing a prank. I didn't want you to drown."

"Then why did you let me?" Frankie asked, offering Roth a silty smile that made his skin crawl.

"Mine doesn't speak," Callan said quietly from nearby. Unlike Roth, she couldn't seem to tear her eyes away from whatever she saw in the water. "Who is it?" Cane asked. "Who are you seeing?"

Callan choked on her answer. "I—I don't know." Her eyes bounced to Cane and away as if even she didn't believe herself.

"It's not someone you've seen before?" Cane asked. Now the two had Fray's attention as well. Callan gave both of them a questioning look before her gaze shifted up to Cane.

"I don't know," she said again. Her brows bunched as she turned back to the lake. "They're wearing a hood. It's the same as last night."

Cane didn't say anything. He walked slowly to the lake shore. He didn't stop there. He walked over the tarry surface of the lake like it really was made of asphalt. The mist danced around his feet. He gazed down at the figure in the water like he was watching a small house spider crawling around on his bathroom floor.

Frankie stared up at him and all the venom was gone. He was a little boy again; his lips and cheeks pink, his eyes twinkling.

"You're sure it's the same," Cane asked.

Callan nodded, but Roth missed it. He was crawling on all fours toward the lip of the lake.

"Frankie?" He whispered. The boy in the water didn't turn. But it was his brother; really him. His lips weren't blue, his skin wasn't bloated and waterlogged. His blonde hair fell in ringlets around his soft, smiling face.

"Roth," Cane said tentatively, his hands out. "Don't move." Roth looked to him questioningly before looking down. His fingertips were in the lake water. It stung. How had he missed that?

He rocked back onto his knees, clutching his burning fingers to his chest.

"Fang, wait. Veronica. No."

Everything that happened next came in stilted fragments of light and shadow.

June

She was love notes scratched on subway walls and peonies in late May. The fizz of raspberry soda and the last five minutes of sunset. She was Monet, Cassatt, and Renoir on his happier days.

And she was Veronica's. For a second.

Amazing really, how long a second could stretch in memories when so much of herself was shoved under loose floorboards and flushed down toilets to nowhere.

June Parker was a meteor painting the sky in blues, and purples and reds. She might not persist in the night sky any longer, but she was still there, imprinted on the backsides of Veronica's eyelids every time she blinked.

There was no world in which June Parker was allowed to die before Veronica. It violated every law of physics. It was good for the world then, that June wasn't dead.

She was floating at the center of the lake without effort, her bare, moon-white arms making ripples in the dark water. Her black hair fell around her face and over her chest, fanning out in the water like lace.

"I knew you'd find your way back to me." Her voice seemed to live within Veronica's mind. It reminded her of sunny mornings in Manhattan with June pressed tightly to her side, whispering about caffeine dreams from the night before. It was the happiest memory Veronica owned. But if it was so happy, why did it make her chest feel like it was about to crack open?

She blinked, and the cracks spread. Images of June's forearms tattooed with bruises in the shape of Veronica's fingerprints. A porcelain bowl shattering against the wall. A note left on her doorstep the morning June left for her winter term, signed "goodbye," not "see you soon." They fought, sure, but only the way lovers do. The only way Veronica knew how to love was loudly. June knew how loved she was. That's why she was here, now.

"I want to be with you," Veronica said. She realized she was only speaking within her mind, but that didn't seem to matter. June was like smoke, passing through the locked doors.

"Come into the lake, V, and we can be together forever. There's no pain here, no suffering. We can just float."

What would it be like to float after kicking so hard for so long? Veronica had been treading water her whole life, and for what? What was all of this without June by her side?

"I'm afraid," she whispered, though she wasn't sure why. Even the creepy lake was no match for June's sunshine. She made the murky water and snow-packed shore feel like a golden hour picnic in Central Park.

The woods, the lake—it all fell away. There was a smile etched on June's lips as she reached out. Veronica stepped forward and she drifted to the edge of the lake, glowing algae trailing her.

"I promise I'll catch you," she said in a soft and conspiratorial voice.

Veronica smiled. The world felt off-kilter. Even gravity seemed to pull her toward June.

June gave her a final, encouraging nod, smiling sweetly.

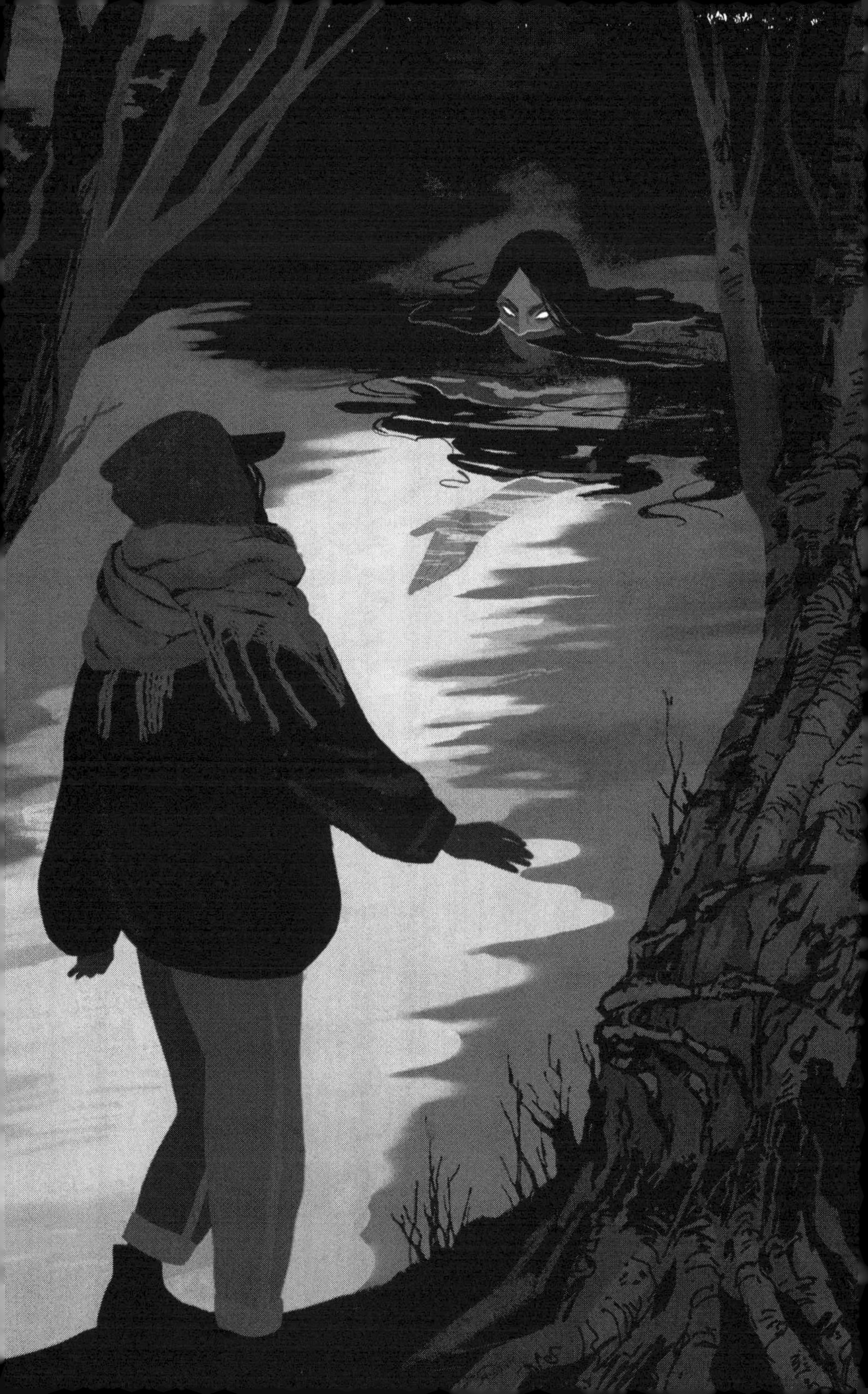

Hell Is Here

Sunrise cracked through the forest in a kaleidoscope of color, painting the world beyond the cabin a cold, hazy blue. Callan had been sitting with her knees hugged to her chest for so long that her arms had gone numb. She was on the sectional in Professor Cane's office, doing her very best to keep her eyes open. She couldn't so much as blink without seeing the way the lake writhed and kicked like it was made of restless bodies instead of water. Why had it spit her out three times while not hesitating to swallow Veronica whole?

It took longer than it should have to recognize the sharp charge that came over the air with Cane's return. She'd been watching the meadow for signs of him. But she should have known he'd surprise her.

"You should be resting," he murmured. His voice was hoarse. His fingers curled tentatively around Callan's shoulders and squeezed out some of the tension she was holding there. She tipped her chin back and caught the icy glow of his eyes. She couldn't look at them for long without falling into the moment when Veronica jumped; the way those glowing eyes had burned as he dragged Callan away from the undulating waves and pushed her toward the cabin.

"Where is she?" Callan asked. The stillness at her back confirmed what she already knew.

Cane stepped carefully around the sofa and took a seat at the end furthest from her. As he settled into the corner, he winced, arching his back and rolling out his shoulders. Callan had never seen him look so human. And yet the aura clinging to his skin couldn't have been further from it.

"I was serving as her escort," he finally said. Callan's hands twisted in her lap. She couldn't stomach the thought of Veronica lost in that lake forever, but it struck her that there might be somewhere even worse.

"Where?" She murmured.

Cane laughed.

The sound was all wrong. It set every hair on Callan's body on edge. She was relieved when it finally stopped and Cane leaned forward to bury his face in his hands. He scrubbed at his hair as he reclined into the sofa, his eyes flicking over her face. Even with that cold, demonic glow, he looked exhausted.

"There is no hell. All the evil in the world is right here with us. The devils too. Who else would tend it?"

Callan considered him. He didn't look like the devils from the stories, yet something told her that he was so much more than the form she saw. Even so, she didn't think it was possible to fear him now. She had seen his face when Veronica jumped.

"Is that what you are?"

At her question, his eyes flickered, then the light guttered entirely as he lowered his head.

"It isn't like they say in that little storybook your father preached over," he said. "There isn't any morality to it at all. Your soul is not from this world. All the rest is. Every ugly thing that hangs from your back belongs to this place. *I* belong to this place." His gaze felt like a physical weight on her cheek. "Your soul is merely a traveler. When it leaves this world behind, it leaves the stuff of this world for the next souls to inherit."

"That's what's in the lake," Callan murmured. "All that's left behind."

"Yes and no," Cane replied. "Places like Pitch Lake are the char marks left on the earth after darkness decimates the land. Something terrible happened here long ago. It left a festering cut in the fabric of this world far too deep to be reabsorbed. It created a monster without a conscience, without a mind. I guard it and feed it, keep it from growing... hope that I can bring some good from it."

"So, she's with June then. Wherever we go next, she's there? She's happy?"

A strained expression came over Cane's face. "June Parker isn't dead," he said. "She may have left her old life behind in a less-than-ideal way. But that's what she needed to do to endure. I assure you, she's alive and well. Better than well. I have a holiday card from her right over there," he said, pointing to his desk.

Callan's chest squeezed. It was too painful, too much. Knowing that Veronica was rushing toward a death that promised reunion with June, only for her to be drifting, alone, the same way she had in life. It was cruel. It frightened Callan all the more because it could have been her end as well. Hadn't she been drifting with the same reckless abandon? Art was the last string holding her, and its hold was tenuous at best. With Veronica's death replaying again and again in her mind, she realized once and for all that she did not want to fade into that abyss she had kept company for so long. She didn't want to float any more than she wanted to sink.

Cane moved closer and pulled her into the warmth of his chest. "This world is made of randomness and chaos, Cal. Humanity gives that madness meaning. Without art to paint the story, all of us are adrift."

This only made her chest heavier, made the quaking sobs scrape at her throat until it was raw and throbbing. Her temples pounded to the rhythm of her heart.

Cane lifted Callan without effort and cradled her to his chest as he settled back into the couch. He stroked her hair, her nape, her back. She listened for the beat of his heart, but it never came. The hushed silence of him was a comfort.

When her sobs had finally subsided, he leaned back to look into her eyes. His had finally returned to their normal assortment of blues.

"You and the others are going to leave today," he said, his face inviting no argument. "I already arranged for plows to work on digging us out. You'll be gone before the shadows return tonight."

Callan thought no more tears could possibly come, but they did. These ones hurt the worst.

"It's almost over," Cane whispered, rubbing her back. How could he not see that she needed to be here? How could he not see that the lake water had smoothed over those old fissure lines in her skin like she was made of wet clay? How could he not see that she needed him as much as she needed to be here?

She pressed her lips firmly to his, taking advantage of his surprise. Cane's hands came to grip her cheeks and wiped away tears that spilled from the corners of her eyes. He made a contented sound deep in his throat as his tongue explored her mouth. His skin smelled like August in Kansas; warm earth, high grass, and the hint of rain in the breeze before a storm. He smelled like home. A version of home that made her chest ache for only the good reasons.

Callan ran her fingers along the muscled planes of his stomach before resting her hand above the place his heart should have been. "I'm right here and I'm staying. I trust you. I'm right here."

He cut her off with his mouth. She might have led the first kiss, but this one was all his. She was gasping, and his touches hadn't strayed past her shoulders. His teeth tugged at her bottom lip, nipped at the edge of her jaw, her earlobe.

His lips were swollen and wine-red when he eventually pulled away. A divot formed between his brows that told Callan he was making a decision.

"Let the others decide," she begged. "Let me talk to Roth and Fray. If they want to see this through, then you let us stay."

His eyes jumped between hers as his jaw worked. "Fine," he said, shortly. "But only if the three of you stay as far away as possible from the lake. And only while the shadows are sated from their kill."

Those words were a cold draft at Callan's shoulders as she wandered the halls in search of Roth and Fray. *Kill.* The lake had killed Veronica.

When Callan fell into the lake, it ached and burned, but the hurt didn't last. In the places hollowed out by that hurt, something else was blooming. She just had to hope Roth and Fray felt the same way.

Finding Fray's room desolate, she wandered down the hall to knock at Roth's door. When no answer came, she pushed the door ajar.

Fray was perched like a gargoyle at the foot of Roth's bed with a purring Schrödinger in his lap.

"What do you want?" He mouthed.

Whether the defensive hold of his shoulders was a threat not to wake Roth or Fray was actually afraid of her, Callan wasn't sure. Glancing over at Roth, who slept fitfully, she did her best to muster her confidence.

"I want us to stay," she said. Fray shook his head once.

"He needs to get out of here. I don't know what it's showing him, but he's becoming a ghost. I haven't even heard him laugh this week. I—" he choked like he couldn't believe he was saying the words. "I fucking hate that he doesn't laugh anymore."

"Leaving isn't going to make him any better," Callan said, careful to keep her voice from rising. Her eyes filled with more aching tears. "He can't go back to pretending, Fray. It isn't fair to any of us to go back to that. We're here for a reason."

"If we stay," he said, his voice quivering. "And it is a big 'if.' Then there are no more fucking games. You tell that fucking asshole that we want to know what the hell is going on before nightfall. No surprises. No tricks. No fucking psychedelics."

"Got it. The road will be clear if you decide to leave after we talk." She looked to Roth and back to Fray. "Meet by the fireplace at two? That will give us plenty of time to get down the mountain if we need to."

Fray nodded once, leveling Callan with a look that said she was dismissed.

No Surprises

If Callan thought she'd nap between her conversation with Fray and the meeting they'd agreed to, she was clearly delusional. It felt like firework fuses were burning under her skin. Schrödinger kept her company as she stared at her ceiling, her mind buzzing like a wasp's nest. Callan's petting became mechanical and repetitive, and he abandoned her for Hilde's company and the possibility of scraps in the kitchen.

Callan went on wearing holes into the wood paneling on the ceiling until a knock came at her door. For a fraction of a second, she thought it was Veronica. Until she remembered that Veronica would never knock at her door again. The person at the door knocked a little louder.

She pulled her half-read book to her lap in a weak attempt at looking occupied. "Yeah, come in," she called. Roth slipped in before closing it behind him soundlessly, keeping his hands pressed to the closed door for a moment. Wearing only a threadbare tee, Callan could see the knobs of his shoulder blades. Pitch Lake seemed to be eating away at his edges.

"You want to stay?" He delivered the statement as a question. There was no fear in his voice, which surprised Callan. When she nodded, he continued. "I thought you of all people would want out of here."

"I don't really know how to explain it. But for some reason, I feel like I need to be here. Like whatever life existed for me before I came won't fit me anymore. Like the only way to find out what comes next for me is to stay here and listen."

"Is it because of him?" At the mention of Cane, shadows slid among the grays of Roth's eyes. Callan shook her head, giving him an imploring look.

"It's about me. It's about us. Don't you—don't you feel like you're on the cusp of something too?"

"I feel like Cane is an absolute lunatic. I feel like I'm going batshit crazy. I feel like if I have to see Frankie's face again one more time, I might actually lose it and just pitch myself into the lake like Veronica. I feel like maybe that would be best for everyone, myself included." He was sobbing by the time he finished. He pulled the collar of his tee up to hide his face. There wasn't much space for Callan to join Roth on the chair, but she stooped to her haunches in front of him and laid her hands on his knees.

"You aren't crazy, Roth," she said, shaking his knees. "Our minds have made us a captive audience here. I've been hiding from it just as much as you. But I think we owe it to Veronica to at least try and listen to what they have to say."

"I think my mind just wants me dead," he whispered.

"No," Callan said. She couldn't believe that was true. Not for herself, and definitely not for Roth. "If that was true, we'd already be dead."

"You don't know what those things say to me," he hissed, his back going rigid as he held in a heavy sob.

The next words were spoken softly, carefully. "If you choose to leave, I'll understand. But I hope you stay. I hope you give yourself one more chance to find a way through this where Frankie isn't the shadow over everything good that comes your way."

Thirty minutes later, Callan and Roth were seated stiffly in the armchairs by the grand fireplace, plates of uneaten food in their laps. Fray joined them, looking tired and irritable, though the scowl on his face softened when directed at Roth. Roth seemed to be doing his very best to avoid eye contact.

The sound of the back door opening and shutting pulled the warm air from the room. Ladon Cane walked into the room with snow layered into his mussed hair and dusting the shoulders of his heavy coat. He stopped short at seeing them seated in the living room.

He glanced between the three of them with a wary expression. His jaw feathered as he crossed in front of them to take the seat opposite the fire, tossing his coat and gloves at his feet.

"The road to town is clear," he said. "My jet is on standby to take you home if that's what you want."

Roth spoke up first. "I don't want to go home," he said. "I want answers."

"Roth—" Fray cautioned.

"No, Callan's right. We're here for a reason. What happened to Veronica is just further proof of that. If I leave—" Roth's voice crumpled. "I can't leave like this. I can't go back to Pugh and pretend like everything's how it used to be."

Concern was still etched into Fray's jaw. But his eyes had softened in a way Callan realized belonged only to Roth.

"What do you want to know?" Cane asked.

"Why did you let Veronica drown? You saved Callan before—"

"She didn't drown," Cane said quietly. "She didn't drown because that thing out there isn't a lake." His eyes came for each of them in turn, lingering last on Callan.

"It felt like water," she murmured.

"It isn't." His words sent a chill through her. "Ms. Fang didn't drown in the lake. She was consumed by it. Like calls to like. The shadow of her soul is the very stuff it's made of. When she jumped, her shadow was torn from her soul the second she touched the surface. She couldn't survive the shock and pain of that loss." Callan could feel the words Cane didn't say. They were woven between the ones he did. That she had gone into the lake three times now and had come out without even a scratch. What made her different from Veronica? And would the same protect Roth and Fray?

When she glanced up, the two of them were already watching her warily.

"Why did she do it?" Roth asked, turning his attention back to Cane.

"Because her shadow was very compelling," Cane said. "I brought you all here because I knew that each of you had walked closely beside your shadows for some time. I was arrogant enough to believe my teachings could silence the call of those shadows. I was wrong."

Callan could all but hear the grinding of Fray's teeth. "If we stay, is that what we can expect of the nights to come? Is that what this is about; annihilating artists?"

"Annihilating artists," Cane repeated slowly. "Everything I do here is for your art. To me, art isn't just a pastime. It isn't frivolous or extravagant. Art is existence. It is persistence. It is hope in the midst of pain. Art is the greatest enemy of suffering. And if anyone has witnessed their share of suffering, it's me." Cane's eyes burned as he considered each of them in turn. "I promise you that what happened to Veronica has never happened before at any of my retreats. Do you really think I could run off with the most promising fledgling artists in the nation and get away with not giving them back?"

Fray made a doubtful sound in his throat. "Doesn't seem any harder to believe than the truth. NDA or not, I can't believe there hasn't been a single person who has let it slip what you do here. What you are." The look he gave Cane could peel paint. Cane's answering look was patient, quiet. It gave away nothing of the monster they knew he was.

"The shadows will be slower for the next several days as they...

digest." Callan coughed to cover a gag. "I don't know what that will mean for their interactions with you."

"And when we confront it, we just cross our fingers and hope it doesn't get hungry?"

Cane sighed, pinching the bridge of his nose. He pulled his glasses from his face and balanced them on his knee. Something about the frustration with which he removed them made Callan think the glasses were just a prop.

"When you stand before a shadow, the shadow mirrors your own, Fray. I don't know how many times I need to repeat it. Whatever you see, whatever it does, it already lives in you. Are you so terrified of yourself that you won't even ask it a question? Are you that afraid to know what you have to say?"

Fray didn't give a response.

"Mine doesn't speak," Callan said. "I don't even know who it is. They're wearing my dad's old ministerial vestments, but the hood is up and it covers their face completely. For some reason, it doesn't feel like my dad." A shiver squirmed at her back. "I—I would know if it was my dad," she amended.

"There's only one?" Cane asked. There was something careful about those words. His knuckles went white from the grip on his knees.

Callan nodded, then, realizing he couldn't see the move, said, "There's only ever been one."

"What about for each of you?" Cane asked.

"There are dozens," Roth said. "They're all drowned looking. Gray and wet. It's probably everyone I've ever met. I think even Callan was among them. Mine don't shut up."

"Same here," Fray said quickly, his gaze darting between Roth and Cane. "It's my dad and mum and loads of others. They scream."

Cane's brows drew down in a concentrated frown. He rubbed at the divot that formed between them like a headache was brewing there.

"What are you thinking?" Callan asked after too many

seconds of silence. The bouncing of her knees was starting to give her motion sickness.

"There is a method I've utilized in the past with other groups of students, but in each of those instances, the students had much more time with their shadows before we tried it. Those students were considerably less complex than the three of you."

"So, they didn't want to axe themselves? How special," Fray deadpanned. "What's the method?"

"We invite them to dinner," Cane said.

"We invite them..." Callan trailed off in confusion.

"This far from the lake, they're considerably less powerful," Cane said. "Inside, with the candlelight, they are much more receptive to your influence and questioning. We can start together, in one room. And if that goes well, we can break out for individual sessions."

"And if it doesn't go according to plan?" Fray asked.

"Another perk of being so far from the lake is that if they try dragging you off, I have the opportunity to stop them."

Anyone There?

Fray let the near-boiling spray of the shower pelt his face until he felt numb. Over the past few days, he'd spent more and more time showering. The sting of the hot water distracted him from the near-painful itch to run from this place until he ran out of ground to run on. And for a few moments, he could clean himself of the memory of the lake writhing as Veronica disappeared beneath the surface, her hand the last to disappear as if her body knew it wanted to be saved even if she didn't.

A knock at the door pulled him back to the room. "What?" He shouted, swiping the water from his face and glaring at the door through the shower glass.

"Hurry up," Roth grumbled back.

"There is another shower, you know," Fray replied.

The shower at the end of the second-floor hall had been claimed by Veronica within her first five minutes in the cabin. Neither Fray nor Roth had dared to use it while she was there. And now that she was gone... Well, now it was haunted for sure. Fray almost smiled at the sound of Roth's sigh on the other side. "I bet you could even use that big jacuzzi tub in there. You probably won't get eaten by a depthless abyss. Or the ghost of YellowFang."

"Too soon, asshole," Roth shot back, banging a fist on the door. There was more color in his words than Fray had heard in days.

He cut off the spray of the shower and toweled off in a cloud of steam before opening the door.

"You could always just join me, Heller," he said, his smirk broadening into a smug grin as Roth's gaze dragged reluctantly over every exposed inch of him. His throat bobbed when his perusal led to Fray's towel slung low around his hips and the muscled lines disappearing behind it.

His gaze made a slow path back to Fray's, warming the skin his eyes touched. "I would rather take a bubble bath in Pitch Lake," he finally replied, eyes twinkling. He checked Fray's shoulder roughly as he brushed past him. "If this shower is out of hot water, I will smother you in your sleep," he called over his shoulder.

Fray turned, getting a glimpse of pale shoulder blades and the strong column of a spine as Roth pulled his shirt over his head. He cut his head away.

"Threat or promise?"

His voice was too strained to serve as a proper taunt. His skin was too tight. He stepped into the hall and shut the door before Roth could answer. Without the loud drone of the ceiling fan, he could hear the pathetic *thud, thud* of his heart as he marched back to his room. By the time he had his clothes on, he could hear his thoughts again.

What had started as an annoying itch in that first silent night spent in the cabin had become a frenetic need for the distraction of sound. Any sound would do. He wanted a room full of people, all speaking over one another; a packed subway platform as a train came in; the cackle of seagulls on a crowded pier. Anything to help him forget how totally and completely alone he was. The silent woods, the hush of the snow, the pitch dark of the night, all it seemed to do was amplify his loneliness.

"Alright, when the shadow arrives, it will come to the chair," Professor Cane was saying from the head of the table. The three of them were on one side of the long table. A single chair sat on the other side. "Heller, Fray, this exercise should help you get closer to the heart of what your shadow is asking of you. Lark, I think the best we can hope for is to identify your shadow in this session. But regardless of what they say or do, you do not leave this room unless instructed."

They nodded in unison. That was one lesson that did not require a refresher. The scene from last night assaulted Fray before he could tamp it down. His eyes screwed shut, but that only made the image more vivid. He inhaled jaggedly.

"Breathe, Fray, Jesus," Roth whispered through his teeth. "You sound like you're having an aneurysm."

Fray forcibly unclenched his fingers from around his fork, doing the same for the muscles in his forearms and shoulders.

"I'm fine," he said, shaking his head.

"Sure."

Fray's eyes swiveled to Roth. Roth's mouth twitched, but it slackened when his eyes jumped to the doorway. Fray watched him tense, bit by bit, as his enlarged pupils tracked the shadows movement to the chair. Fray refused to give the thing his attention.

"What do you see?" Cane asked the group. He'd left his chair and now paced behind the three of them slowly, his steady footsteps the only sound in the room. At least, to Fray.

Fray turned his eyes to the chair. The empty chair.

"It's my dad," he said. *Lie, lie, lie.* His heart was a relentless lie detector, tattling on him with every erratic thud against his ribcage. He imagined what it would look like for Aemon Fray to sit in that chair; what it would feel like. He even visualized it, in case Cane could see his thoughts.

"Are you sure," Cane said from his shoulder. His heart

tripped over itself. His mouth filled with cotton. "Look closer. Does he change? Is there anything off about him? What does his expression, his dress tell you about him?"

"M—mine is Frankie. Obviously. He. He's wet. He drowned. He says it was my fault."

"Do you believe him?" Cane asked, turning the heat of his attention away from Fray. "Why was it your fault, Mr. Heller?" Cane pressed.

"Because I should have gotten to him in time," Roth said slowly, entranced. "I was so close. I should have jumped in. I shouldn't have left him alone. He was mine to take care of. Instead, I laughed. I fucking laughed when he fell."

"The current in that stream you were fishing on was extremely strong with the ice cover, was it not?" Cane asked. Roth didn't respond. His head ducked against his chest. "And you were miles from home in sub-zero temperatures. Even if you had dragged him from the water without drowning yourself, you would have frozen before finding a way home. What if you brought logic to this conversation with your shadow?"

"He wants to be alive," Roth said miserably. "I'm alive and he's dead. It's not fair."

"Would it have been fair for you to die and him to live?"

Roth's throat worked on a swallow, but he didn't speak.

"Do you wish you had died instead of him?"

Roth's head bobbed.

"Then tell him that. Tell him everything you wish you had said to him before he died. Everything you wish you could say to him now. Don't leave anything out."

"How will that help?" Roth asked, his voice breaking. "That thing isn't him. Frankie is dead."

"You're right. That thing is the darkness inside of you. Don't let it corrupt what you have left of Frankie. All this time you've avoided the thought of Frankie, your mind has made him into a monster. The only way to unmake that monster is to shine light on him. Talk to him, talk about him. Say his name without fear. Give your grief air to breathe."

Tears tracked lines down Roth's cheeks. Cane placed a hand on his shoulder.

"Why don't you take the lecture room down the hall, Roth? I think it's about time you gave Frankie an audience."

Roth sniffled as he rose. His head seemed heavy on his shoulders, but his lips lifted in an uneasy smile as Professor Cane ushered him down the hall.

"Lark, any progress?" He asked, coming back to the table.

Callan didn't answer.

"Callan, what do you see?" He prompted calmly. "Callan."

"It isn't anyone," she finally bit out, her voice barely a breath. "It has no face."

Cane's face tightened as he took the seat Roth had just vacated, his knees framing her. "What do you mean it has no face? You can't see it, or it's shadowed over?"

"Under the hood," she answered. "It's just blackness. There is no face. There's no one there. It's no one." Her serrated breaths were deafening in the silent room. "What do you want?" She screamed at the empty chair. When it didn't answer, she repeated the question, desperation in her voice.

Slowly, carefully, Fray pushed his chair away from Callan's, wanting to be nowhere near her if the shadows tried to claim her again.

Professor Cane wrapped his hands around her upper arms as she continued screaming. "It's okay. This is enough for tonight. We can try again later."

Cane continued trying to pull her away from the table.

"No!" Callan yelled, struggling against his hold. "I need to know what it wants." She turned pleading, tear-bright eyes on him. "Please. Please just help me. Why can't I see its face?"

"I don't know," he said. "I've never heard of an encounter where the manifestation remained faceless. You said it's wearing your father's old vestments?"

Callan nodded, looking at it over her shoulder. Fray turned to the space she stared at. He still saw only an empty chair. Why weren't there any monsters around to torment Fray? Surely, he deserved it more than someone like Callan. He had caused plenty of heartache in his life, disappointed just about everyone worth disappointing, made enough mistakes for an entire miserable lifetime. And yet, the only monster he faced was more of the silence he'd struggled against since he arrived. Maybe he was defective.

"Fuck this," he muttered, pushing away from the table.

With Cane and Callan engaged, Fray was all but forgotten. He used their distraction to make his exit, heading straight for the front door. If the shadow wanted him surrounded by silence, if it wanted him alone, then he would give himself over.

"I'm here, fuckers!" He shouted into the night air, raising up his hands in surrender. His yelling shook loose some of the snow on the branches overhead and it dusted his neck like spidery fingers. He sidestepped a pair of sparrow wings that had been pinned down on the path. The blood still steamed at the severed edges. A few yards ahead, he found another deer leg. "You can stop killing Bambi's friends on my behalf," he yelled. "I'm right here. Come out and fucking face me."

Silence. Vacuous, sticky silence was all Fray received in response. Even with a foot of fresh snow covering the path, he reached the lake with startling speed. He checked over his shoulder to be sure the lake hadn't crept closer to the cabin. It was the exact same as the last time he'd been here to watch it devour Veronica. Just thinking of it triggered a visceral magnetism, dragging him by the stomach toward the edge of the darkness. He resisted it by planting his ass firmly on the ice about ten feet away. If his shadow wanted to drown him, it would have to show itself eventually. It would have to at least try to be convincing.

"Here I am," he called again, though this time it came out in a guttural, cracking mess of nerves. He wet his lips as his fingers tightened on the uneven knobs of the ice beneath him. "Do your worst. Fuck me up. I can take it."

His scream echoed off the unrelenting surface of the lake. Nothing moved, not even Fray.

He almost laughed with relief as the dark, bald crown of a head pushed through the tarry surface of the lake.

"You always were tripping over yourself to get my attention," said the thing in the water. The shadow had nailed the precise tenor of his voice; the overworn arrogance, the cloying condescension.

"Hey, Pop," he said, sitting up a little straighter. Even if his mind knew this wasn't his father, his body didn't. There was always a tightening, a straightening, in Aemon Fray's presence. He turned all his favorite toys into plastic. It made them so much easier to play with.

"I thought you would eventually give up and go home. You're such a good little quitter that way." He pulled a hand from the murky water to check that his fingernails were perfectly manicured; a move that sent a zing of alarm through Fray. It was so... real.

"I'm not giving up this time," he shot back. His voice was so much *less* when his father was on the receiving end. "I'm making a name for myself."

"You aren't making a damn thing," his father said viciously. The lines of his face drew up in mocking malice. "Everything you think is yours, belongs to me. Everything you create, everyone you trust, everywhere you go. It's all mine."

"That's not true," Fray said, even as his mind screamed that of course, it was. He said the words he wanted to be true. "That's why I'm here. You have no control here. You have nothing to do with this. This is all mine."

His father gave him a lopsided, falsely empathetic smile. "Oh, come now, Bennie. I know you've been hand-fed from a golden fucking spoon since you were an infant, but surely you aren't that stupid. Why would Dr. Ladon Cane want Benedict Fray at his little arts and crafts slumber party?"

He raised a heavy brow. It was a taunt Fray had mimicked so many times, he almost forgot that even his facial expressions were his father's.

"It couldn't possibly be that he hopes to take credit for the art that comes from you. Art, I will add, that I coaxed out of you like a fucking maestro, all the while listening to you whine about missing football practice and school dances. Anything you make here, anything you make anywhere—it will only ever be mine."

"You'll die someday," Fray said through his teeth.

"Of course," Aemon said. "But as long as you're alive, my name will live through you. As long as you make art, you will live in my shadow."

"I fucking hate you!" Fray screamed. "I'd rather drag your name through the mud than make a single cent off of you. You disgust me."

"You'd never say a single foul word to anyone," Aemon replied, his smile deepening into a feral grimace. "You're too afraid of what it would mean. I don't just control your trust and assets. I own your mother. I own your friends. I own this precious little life you pretend is yours. Hell, you and I both know, you'd never be here if it wasn't for the name I gave you. That's why you throw it around so much, isn't it?"

"It's my name," Fray growled.

"I think you'll come to find that it's not. That name means nothing without me. You're nothing without me. This messing around needs to end."

"No," Fray spat back. "I won't let you ruin another second of my life. You think people admire you, adore you? They fear you. They hate you. You're an arrogant, self-important prick with an inferiority complex. You can't even enjoy your own success because you're too busy tearing everyone around you down. You must be so fucking miserable. All alone at the top of your castle.

You must hate yourself to be so goddamned awful to everyone else."

"You would know, wouldn't you?" Aemon replied, pinning Fray with a cold look. "Maybe that's why I keep clipping your wings."

Slowly, so slowly Fray hardly registered it was happening, Aemon began to slip away. The dark sifted away his shoulder, his hair, like the wind dragging at a sand dune. The last thing to go was his smug grin. The lake rippled around the imprint he left. When Fray was sure he was gone, he scooted to the edge on hands and knees. Glancing down at the surface, he saw that Aemon was still there, staring up at him. But as Fray glared down and his eyes sharpened on the details of the man's face, he realized it wasn't his father entombed in that watery grave.

It was him.

What Was Left in the Fire

Its face was made of the same darkness as the lake. It glinted in the candlelight like liquid obsidian, taunting Callan. It wore her father's clothes. It sucked all the air from her orbit. It had to be him. There was no one else it could possibly be. Yet, he hid behind masks. Did he really have nothing to say to her?

"I know what you did," she spit at him from across the table, pointing an accusing finger. Her other hand was pinned to the table by Professor Cane, who looked warily between her and the chair where her shadow sat. She might have imagined it, but she thought the shadow tensed. She wondered what the stain seated in that chair looked like to Cane. Surely, it must be uglier than the others. The thing didn't respond, of course. That wasn't surprising. He was the one confessions were made to. He never would have confessed to a damn thing.

"Why? Why did you do it? I need to know." She was beginning to shake violently. Every second of silence added to that ancient weight on her shoulders.

"Callan, you're freezing," Cane said beside her. His free hand tugged gently at her chin. She yanked herself free of him.

"I don't know what to do," she said, turning this comment on

Cane. His face was clouded with concern and pity. She had to look away before the tears clinging to her lashes poured over.

"It isn't your fault. None of this is your fault," Cane said, rising to his feet. He held out a hand to her. "There's something I need to show you. Or, rather, something you need to see." Callan didn't recognize the pleading look in his eyes. She swore there was even pain there.

He led her away from the dining room and the watchful, eyeless gaze of her shadow. When they reached Cane's office, he didn't bother to light a candle. He just led her to the center of the room and dropped her hand.

"Don't be frightened," he said, slowly unbuttoning his shirt. "This is how I ferry souls. It probably won't be pleasant for you, but we don't have to go far."

"Where are we going?" She asked, watching curiously as Cane went to his desk and pulled something free that glinted in what little light came from the hall. Looking closer, Callan realized it was a jagged, black blade as long as her forearm, engraved with symbols. She exhaled shakily, taking a step back.

"Not where," Cane said, advancing toward her. "When." For every step he took, she matched him with a step backward. "I'm not going to hurt you, Callan. Please. I could never harm you. That's always been the problem."

Every nerve in her body screamed to run. "Explain," she blurted.

"When you were a child, you started a fire," he said, continuing to prowl forward. "That fire left a stain, very similar to the one in the woods out there," he continued, tipping his blade at the wall of windows and the dark, snowy meadow beyond. "When I came to ferry the souls lost that day, I found you there."

"No," Callan breathed, shaking her head. "I don't believe you." Her back hit the bookshelf beside the door. Before she could flee, Cane had her pinned, his body making a cage around hers.

"You need to see, Callan," he whispered. "You need to

understand what happened that day, or you won't be able to move forward."

"Please don't hurt me," she whispered back.

Cane laughed against her temple before stepping back from her. He held the knife aloft. "This isn't for you, love. Just watch."

She did. She watched as he used the knife to carve precise lines into the side of his abdomen. The slashes were practiced, and deep, forming a rune-like shape. It didn't bleed. As he continued to cut away at his skin, a pale blue light fractured through the cuts. There were marks all over his body, scars so fine and pale that she hadn't noticed them on his skin before. Now, they all glowed with a twinkling energy, as if he was made of stars. Cane took her shaking hands in his, letting the knife clatter to the ground. "Look at me," he instructed. Her gaze lifted to his. The churning glow of his irises was ancient and cold.

The room around them began to crumble. Darkness crept in through the cracks until they were consumed by it. The only light came from the runes carved into Cane's body, and Callan watched that mesmerizing light coming from them as her own body was whipped around violently like she was being tumbled in a washing machine.

"Almost there," Cane said. But his voice only existed in her mind. The roaring, vacuous absence surrounding them sucked up all sound until her ears popped from the pressure. As soon as it began, it ended. Her eyes were screwed shut, but she felt sunshine on her skin, heard the grass murmuring at her knees. She blinked through the buzzing, late afternoon light of a September day. The burning church stood before them; a pillar of fire reaching toward the sky. The pop and creak of embers, the woosh of flames, almost felt peaceful with the grass swaying in the backdrop.

Cane squeezed Callan's hands, and suddenly she remembered their reason for coming. Her gaze lifted to his. His eyes were already burning into her.

"This is a memory," she said.

Cane's lips tightened and he nodded. "But not yours," he

added. His thumb swiped the underside of her wrist before he released her. He walked purposefully toward the door. But Callan remained frozen, watching his back. He spoke without turning. "Not seeing it doesn't stop it from being a reality, Callan. Have courage. It will be over soon. We only have minutes before time drags us back."

Callan trailed a few paces behind Cane as he marched up the smoldering church steps and wedged the heat-swollen door open. The charred backside of the door nagged at something deep in her mind; one of those locked doors she'd left untended for years. Cane walked slowly up the pews, the thick gray smoke eating at his figure.

"You tried the front door first," he said quietly, his voice almost inaudible over the burning of the church. "It was jammed shut and you wasted most of your energy trying to peel it open. When it didn't work, you went for the cellar."

"There's an exterior door in the cellar," Callan said, recalling the glowing outline of it from memories of being locked inside. The thought of her own escape from this charred wasteland made her heart flutter.

"Yes," Cane replied. He took the cellar stairs reluctantly. When he glanced back at her, the expression on his face turned the fluttering in her chest to a sick twisting and churning. "And you almost made it."

The cellar was still cold and dry, despite the fire raging above. The smoke hadn't made its way in either. It was dark the way she remembered, and smelled like soil and dust. Cane stopped abruptly, blocking her view of the exterior door.

"This will be hard to see," he cautioned, taking her by the elbows. She craned her neck to see around him. But there was no younger version of her beating against a locked door, or waiting to be let out by firefighters. Cane stepped to the side, giving her a view of the floor.

Her heart kicked around uselessly as she stared and stared.

There was a small, sad lump on the ground. So much smaller

than Callan remembered, so much smaller than a fifteen-year-old should be. The skeletal wrist and dirty, torn-up fingers reaching for the closed door couldn't be hers. Her gaze inched up to the fabric covering her, made of deep purple satin inlaid with religious embroidery. It was singed through in places, still smoldering in others, and blackened with soot. She must have stolen her father's liturgical vestments to protect her from the flames.

She looked questioningly at Cane. Instead of speaking, he pointed at the dewy, phosphorescent globe of light suspended above the younger Callan's unmoving body.

"By the time I arrived, you were barely clinging to life," Cane said at her shoulder. "Your soul was already separating."

As he drew closer to her younger self, she jerked away. As if she recognized him, what he meant, and wasn't ready to accept him.

"You had so much fight left in you," he said with a tight laugh. "Even as I watched your soul take shape before me. The soul I was supposed to ferry with those of your parents. You—" His voice faltered. He trailed his fingers through her hair like he needed a reminder that this was only a memory. "You died," he said, voice guttering. "But I refused to take you. I just... fucking... couldn't. I could tell with one look at you that you had already lived through hell. You'd been living it your whole life. I should have put you out of your misery. But you were still so full of hope, so full of love. I saw your mind, and it was curious and artistic." Cane cut himself off abruptly, inhaling. He drew further into the shadows of the cellar. "I was selfish. You intrigued me. I couldn't let the shadows have you."

He exhaled shakily before he lowered himself to his knees. From Callan's vantage, he looked every bit the archangel from the stories. All he needed was a pair of wings.

She watched as he breathed her soul back into her. One hand cupped the back of her head, the other grasped her soot-stained jaw. As he forced her soul to rejoin her body, bit by bit, the shadows crept from the corners of the room. Their reaching fingers grasped for the younger Callan's body. Cane banished them with a single flick of his glowing fingers.

"You're a god," she whispered. Cane rose with the younger Callan still clutched to his chest. Color was back in her lips, and shallow breaths scraped over them.

"I've been called many names over the millennia," Cane said. "They never stick, and they never capture the whole story."

"Then what are you? What are you really?"

"Does it matter, Callan?" He searched her eyes like he might find the answer there. "I do what is within my power. Sometimes I overstep that power. The universe seems as disinterested in my suffering as any other. Maybe I'm nothing more than a man."

"You're more than a man," Callan said, in awe of him. "You saved me. You brought me back to life."

"What I did here upset the natural order of things. I didn't understand just how much until I found you again and I saw how the shadows act in your presence. I shouldn't have interfered."

"But I didn't want to die," Callan protested.

The church was beginning to crumble around them in earnest. The rafters were breaking free and cascading onto the pews. The stained-glass windows popped in quick succession like popcorn kernels.

"Your mind cannot even comprehend the vastness of the universe. You cannot know the consequences of what I've done."

Once outside, Cane walked up the road to an outcropping of apple trees. He lowered her younger self to the ground, carefully arranging her on her side to avoid the worst of the burns on her back.

"Whatever you may believe, I'm grateful you saved me," Callan said. "I'm grateful for the life I have, even if it's meaningless to you."

Cane rose and pinned her with a look that had her backing into the hold of the apple tree. He grasped her face on both sides, bringing his face even with hers. "It means everything to me, Callan. But it isn't your life I worry for anymore. It's your soul."

He offered his hand. "Come. This wasn't all I needed to show you."

She took his hand and allowed him to lead her back toward the inferno. "It took forty-seven minutes and eighteen seconds for the fire department to arrive," Cane said as they watched the fire tear through every beam. He led her around the backside of the building, where a wide, grassy clearing separated the church from a grove of towering elm trees.

But when they reached the clearing, they were forced to stop short. Water was rising in the dense grass, dark and brackish and cold as ice despite the heat of the day.

"Is this all because of me?" Callan asked.

"I don't think so," he replied, sinking his hands into his pockets. "But I do wonder—" He trailed off, his brow bunching as he concentrated on the rising waters.

"What?"

Cane considered her. "I think when I gave your soul back, it had already fractured from your shadow. I think that's why Pitch Lake didn't claim you."

"Because I already have no shadow?"

"You have a shadow, Callan. Every human does. I just think, perhaps, yours has been separated from you."

"Good," Callan said. "I don't need it. I don't want it."

"You don't know what you're saying," Cane said, shaking his head.

"I do," Callan said, refusing to look away from his glowing, imploring eyes. "My shadow is the worst of me. It's everything I inherited from the man who caused all this. Even if it was my doing, it was his evil. He hurt those people, he hurt me and my mother. If I killed him, it's only further proof of how like him I was. I don't want any of that back if it will make me more like him. If it will make me a monster."

"Your shadow isn't the worst of you," Cane insisted. "It's what makes you human. It's everything that you can't take when you leave this world behind. It's beautiful and fleeting and mortal.

Your human life is already short enough, and you would allow yourself to live it feeling *nothing*?"

She stepped into him, gripping his shirt. "I feel, Ladon. I feel too much already. What do I need to do to show you just how much you make me feel?"

She lifted to her tiptoes, seeking the warm press of his mouth to hers. His lips brushed hers, but he stepped away before the heat could comfort her.

"I will not have you in bits and pieces, Callan. I don't want you to be the watered-down imprint of that fiery soul I saved. I want you whole. I want you, monster and all. Stop fearing yourself."

"What if that's all that I am? Fear."

"You are so much more than your fear. I saw it. I saw how you fought here. I know what is in your heart." His eyes were like blue granite. "It's you that doesn't. You don't remember what happened here. Not really. Am I wrong?"

"I know—"

"You know what you read in the papers about this day. You know what you read about your father, accusations from his victims. You know what the foster homes whispered about him, about you, while you were growing up in his shadow. But you don't *know*. You don't have the memories yourself."

Of course, she had memories. She knew what her mother's perfume smelled like, and the feel of the wind through the window of her father's truck. She remembered. She remembered everything worth remembering.

"That's what I thought," Cane said, taking her silence for acquiescence.

"What do you want me to do," Callan demanded, her chest heating. "I didn't choose this for myself. I can't just decide to remember. I can't just make my shadow come back."

"I know," Cane said, but his frustration was evident. "I know that."

But it didn't feel like he understood. The rising of the water before her, the pity in Cane's eyes beside her, it made her head buzz like a hornet's nest. She turned on her heels, prepared to march back to where they had arrived, and hope it might suck her back through time.

But it seemed that time was already growing impatient.

The sky began to split down the center. Darkness spilled through the cracks like ink pouring into water. It blotted out the day; blotted out all the color around them. The only light that remained was the bottle green of the minutes before a tornado touches down.

"We have to go," Cane said, yelling over the howling wind. His feet dragged, and he teetered as he led her away from the newly formed lake. "It's going to be rough. I always lose some control with the return journey."

They reached the dark indent in the earth that marked their arrival. Cane gathered Callan close, gripping her around the shoulders. He didn't have a pulse, or even breathe, from what she could tell. But she knew he was fatigued. He swayed into her as he checked the watch on his wrist. In front of them, the church continued to burn as the memory crumbled in on them. Cane cursed as he looked up to the cracking sky.

"Hold on," he said. "You can't let go of me in the void." His words were slurred and slow. His gaze darted around them frantically as cold dread pooled in Callan's stomach. "We're going to need to improvise."

"Are we stuck?" She whispered the question. Cane's response was a frustrated huff. He bit hard into his lip and spit the glowing matter that poured forth at their feet. It was still shimmering on his lips when the ground gave way beneath them. Cane held her so tightly she knew it would leave bruises. She held on to him with the same force. If she thought their flight to Montana was turbulent, this was like the epicenter of an earthquake. Even the light from Cane's runes was muted, growing dimmer with every second that passed. She felt his hold on her loosening. His head fell back. Phosphorescent blood was dripping from his nose now.

She tried to scream, but the vacuous darkness stole his name before it had even left her lips. His eyes flared, glowing brightly, and his grip tightened again.

"Brace your knees," he murmured into her mind. She did as she was told, just in time for them to make a rolling entrance back into Cane's study.

The jarring quiet of his office made her ears ring. Callan ran for his desk and emptied the contents of her stomach in the trash can there. Every time she shut her eyes, it felt like she was back in that in-between world.

Cane stumbled into furniture as he shuffled toward the door.

"Do you need help?" Callan asked, still hunched over the trash.

"I need rest," he said as if every syllable was a torment. The glow of his scars had receded until it barely pierced his skin. He shrugged a blanket over his shoulders and winced. "Come to bed with me. We can talk in the morning."

He didn't give her time to object. But he didn't accept her help getting back to his room either. When they reached his bedroom, Callan set about lighting candles while he cleaned himself up in the bathroom.

Callan was overflowing with questions. But at the first sight of his hunched shoulders, his lowered head, she knew it would have to wait for morning. He was so human in this state. His vulnerability was unsettling.

"I can smell your fear from here, Callan. I promise I won't bite," he said. He threw himself down on the bed, curling in on his abdomen.

"I'm not afraid of you," she said, lowering herself carefully to the bed to keep from jostling him. "I'm afraid for you."

This made Cane laugh, though the sound was weak and dry. "Don't be. I just need rest. I'll be fine in a couple hours."

She watched the tightness in his features soften with sleep. He didn't breathe, but there was other evidence that he had finally relaxed. The smoothness of his brow, the softness of his eyelids, twitching with what could only be a dream. The bite on his lips only made them plumper, the color a deeper wine red. He was devastatingly, cataclysmically beautiful. And he was going to hate her for what she planned to do next.

She waited a half hour until she was sure he wouldn't wake. Then she slipped from the bed, pulled on her coat, and waded out into the still, black of the night.

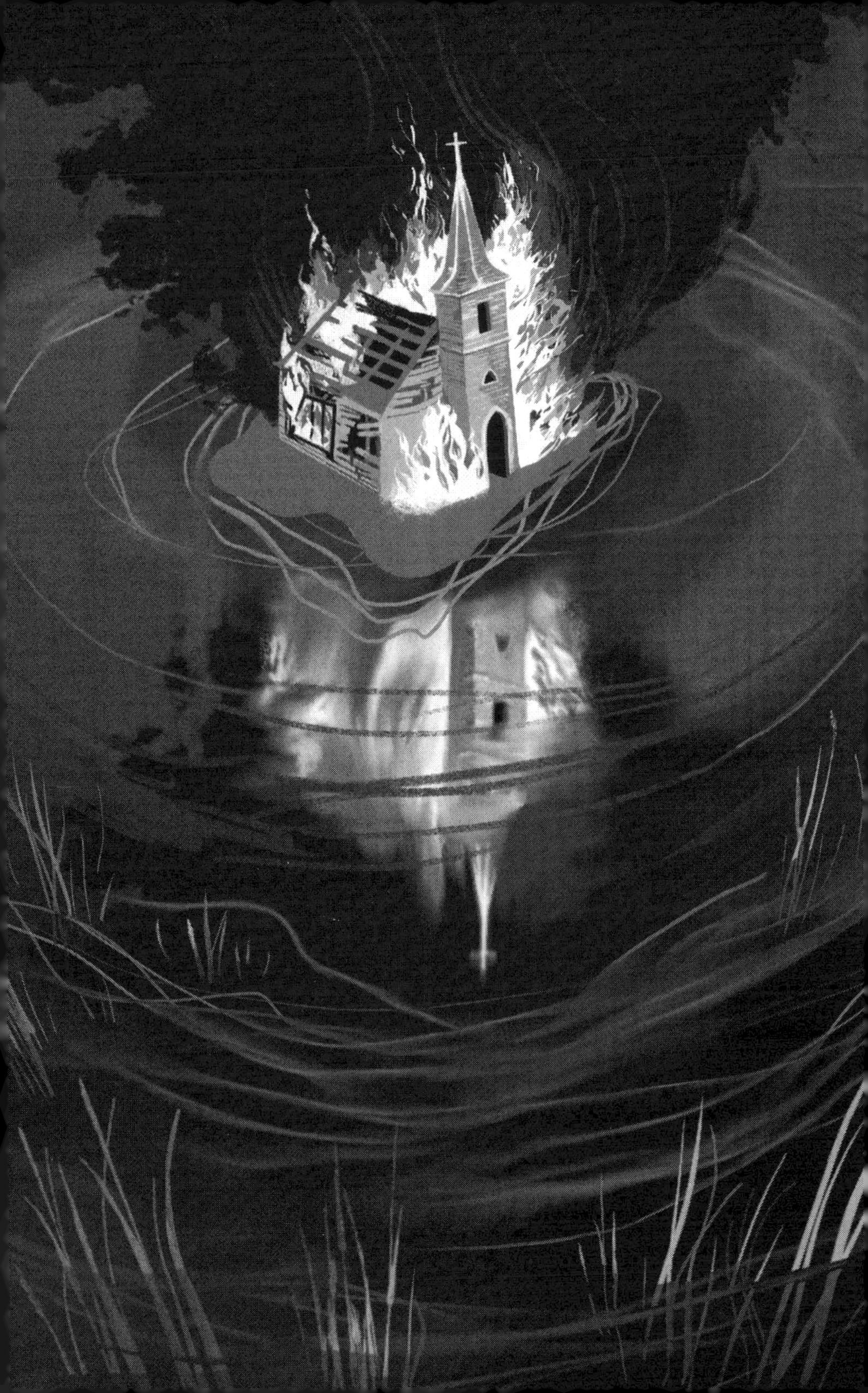

Baptism

The flickering hurricane lamp at the center of the conference table was the only light in the room, the electricity long since sputtered out. The door clicked open on the conference room, just as a perfect replica of Roth's own body disappeared from the seat across from him, the phosphorescent imprint of him still clinging to the air particles. It was Fray who entered, his feet dragging. The faint light caught on the water dripping from Fray's face, glistening on his coat. Fray flopped into the chair Roth's shadow had been sitting in, earning another small jump from Roth.

"Are you one of them?" Roth asked quietly. He was surprised he didn't sound afraid. He felt it. His hands gripped the undersides of his chair. His nerves were ice-thin and electrified. Fray didn't seem to notice. He set to work pulling off his wet boots and socks.

Fray returned the question. "Do I seem like a shadow to you?" He glanced up briefly when Roth didn't answer. "Why would your shadow come in the shape of me, Heller? Are you afraid of me?"

"I'm not afraid," Roth said through clenched teeth. Fray had that effect on him; winding him tighter and tighter with every word out of his stupidly perfect mouth. There was a knife edge of thrill in never knowing exactly what Fray would pull out of him. At least it would be cathartic. Fray never let him have his numbness.

"It seems like you're afraid of me," Fray said, now stripping off his outer jacket. "If you think I'm one of your shadows, that is."

"It's not—" Roth cut himself off with a frustrated sigh. "You're wet." He shoved a hand at Fray over the table, as if it was insurmountable proof that he wasn't real.

Fray lifted a single brow, his fingers starting at the buttons on his shirt. The movement made Roth's throat tight.

"I'm not another drowned thing that crawled from the lake to torment you, Heller. I went looking for my own monster in the snow. Found him too." He shrugged but Roth didn't miss the way his fingers fumbled the next button.

"Why are you stripping in here?" Roth asked. He hoped his voice didn't sound as strained as he felt. Fray pulled the soaked shirt from his skin and let it fall to the carpet with a wet thunk. The muscles that corded Fray's chest bunched as he crossed his arms.

"Does it make you uncomfortable?"

Roth ignored his question. "Why don't you go strip in your room then?" He was unconscious of the way he mirrored Fray as he crossed his own arms. Fray inhaled slowly as he reclined back in his seat. Roth's eyes followed the tightening of his abdominal muscles entirely against his will.

"Because then I couldn't watch after you," he said. Roth had to repeat Fray's answer in his mind a few times before it made any amount of sense.

"I don't need to be watched," he said, feeling the sting of a blush creeping up from his collarbones. "I'm not going to throw myself into the lake like Veronica."

Fray lifted a shoulder that said it made no difference. He wasn't going anywhere.

"You think I'm full of shit? Okay. Right. I'm not the one lying about what the shadows show me."

"I didn't lie," Fray said, stiffening. "I did see my dad. Eventually."

"What did you see before?"

"What did you and Frankie talk about?"

Roth's nostrils flared around an exasperated sigh. "Fine." He kicked away from the table and rose, realizing too late how exhausted he was. He caught himself on the edge of the table and Fray jumped to offer his help. "I'm fine," Roth insisted, tearing his wrist away from Fray's hold. "As you can see, the shadows are gone. Please leave."

Fray didn't speak. He didn't leave either.

"I'm sorry," he finally whispered. "I didn't mean to hurt you. I thought those were party drugs in your bag. If I'd known you needed them, I never would have said anything." His eyes were earnest, imploring in the dark.

"Bullshit," Roth said without malice. "Even if you knew I needed those drugs, you'd have stolen them yourself. You'll do anything in your power to get ahead. Which is hilarious because you're already leagues ahead of everyone else. I guess you're like your father that way."

Fray stepped into Roth's space. "Don't compare me to him," he said, nostrils flaring. Roth stood his ground. He'd been bullied around by his dead teenage brother all night, he wasn't about to start over again with Fray.

"Then don't act like him," Roth replied. Fray blinked. Eventually, he stepped back, averting his eyes.

"I did it because I couldn't stand the thought of Cane figuring out that you're better than me. I thought if he found drugs in your room, and started questioning whether you deserved to be here, he wouldn't have as much time to wonder what I did to deserve my place here, except have a famous dad."

"How lucky for you that your plan worked perfectly," Roth said bitterly. He'd barely gotten his footing here before every rotten secret he'd been keeping was aired for the whole group. Fray hadn't just embarrassed him; he'd made his life misery. But if Fray hadn't ratted on him, he'd still be drifting through his life in varying textures of grayscale, a ghost in all the ways that mattered. He wasn't about to thank Fray. But if given the opportunity to go back and do it again a different way, he wasn't sure he would.

Fray swiped a hand over his neck, and said, "I'm sorry that I hurt you. I'm sorry for what I put you through."

He left before Roth could say another word. The room felt colder without him in it. Roth didn't linger long. He trailed up the stairs, keeping as quiet as possible so none of the shadows in the house would peel away from the walls and stalk after him. He crept past the sliver of buttery, dancing light coming from beneath Fray's door, and returned to his room.

The cold that had set in downstairs slipped deeper as he stripped off his clothes and put on his pajamas. Outside, the wind howled, throwing branches against the siding like fists. Roth knew that as long as night held, so could the shadows. Even after hours spent in Frankie's company, he shivered at the idea of spending more time in his presence tonight. Frankie himself wasn't so terrifying anymore. But the thing under his skin, the thing that wore Frankie like a Halloween mask; that dredged up the kind of fear Roth thought he'd outgrown. The kind of paralyzing fear that made his throat ache with a scream he couldn't let loose.

He'd meant to go to bed. At least if he slept, the monsters of this world couldn't chase him into his nightmares and join the monsters haunting him there. But sleep would not come. He paced around his room in tight, methodical circles, but all it did was pull the anxiety taut within his stomach.

"You're going to make yourself dizzy," Fray mumbled from the door. Roth had been so lost in thought, he didn't even hear the door open. Fray was idly scratching at his bare chest while leaning against the door frame.

"What are you doing here?" Roth demanded. He knew he

must look gangly and childish in his tattered pajamas, his hair standing at angles from all the times his fingers had passed through it. Even the shape of his long, bare feet against the hardwood was embarrassing.

"It's a bit hard to sleep hearing the floorboards squeak with every single step you take," Fray answered.

"I'm thinking," Roth said by way of explanation.

"I can hear that," Fray said. "But maybe you can think with your head against your pillow instead." He nodded at Roth's bed. It was in a state of comical disarray. Roth swallowed, eyeing the bed like it might bite him.

"I can't," he said.

"You can't what?"

The thought of being back in those sheets he'd sweated through night after night, drowned in over and over, made his skin crawl all over again. Fray, who had been observing Roth for far longer than the weeks they'd been at Pitch Lake, caught on quicker than Roth thought possible. He felt a slight tug at the hem of his shirt and looked down to find Fray's fingers delicately wound into it.

Fray didn't say anything, which was good. Every time he spoke, Roth's mind looked for a fight. Instead, Fray led him to his own room, never letting go of Roth's shirt.

The door shut behind them and Fray was everywhere. His cologne hung on the air and the fibers of the sheets. Roth quickly clocked the details; books strewn about in various stages of being read, the neatly made bed, the clothes folded and waiting for tomorrow's lecture. None of it mattered the second he felt Fray's fingers sliding over his ribs as he tugged Roth's shirt off.

"Get in bed," he said, discarding the shirt on his clean, uncluttered floor. It was Roth's first intrusion into Fray's tidy, alien world.

"You know, I still hate you," he said, his eyes lingering on his shirt on the floor. He, like his shirt, was out of place. He could feel the precise shape of every awkward inch of himself as Fray looked him over.

Fray moved around the far side of the bed and crawled under the blankets. He tucked his arms behind his head in a move that put every inch of muscle on display. "Good. You can keep hating me from the bed."

Reluctantly, Roth settled into the bed, wadding a pillow into the crook of his neck and giving Fray his back. If he leaned forward at all, he would fall out of the bed.

The bed jostled as Fray leaned over to blow out the candle. Roth's legs and arms felt heavy with the silence hovering between them. He kicked his legs into the cool space at the bottom of the mattress only to accidentally brush against Fray's bare foot. The contact sent a shock of heat through Roth. His breaths shallowed.

Beside him, Fray was perfectly still. Roth couldn't even hear him breathing over the insistent *thump, thump, thump,* of his own masochistic heart. He was certain Fray wasn't remotely bothered by him. Certainly not the way he was bothered. And, god, was he bothered. He focused all his energy on making every inhale and exhale sound normal, even if they felt electric and forbidden. He buried his face into his pillow and prayed for the relief of sleep.

Minutes, maybe hours later, Fray put him out of his misery. Or, maybe, just added to it. Cool fingers tightened around the waistband of his pajama pants, pulling him back towards the center of the mattress. The thumping of his heart became an erratic staccato that made sweat bead on his palms.

The heat of Fray enveloped Roth in waves as he aligned every inch of their bodies with a practiced efficiency. A hand wound around his waist, pressed into the top of his thigh.

"Still sticking to your story, Heller?"

Roth's back arched as Fray's fingers teased at the band of his pants. They hovered there, brushing back and forth over the sensitive skin of his stomach.

"I do," Roth said breathlessly. "Hate you."

Fray hummed into the back of his neck. The rumble in his chest sent a shiver over Roth's skin. Fray's fingers slipped lower, forcing a desperate sound out of Roth.

"Say it again," Fray murmured, trailing kisses down Roth's vertebrae. Roth's eyes fluttered and then squeezed shut. "And this time you'd better mean it. Or I won't make you come."

He moved then, inching down the bed and stealing Roth's pants in one smooth motion. Roth's breath grated at the silence. He didn't look down, he couldn't.

The warm, wet flat of Fray's tongue over the crease of his cock forced his back away from the bed like something possessed. He whimpered when the first lick was not followed by a second. "Please."

Fray chuckled. His free hand trailed lazily over the quivering skin of Roth's stomach. "Is there something I can do for you, Heller?" He taunted. "You know the rules."

"I hate you," Roth said to the ceiling. It sounded like a prayer. "I fucking hate you," he ground through his teeth. Fray's fingers wrapped around his base. "I need you." The confession crawled out of him before he could bite it back. He could feel the smirk come over Fray's face from between his legs.

"I think I like the sound of that even better."

Fray took him into the very back of his mouth. The flick of his tongue made Roth's eyes roll back. He pulled away with an obscene pop of his lips. "Eyes on me, Heller. Whether you hate me or need me, it's going to be my name on your tongue when you come."

"Arrogant prick," Roth said, rising up on his elbows. The words had no bite when they came out so breathy. Fray didn't give him a chance to protest further. Once Roth was watching, he set to work again. If Roth was being honest, he didn't want to look away. He wanted the image of Fray between his legs to burn into his irises so he saw it every time he blinked.

The pleasure was a jagged, near-painful thing as it swelled under Roth's skin. He gripped the sheets and let his head fall back against the headboard. His eyes were heavy, but they stayed on Fray. Fray's amber gaze flicked up and his free hand went to Roth's balls. If he was looking for permission, he found it.

"I'm— I'm—" Roth helplessly let out the cries he'd been biting back. Fray's hand settled on his stomach, pressing him back to the mattress.

"Then do it, Heller." Fray's voice was hoarse and pitched so low it sent another thrill through Roth. His hands flew to Fray's hair to steady him as the flood of pleasure finally washed over him.

Fray groaned appreciatively. "I'll get my name out of you next time," he said, climbing up the bed and tossing an arm over Roth's wrung-out body.

"Not a chance," Roth murmured, grinning up at the ceiling.

That night, he didn't drown.

This Body, a Tomb

The black woods wrapped their spindly fingers around Callan as they welcomed her into an embrace that should not have been so familiar. With her mind made up about the course forward, she thought the woods, the lake, might try to test her further, coiling up like a labyrinth. But the lake found her without effort.

Her toes were wet with the water at its edge. She hardly noticed the sting. She was searching the dark swathes beneath the fog for signs of her shadow; and finding none.

She sent a whispered intention through her mind.

The fog danced and trailed around the head that slowly breached the surface in answer. Though it was cloaked and shadowed, she knew it. It wasn't her father like she'd always expected.

She teetered on the edge of the lake as the shadow remained motionless. Without looking away from the figure, Callan stripped off her outer layer, tossing it into the snowbank behind her. Her hand went to the cross at her throat, fisting it tightly.

"Are you going to hurt me?" She asked the lake, the shadow at its center.

It didn't respond. It wouldn't, she knew. If she wanted to

understand, she would need to be the one to jump. She would have to want to know.

Its phosphorescent blue eyes jumped to the opposite shore of the lake just as a distant roar split the silence of the wood.

"Callan!" Cane roared from somewhere in the woods. *Shit.* Callan's hands flexed as she stared down at the waiting water. Her heart sputtered and sped. "Callan," Cane yelled again, his voice closer this time. He would be to her in seconds.

She coiled her legs beneath her, taking in a deep inhale of wet, loamy forest air. Maybe it would be her last. For the first time, that idea struck her as tragic. She didn't want to die. She didn't want to fade away either. So, she jumped.

Her surrender came in waves. It burned, consuming her just like the fire had. She couldn't see through the agony, couldn't breathe. All she was, all she thought she would ever be, was pain. She held her breath until the pinpricks of blackness in her vision overtook the very real blackness surrounding her. Finally, she let it go too. The breath was hot and weighty, but it didn't drown her.

In fact, the more she breathed through the stinging pain, the more she realized that the lake wasn't killing her, it was cradling her. As her eyes adjusted and the surroundings sharpened, so did the figure floating before her.

She watched as the figure's fingers, burned to the bone, wrapped around the hood of the violet vestment, peeling it back inch by inch. Callan didn't recognize the version of herself beneath it. The dull, flat sheen over its—or rather, her—eyes; the cowering hold of her bony shoulders. She looked like a mistreated old doll, matted and melted with singed hair.

Her hand drifted to her cross. The eyes of the shadow followed, widening. Her lips opened, but only a flood of bubbles and garbled sounds came out. It was too late.

Touching the cross, Callan's vision was painted in golds and oranges. The heat-swollen door to a long-smothered memory finally came unstuck.

She was on her hands and knees in the apartment above the

church. It was burning. She crawled toward the shining gold knob that marked the door, her hands stinging with cuts and burns, only for something to grip her calf and yank her back. She cried out as panic tore through her chest. She scrambled forward, but her father's hold was too strong. She attempted to kick out, but he caught her easily.

"You can't go, Callan," he said, a thin, bloodied smile spreading over his ash-covered features. His eyes were black as coal and shimmering with the light of the flames. At his throat, a golden cross shone with the same flickering light. "You have to burn too. You have to come with me. We're monsters, you and I. I thought I could make you better, but I was wrong. We can't help but hurt people. See what you did? All you'll ever do is hurt people."

Callan's gaze darted around the room as she searched for some proof that he was wrong. She wasn't a bad person. She wasn't a monster. Her gaze dragged to the lump on the floor behind her father. Her mother. Her mother's body. Callan's shoulders slumped as a brittle cry broke her lips. She had done *this*. Maybe she was a monster.

"I don't want to go to hell," she whimpered, backing away slowly on her butt. Above her, her father teetered on his feet as a wet cough tore through him. He gripped his bleeding abdomen with one hand and steadied himself against the wall with the other.

"Do you have so little faith?" He demanded weakly, wheezing on every exhale. He pulled a handkerchief from his pocket and dabbed it to his mouth. "Our father will come for us. He has already forgiven us. He knows how we sin."

Callan wasn't prepared to take that chance. As he doubled over in another fit of coughing and gagging, she kicked her feet to slide herself closer to the door.

"If you run," he said between gurgling breaths. "You are spitting in the face of your creator. He will not have you."

Callan shook her head, shaking free her tears. "I don't want your god," she said. Her father's god was a poison. His face twisted in rage as he took a bounding step forward, reaching out for her as a string of curses left his mouth. He only made it a half step. The wood floor gave way beneath him just as the ceiling caved. Debris came loose, hitting him over the head and knocking him unconscious.

Callan stared and stared. But her father never rose. It seemed impossible that a man like him could have been killed by his own church. Maybe, he'd been killed by his own god.

No, she countered. *He was killed by me.*

There was little time to get out of the church. Already, her breaths were dragging raggedly through her swollen, dry throat. But she couldn't leave yet.

She crawled back to him with her heart in her throat, the beat of it drowning out the roar of the fire. She pushed his head back. As she watched the gold cross at her father's throat continue to glint, rage ate up all her pain, all her fear. Huffing, she tore the cross from his neck and squeezed it tightly in her stinging, cut hands. She closed her eyes in a silent prayer, hoping his god had seen all of this, and that he was practiced in vengeance.

When her eyes opened next, she was back in the lake. Her shadow floated before her, her father's cross clutched in the girl's injured hands. Her younger self watched her with concern, even pity. What could this young girl who had suffered so much possibly have to pity her for?

I am you, her eyes said. But still, that truth would not wedge itself firmly into Callan's mind. She watched as her shadow lifted the hand holding her father's cross. Watched as her fingers spread, allowing the chain to sift through, and finally releasing it to the lake. It sunk quickly, swallowed by the darkness below them in a heartbeat.

When Callan's gaze rose again, that hand was still poised in the dark space between them. An offering. As she stared at that battered hand, ghosts began to rise in her periphery. Faces that would not have been familiar before. But here, in the lake, those faces told stories. Those stories were tangled up in her like the sinew of muscle. They were as much her as the girl floating before her. She knew them the way she knew how to breathe and think. She knew, instantly, that they had never left her, even if she had lost them. They had always walked beside her.

Slowly, Callan fitted her fingers into the hold of her younger self, lifelines and heartlines aligning. When their gazes collided, the younger's eyes said, *this will hurt.*

Suddenly, the warm, sure hold of her hand was gone. As was the reassuring glint of her green eyes. She was washed in the dim, green glow of the girls' bathroom in her high school in Kansas. She was standing in a stall, and she wasn't alone. A girl stood before her. They were the same age, but this girl's eyes were old, tired. Desperate. The memory of her bloomed in Callan's mind in the same instant her name bloomed on Callan's lips.

"Haley, what is it? What's wrong?" Her voice was so young and bright, not yet sanded down by life. "Tell me, I can help you." Haley's eyes were heavy with unshed tears as she shook her head, sniffling.

"You can't help me," she whimpered, hiccupping. "No one can help me." Haley's tears came in earnest then, and Callan felt the familiar sensation of her chest cracking. She grabbed Haley's cold hands and held them tightly. Distantly, the class bell rang. Haley flinched, her shoulders coming up around her ears.

"We can stay in here," Callan reassured her. "We can stay in here as long as you need." They stood in silence as the halls filled with the noise of students shuffling by and using the stalls of the bathroom around them. Haley crept so close that Callan could smell the cherry scent of her lip balm.

"Pastor Lark hurt me," she said on the barest breath. Four words that felt like the yellowing of the sky around a twister. They were cataclysmic; the beginning and the end. Callan didn't need to hear the rest of the words. The memory of them sank into the pit of her stomach like heavy, cold stones.

When her head rose, she was alone in that bathroom stall.

Now, the tears falling were her own. It was only a few days later, but Callan's world could not have looked more different. Haley would never share another secret with her in the bathroom stalls again. She would be lowered to the cold, damp earth on a Sunday in September. Pastor Lark would preside in his pristine violet vestments as they threw soil over Haley's wasted body; a body she could no longer stand to inhabit because of him.

That day, she left school early. There was no point pretending the world continued to spin when it had so clearly stopped with Haley's heart. A numbness spread through Callan's veins as she set about her plan. There was very little emotion to any of it. She would douse the whole building in gasoline, then she would wait. When he came home, she would let him burn.

Callan thought maybe she really was a monster if killing him came so naturally. But then she heard her father's roaring yell from below.

He had her by the neck before she had time to form a single thought. He dragged her down the stairs of the apartment, through the pews, down the hall leading to the door in the ground.

"No, no, no," she whimpered. He fumbled with the latch on the door, cursing, his fingers painfully tight on her neck. Then he shoved her into the dark.

"You will clean this mess up after you've thought long and hard about your sins," he hissed. "You're lucky I don't kill you right here and now. God would thank me."

Callan's hands trembled as she searched the shelves of the cellar for a weapon. Above, she could hear her father stomping around. Eventually, her mother's softer footsteps joined the mix. Then the yelling started up again. Callan wasn't the only one hearing secrets in town. Her mother wasn't backing down from this fight, even if Callan wished she would.

Her chest swelled with a mix of hope and fear at the fast clip of her mother's approaching steps. But she never made it. Callan flinched as she heard the crumpling of limbs against the floor and the silence that ensued. She blinked back tears to keep her vision clear. Her father paced back and forth for what felt like hours. Callan's eyes followed the sound of his steps, back and forth, dread tightening into knots in her gut. She knew his mind had been made up when his steps came for the cellar door.

"Change of plans," he said, swinging the door wide. She could smell smoke as he grabbed Callan by the hair and dragged her out. He marched her up the stairs to the apartment and threw her onto her bed. "Stay." Mind blank with fear, realizing he had hijacked her plan, she did as she was told.

All she could do was listen to the slow, stilted drag of her mother's body up the steps, her father huffing and cursing the whole way. He kicked the door shut behind him, startling a few more tears free of Callan's eyes. She twisted her hands in her lap as she surveyed her small, spare bedroom for anything to use in self-defense. The best she had was a lamp, a thick bible, and a hand mirror.

She sprang forward and threw the mirror to the ground, gathering up the splintered pieces. Her hands were dripping blood by the time she rounded the corner of the living room and lowered into a crouch. She hardly felt the sting.

The first thing she saw was her mother on the floor, arms and legs splayed carelessly. Her father had barely gotten her through the door. The next thing she saw was the fire. It had started in her parent's bedroom but, thanks to the gasoline, had begun to spread quickly. Her father emerged from the room like an omen, framed by creeping flames and black smoke.

"Get back in your room," he barked, dragging Callan's mother like a sack of soil towards the fire.

"Don't touch her!" Callan screamed, the words coming out wet with her tears. She rushed forward, falling onto her mother's body.

"I hope he makes you suffer, you little devil," her father hissed, yanking her mother's body away with a single violent tug. Callan fell, landing on the fistfuls of broken glass.

"You hurt Haley," Callan bellowed. "You hurt mama. You hurt everyone." Her father's eyes widened, then narrowed to slits. He lunged for her, wrestling her against his chest as he dragged her back toward her bedroom. She took her opportunity to jab the shards of glass into him, slicing at his stomach. "I hope *you* suffer," she spit as he screamed. He released her, but she was shaking so violently she didn't think she could walk, let alone run. "I hope you die. You're a monster! God won't have you. You're going to hell." She continued to shout uselessly, as he doubled over, picking pieces of glass from his skin.

Callan continued to shiver as she backed toward the door, the fire building around them. In the commotion, she'd forgotten her mother's body behind her and she tripped, falling onto her injured hands. Despite the pain, she dragged herself forward on her elbows. The door accordioned away from her. The space stretching impossibly. The door's golden knob called to her like a holy beacon, but she would never reach it now. Her father would catch her. Her father would always catch her. He was right behind her, his breaths hot in her ear. His hand was a manacle at her ankle, dragging her back. She reached one last helpless, hopeless hand for the door.

This time, it sprung open. A palm with silvery scars matching the wounds on her hand reached through. She took it.

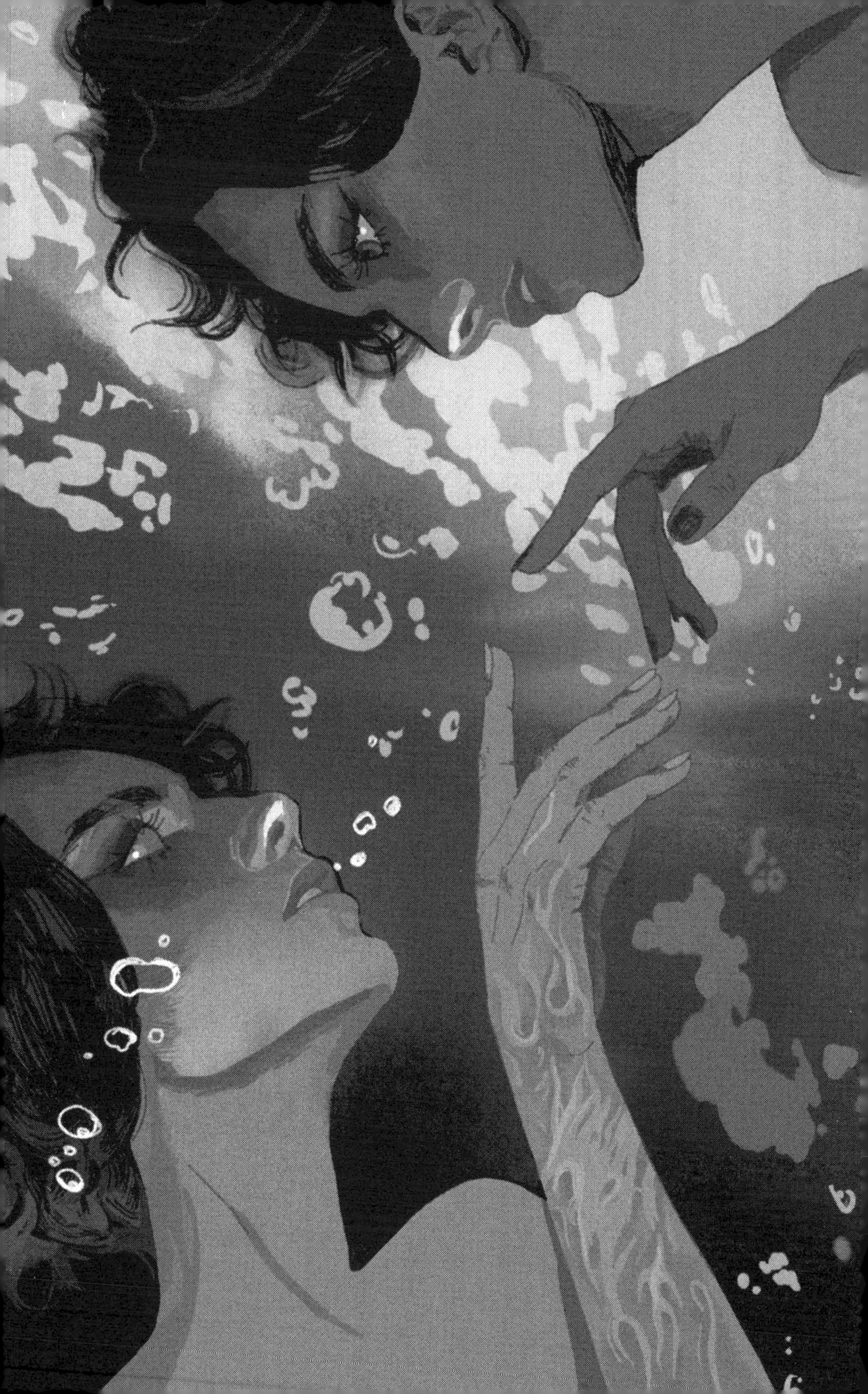

Float Plan

Water expelled violently from Callan's mouth as they rocked forward onto hands no longer stinging with fresh cuts. They were back beside the lake, the sky clear overhead with a scythe moon hanging in the center. The smoke was gone. Their father too. But their ears were still ringing with adrenaline. Callan's hands shook as they turned them over to inspect their wounds. The scars shone silver in the moonlight. Old, but new to Callan. The burn scars made wave-like patterns of varying shades over the backs of their hands and forearms. It was impossible to know where skin ended and scar tissue began. A forgotten masterpiece.

"Callan," Ladon bellowed through the trees, closer than he had been before they jumped. What had felt like a lifetime in the lake had been only seconds.

"Here," they said weakly. Even their voice sounded different. It wasn't that it was wrong. It was just... *more*. Ladon broke through the final row of trees and froze. He seemed to gather himself, collecting his feral, frayed edges as he registered that they were safe. That they were changed. He stepped stiffly, slowly into the clearing of the lake.

"Hello, Cal," he said carefully, the glow of his eyes narrowing as he assessed them. He moved like he was unsure; like Callan was the predator rather than him, the god. "What has the lake shown you?"

"Everything," they whispered hoarsely, lungs still heavy with the soul stuff that made up its depths, hair dripping with it. Ladon drifted forward silently as they rose. He stripped off his coat and offered it, careful not to touch any part of them. Callan stared at his stark, sober features as they pulled it around their shoulders.

"When I told you I would only have you whole—" His voice broke off. He tipped his head back to the night sky. The column of his throat glowed in the moonlight. "I never meant that you were broken. You've always been exactly what you were supposed to be. You did what needed to be done to survive. I'm in awe of you. You're perfect, however you are. And I hate to think that I pushed you too hard."

"I didn't do this for you," they said. "I couldn't have done it without you. But it wasn't for you. It was for them," Callan said, opening their palms so he could see the patchwork of silver threading through the lifeline and heartline. They took a step forward. "You saw them all along, didn't you?"

He gave a slow nod in response. The glow of his eyes intensified.

"Why didn't I?"

"Your mind wasn't ready to confront what they meant; the memories they held," Ladon said, seeming relieved to relax into his therapist talk. "If we had continued with hypnosis and our other protocols, you would have eventually unlocked them yourself."

Without the lake, he didn't need to add. Callan didn't exactly believe him but nodded stiffly. A part of them had been in the lake all along; ever since that day in September. The longer they stood, the heavier their head felt. "You need rest. Whatever happened in the lake, it drained you."

He offered Callan his arm, which they took, and he led them back toward the cabin.

Cane pulled them closer into his warmth as they walked, "Your eyes are glowing like mine," he murmured near their ear. Callan stiffened, but Ladon only laughed, tugging them along. "It will go away. Probably."

"But I'm not—I'm not like you. Am I?" The sight of the cabin was such a relief their knees would have buckled without Ladon's support.

When they hit the porch, he began removing their cold, wet layers, dropping them on the stoop and pulling Callan into the warmth of the living room. "I think only time will tell exactly what the lake gave you," he said finally.

Callan decided they needed a full night of sleep and a good meal before attempting to give those words meaning. They were still shivering in a wet tank and leggings, but they didn't make for their room or Ladon's. Ladon stopped Callan with a gentle hand.

"You need to warm up and sleep," he said, inviting no argument.

Images splintered in Callan's mind. "Not yet," they said. "There's something I need to do first." A scene to get down in acrylic before they fell asleep and risked losing it again forever. Ladon seemed to understand implicitly. He watched them climb the stairs and head down the hall toward the dark studio. He didn't follow.

Not until hours later, when the first light of morning was fracturing through the thick cloud cover in watery yellows and oranges. Callan stood in the center of the room before their creation, feeling as thin and ragged as an old, hole-riddled dish towel. Ladon entered the studio without a word, coming to stand behind Callan and placing a hand at their nape. They drooped under the gentle ministrations of his fingers.

The painting had felt like an exorcism; a thing dredged up from Callan's soul rather than from a collection of paints on a palette. It was far from finished, but already Callan felt lighter without the full weight of it on their soul.

Ladon stripped the paintbrush from their fingers, depositing it on the easel. Without it, Callan felt weaponless and numb. They had no power over the waves crashing through them. Their vision swam with tears as Ladon pulled them into his chest.

"Let me take care of you," he murmured into their hair. "You don't have to hold all of this on your own."

Callan stared up at him through wet lashes, marveling at the icy blue of his eyes. "How can you even look at me knowing what I've done?"

Ladon scoffed, pulling away so he could pin them with an imploring look. "What have you done except survive, Callan? You escaped. You found your way to me, just as your soul did. I'm keeping both. If you believe I'm a god, then let me be the one to weigh your sins."

Callan ducked their head as tears spilled free. Ladon turned them so he could rub the tight muscles in their back. With expert precision, he loosened the knots between their shoulder blades. The reverence of his hands made it seem he'd been aware of these hurts for some time; the kink in their neck, the constellation of knots in their shoulders, the ache under their left arm. He found them all. By the time he was done, the only thing keeping Callan upright was Ladon's palm at their hip.

"Let's get you into bed," he said finally, pulling them toward the door.

Despite the tiredness of their body, Callan's blood hummed. The warmth forged by his hands was a welcome replacement for the numbness that had settled into their bones. The desire to *feel*—to feel anything—overwhelmed them. Their fingers caught in Ladon's belt loop before they lifted their gaze to his, searching.

"Not tonight," he said with a single shake of his head. The rejection was like a slap. Callan let their hand fall away, turning to hide the traitorous swell of tears that followed; hating that he would know they were crying whether he saw their tears or not.

They would have to get used to the emotions coming so easily, even when unwanted.

Ladon pulled them into his chest in a possessive hold. He nipped the edge of their earlobe before saying, "Don't you dare hide from me, Cal. I see you. And I will have all of you when you are ready. But the things I'll ask of you will require your full strength and attention. Have I made myself clear?" He shook them slightly when they didn't answer.

It took considerable will for Callan to pry free of his hold, to face him with their chin held high. They could feel the glow returning to their eyes as they said, "I'm tired of being told what I'm ready for. I think I've proven I'm stronger than you think. I'll decide when I'm ready." They placed their hand back on his chest, eyes staying level on his. "Please, Ladon. I want you."

"You don't know what you're asking for, love," he said so low it sounded like a threat. "I told you I wouldn't be gentle."

He was close enough that Callan could feel his unsteady exhales on their cheek.

"I don't want gentle," Callan replied.

He didn't reach for them yet, but the absence of his touch had its own weight. It fluttered on their skin like phantom hands, desperate and grasping. His shadows, Callan realized. He was struggling to control them. Callan reached out a hand for him and his shadows twisted up from the floor to hold Callan's hands in place.

"Final warning," he gritted out. "In this state, I'm mostly instinct. There is very little of the professor, even less of the shrink."

"Good," they said, hands flexing against the silky hold of his shadows. The shadows eased Callan back until their hip hit a workstation table. "I don't want the professor," they added, gazing up into his glowing eyes. "I want the monster."

His restraint snapped. His hands grasped either side of their face as he captured their mouth in a demanding kiss. There was nothing teasing or sweet about the kiss, even as it went on and on.

His shadows hoisted them up onto the table, spilling paints and brush water in the process, and pinning Callan exactly where he wanted them so his hands could explore their body. He stepped away with a frustrated groan, undressing efficiently while continuing to devour Callan with his eyes. His shadows worked in tandem to remove Callan's clothes, exerting the same frenzied impatience. The shadows spread Callan's legs wide and he stepped between them, fingertips whispering over their skin as they came to rest at their throat. The jutting length of him filled the distance between their bodies. The closeness sent a shiver through Callan.

Ladon growled low, tightening his hold on their throat. "Move like that and this will be over very quickly." His mouth traced the path of his fingertips with a slowness that had Callan panting and writhing. He nipped teasingly at their lips, chin, and collarbones.

"Ladon," Callan whimpered, their body trembling with tension. Ladon lowered to his knees and trailed his fingertips idly from their sternum to their navel. As those fingers drifted further, Callan's eyes fluttered. They gasped.

Ladon's thumb settled over their clit, exerting the barest pressure. "I want to eat every sound you make before it leaves your lips," he mused. Callan bucked away from the table but his shadows captured them quickly, holding them still. "I want every ounce of your pleasure," he said, his gaze lingering on his thumb as it worked slowly. "Every speck of your fear. I want those eyes, that mouth. Every freckle and every fucking scar. This body is mine." His gaze lifted to theirs, trailing his free hand up their quivering body to tweak their nipple. They cried out, writhing against the soft hold of the shadows. "You. Are. Mine," he growled.

Callan watched with rapt attention as he ran his nose up the inside of their thigh, planting kisses over the sensitive skin. Then, with one long, slow, stroke of his tongue, their vision was painted white. There was a low rumbling of approval from below as

Ladon's shadows tightened on their thighs. Then he did just as he'd promised, and devoured them. He brought them, over and over again, to the precipice. Teasing and toying with them until they were drawn so taut they thought they might snap in half.

"Ladon, please," they gasped.

He chuckled. "You'll have to do better than that to rush me." His hot breath on their inner thigh sent pulses through their nerves. His finger trailed softly up to tease at their entrance. They cried out, chest heaving even as the shadows forced their body to remain flush against the table. His mouth returned to its taunting rhythm. Callan freed an arm from the shadows' hold to grab a handful of his hair. His gaze flicked up, though his mouth didn't stop working. His fingers pumped into them as he sucked lightly. Tighter and tighter he wound them, as their breaths grew shallow and their core tensed. With a single, knowing flick of his tongue, pleasure washed through them in all-consuming waves. Their heart roared in their ears, drowning out everything else.

When they came back to earth, Ladon was sitting back on his knees, staring up with a wolfish grin on his glistening lips. He brought his fingers to his mouth and sucked them.

"Fucking beautiful," he growled. "And all mine too."

Callan had never been happier to concede to him. They gave him a sated smile as he rose to his full height.

"If I'm yours," they panted, "then take me."

They struggled against the hold of the shadows, but they were unyielding as they spread Callan wider for him.

His nostrils flared. "Give me a moment," he said. "I don't want to hurt you." There was a distinct warning in the black of his irises that Callan ignored as they wet their lips.

"I want whatever you have to give me," they said, gaze eating up every muscle on display. Callan was feverish with need, even after their own release. This need was for him. They needed to watch him come undone, needed to know that he was as deep into this as they were. They stared up at him, willing his surrender, and shivered as they realized the barely restrained violence in his eyes. Shadows tugged at every inch of Callan's skin like they wanted to play but didn't know where to start. He was so near to snapping. Callan was desperate to see it.

They attempted to reach for him through the hold of the shadows, and this time he didn't deny them. Their hand fisted his length as all the air in his lungs evacuated. When his eyes fluttered open, they were all animal.

"Monster and all," Callan whispered against his lips. His tongue darted out to capture the words. Then his mouth slanted over theirs, taking up a bruising, desperate rhythm. He lifted them from the table and drove them back against the wall, art supplies toppling from the shelves around them. Powerful thighs braced beneath Callan's as he brought their hands above their head.

"You're going to be a good little monster, aren't you?" He asked, his voice taunting. "You're going to come for me. And when you think you can't possibly continue, you're going to remember what you just begged me for, and you're going to come again." he positioned himself at their entrance but didn't move any closer. "I don't stop until I hear you scream," he said. Callan whimpered as just the tip of him caused a delicious stretch. He took his time, eating up the distance between their bodies inch by inch. He used his shadows to hitch up one of Callan's legs so he could angle himself even deeper. Then, with a desperate sound, he thrust himself to the hilt. "Fuck," he groaned, pulling all the way out before slamming home again. His head fell back as obscenities poured from him. "You won't ever move again without feeling me," he growled. It was almost too much. Callan's eyes squeezed shut as they adjusted to the pressure, his demanding rhythm. "You can take it," he whispered hoarsely. "Look at you. Made. For. Me." He rose up, flattening a palm between their breasts as he brought them to the edge once again. Around them, all the light from the candles Callan had lit was blotted out by his shadows forming a dark, beautiful tapestry at his shoulders.

"God, Ladon, please," they whimpered, needing something they weren't capable of articulating. He understood perfectly. His fingers found the place where they were joined, his thumb flattening over their clit.

"I sure hope the god you're referring to is me, Callan," he warned, grinding down his thumb as his other hand went to their breast. "You don't want to see me jealous."

With a tweak of his fingers, they cascaded into another orgasm. He fucked them through it, refusing to slow his pace. "If you want this to end, you'll need to scream for me," he said, continuing to torture them with his fingers. "I want everything, and I won't stop until I have it."

"More," Callan panted, though they weren't sure their body could take it. Their mind had never been so blissfully quiet.

"Good," Ladon growled, the dark pits of his eyes betraying just how far gone he was. In one fluid motion, he pulled out and flipped them around so they faced the wall. Before they could take another breath, he was back inside, his hands caging their hips as his thrusts became erratic. A hand moved down their back, tracing the curves of their scars until they shivered. The hand snaked around their side and squeezed their throbbing clit. Another orgasm ripped through them. "Sing for me, Callan."

"Ladon, I— I— can't," they cried, breathless.

"Oh, sweetheart, you should have listened earlier," he murmured, draping himself over their back. He wasn't winded in the slightest. He stroked lazy lines up and down their quivering stomach and began to set a slower, deeper rhythm that, impossibly, bloomed heat in Callan's core once again. "You know when this ends. Give me everything."

Hours later, they lay on the floor of the studio, cradled by Ladon's shadows. Callan's head was nestled in the crook of his shoulder, eyes fluttering as dawn washed over the mess they'd made of the studio.

Ladon disentangled himself from Callan and stood,

wandering to the easel at the center of the room. "Incredibly unsettling," he commented, glancing back. He drifted closer, peering at the details of the self-portrait. Its eyes seemed to follow him as he circled it.

Before, Callan had been unsure what emotions lived in those eyes. Fear? Delight? Defeat? Now it was clear to Callan, even if it was impossible for anyone else to understand. The point wasn't for the world to understand. The point was for the world to witness what could not be understood, to make space for the questions even if no answers followed, to accept the dark spaces between understanding for the art that it was.

"What will you call it?" Ladon asked, returning to Callan's side to offer them a hand up.

Callan gazed into the eyes of the monster on the canvas. It gazed back. "My soul."

Icarus

"Don't be a prude, Fray," Roth whined through the crack in the studio door. He'd been pacing outside for several minutes. Fray wasn't sure if he was nervous or excited to reveal what he'd been working on. It was certainly... different. He took a step back from his work, taking off the protective eye mask he'd needed as he welded the metal pieces.

"I can hear you in there, you little shit. I showed you mine, now show me yours," Roth continued with a smile in his voice. If anyone got the idea to wipe it off Roth's face again, Fray would be happy to inflict any manner of violence to make sure they suffered for it.

If Fray was being honest, he had very little hope of competing with the masterpiece Roth had shown him. He had very little hope of keeping up with Roth at all. Perhaps most unsettling, he thought he might be okay with that, eventually.

Baptism was the name that had sprung to Fray's mind as he poured over the details of Roth's sculpture. A young boy suspended in water, reaching for the surface. The details were almost too realistic for something set in stone. Air bubbles floating up from his mouth, the strain in his muscles, reflections from the surface in his eyes. But the way he reached for the surface, the insistent set of his face told a story of survival and potential. He wasn't drowning. He was pulling himself from the depths. He was being reborn.

Fray's work held none of the innate motion of Roth's sculpture. If anything, the piece was arresting. Quiet. Desperate. But there was hope in it nonetheless. Fray wasn't sure if he needed Roth to see the truth of it, or if he couldn't stand for Roth to know just yet. Roth pounded against the door again.

"For Christ's sake, Fray, open this damned—"

Fray swung the door open and immediately returned to his workstation.

"It's not done," he grumbled, already offering excuses as Roth walked a slow circle around Icarus. When Roth finished taking in the sculpture, he sat on the ground and quietly asked, "Have you seen it from this angle?"

Fray kept his gaze averted as he shook his head.

"Come here then."

Fray reluctantly went to Roth's side, sitting so close their legs touched. He swallowed around a tight pain in his throat. Then he lifted his gaze to see what he'd made from Roth's perspective.

A pair of pristine, white wings poised in flight, held together by the brutal grip of a melting, golden fist. From below, it looked like the wings were fighting toward the sun, struggling to melt away the hold of their captor. Fray didn't have the heart to convey in their depiction that there was nothing beneath the fist. If it melted away, they would be directionless, tugging in opposite directions. If that fist fell apart, so did they. But there was a defiant hope to their flight. Was it better to fly steady or to be free? Was there even a difference?

Roth reached over and gathered Fray's tears onto his thumb. "You're brilliant," he whispered. "Absolutely fucking brilliant, you bastard."

Fray laughed wetly, twisting his hands into his pants.

"When I was a kid, my dad was my biggest fan," he said, his voice poked through with holes. "Aemon loved the idea of a minime. He used to tell people I was a protégé. He sold my first piece when I was six. But then, all of a sudden, I wasn't small. I was a man like him. An artist like him. People wanted to talk to me and not him. In a split second, he stopped being my dad and became my competition. But I could never quite stop being his son. Maybe I'm still asking for his love with this," he said, gesturing at Icarus. "Maybe I'll never stop asking."

Roth leaned into Fray's side, nudging him lightly. Fray's hand settled around his shoulders, tugging him in closer.

"I don't think it's his love you need," Roth said. "But I get it. I can't imagine being his son."

Fray traced the wavy pattern at the base of the fist that gave it its melting effect.

"He built his empire, but he didn't teach me any of the things I'd need to build something for myself. All I ever learned from him was how to tear people down. And even if I did make something of myself, I'll always be a Fray. Everything I'll ever make will be compared to him. Anything I do outside of art will be to spite him."

"Let them compare you," Roth insisted. "Let them stand you up side by side and let them see him for what he is. Stop playing small, that's his game."

Fray rested his head on Roth's shoulder as they continued to look up through the luminescent wings. In that moment, Fray knew he had the answer to the question at the heart of Icarus. It was always better to be free than to be safe. It was always better to have someone there to catch you when you fell than to have someone carry you towards the things you thought you wanted.

Sometime later, the door creaked open. Callan poked their head in, Schrödinger cradled in their arms. They smiled at Roth and Fray before staring in open-mouthed wonder at Icarus.

"Holy shit, you finished it," they said, creeping through the door. Fray stiffened, but Roth rubbed the tension out of his shoulders with an encouraging shake.

"Isn't it incredible?" Roth asked. Callan nodded as their eyes poured over the details, hand skimming the surface of the gold fist. "Any bets on whose will sell for the most?"

Fray and Callan groaned in unison.

"Fine, fine. We all know it'll be me anyway," Roth said, his face brightening on a smile. Fray swatted at him, but he couldn't help the mirroring smile that spread over his features. It seemed Cal was susceptible to the same influence. Soon they were all grinning like idiots.

"Ladon is ready for us," Cal said. "He's at the lake."

"Ladon, huh?" Roth teased, wedging his tongue into his cheek and eliciting a blush from Callan. It was old news that Callan and Cane were shacked up. For the first week, they kept quiet about it. But after sharing a very unprofessional kiss on New Year's Eve that rivaled the R-rated one Roth and Fray had shared, the cat left the metaphorical bag. "First name basis for the teacher's dirty little pet."

"I will kill you," Callan deadpanned. "I know where you sleep." Roth raised his hands in surrender, laughing.

"After what we've all been through, I think we can call him whatever the hell we like," Fray chimed in. "It's not like he's actually a professor."

"Well, he's a professor," Callan said, tipping their head from side to side. "He's just *also* a god. It must make for very complicated tax filings." They paused, like a dog hearing a distant whistle, then groaned, rolling their eyes. "He says we're stalling."

Roth stared like they had grown a third eye. Whatever had happened to Callan in the lake, they were... different now. It wasn't just their art, though the transformation there was remarkable. It was Callan. There was something distinctly unknowable about them now. He shook his head, "I will never get used to that."

The three of them rose from the floor and made their way outside. The sun was high in the sky, making the icicles lining the porch gleam and drip into the snow drifts below.

As they traversed the trail to the lake, the hole Veronica left seemed to hold space for her. She was there, walking behind Callan and in front of Roth. She was kicking at the snow, and cursing the cold. As they rounded the last bend in the trail and came into view of the lake, Fray knew there was even more of Veronica here. Fray could feel that shadowy part of her soul just beneath the dark surface, winking up at him. There was no sadness to it. Only peace.

They came to where Cane waited, hands deep in his pockets as he stared into the lake. He nodded at each of them as they approached. The lake looked as it had on their first visit; a black eye rimmed in barren Tamarack lashes. There were plastic sacks at the shore, this time only three instead of four. Cane waved them forward.

"We've come to the end of the retreat," he said. "As I promised, our adventure will end here. Look into the lake, and tell me what you see."

Fray kneeled down and braced his hands on the lake's lip, peering over. No longer was the lake opaque and reflectionless. Now, he stared down into his own face. It wasn't his fear, or his father, or any other devil waiting in those depths for him. It was only him. It had only ever been him. He glanced to the side at Roth, who tipped his head up at the same time, a hint of a smile playing at his lips despite the sheen of tears in his eyes. Beside him, Callan was smiling down at their reflection.

"Amazing isn't it, how your mind can make itself into a monster. How you can grow so far apart from yourself that you don't even recognize a piece of your own soul standing before you."

As Cane drifted toward the lake shore, Fray watched for his reflection on the surface. Fray saw the first tendrils of shadow, the start of bone-white skin, of pitch-black veins and... horns. Cane paused and, seeming to realize himself, paced away from the lake and Fray's watchful gaze. When he turned to face Fray, his navy eyes were swimming with mirth and an ancient secret. He gave Fray a wink.

"I hope as you return to your life, you don't lose sight of yourself. I hope that no matter how crowded a room becomes, you're always able to recognize yourself in it. That you find a home for every facet of yourself in this body of yours, temporary as it may be. Our monsters are many, but at their core all they are is us."

Fresh Cuts

Ten months later.

A tingle spread over Ladon's skin just before his phone buzzed in his pocket. He pulled the newspaper from the table and leaned against the wall.

"*Cal Stuns Fans with Latest Pop-Up*," he purred into the phone, reading the headline story of the *Times*. "I told you auctions and openings were antiquated."

"I didn't say I needed an auction," Callan replied, sounding half-distracted. "I just said the prep for these pop-ups will give me a coronary, and I stand by that observation. It's not a matter of if, it's a matter of when." Ladon smiled at the sound of Callan's grunt, the clatter of a suitcase bumping into the stairs. He checked his watch.

"There will be consequences if you miss your flight, Cal," Ladon said with just a hint of what he had planned for them when they finally returned home. He set the paper on the table and paced to the window, looking out over the gold and crimson meadow. In another two weeks, it would all be covered in snow.

"It's too early in the morning for dirty talk, Professor," Callan said, voice edged in a smirk that Ladon could picture in perfect detail. Over the symphony of Manhattan traffic, he heard Callan greet their driver and settle into the backseat. "Roth's opening was absolute perfection, by the way. There wasn't a dry eye in the building. He said to say, and I quote, '*Hi dad, are you proud of me yet? Can't wait to come back to hell house.*'" Ladon chuckled. Callan wasn't the only one joining him for another winter term. Roth would come after his series ran its course in New York. From there, he'd be moving to Los Angeles with Fray. Callan would stay here, with him. Permanently. The thought made the shadows tangling around his legs settle a little, though he knew they'd never relax entirely without Callan nearby.

"Hey, did you get a chance to look into that plot of land?" Callan asked casually. Ladon knew that casualness was only a ruse. But it was one he would give them. For now.

"I did," Ladon replied, returning to the table, where the land sale contract already listed Ladon and Callan as co-owners. "The owners were... surprisingly motivated to sell. I heard a rumor that the locals think the marsh that formed behind the abandoned church has zombies in it. They only seem to come out in the dead of night."

"Zombies? Oh, how monstrous," Callan teased. Their voice darkened over the next words, the anticipation a physical weight. "When can we go?"

Acknowledgments

What Feeds the Lake is the answer to a question I posed to myself in the darkest, loneliest days of my existence. I was in my second year of law school, sitting through a lecture on law and economics when the first panic attack hit me. As with all struggles that came before, I thought I could reason and study my way through it. Or, at least, ignore it until it went away. But time and time again, those phantom fingers wrapped around my throat, and plunged me into dark, cold waters that stole everything. I drowned in those waters for over a year. In that year, I existed within my own stomach, watching my body and my mind wither around me with no tools to stop it, lighting matches to keep off the darkness crowding in. All those matches seemed to do was burn my fingers. And eventually, even those ran out. As I sat in the dark, waiting for the monsters to slink forth and devour me, I finally began to understand the nature of those monsters, the nature of the darkness too.

But that wasn't when the answer came. It took years, and many loves of many natures, to realize that the answer had been hidden in the question. It is those loves I must thank here. Funny really, how words have become my greatest weapon against the dark, and yet they feel wholly inadequate to capture my gratitude for the people that chased off that darkness to begin with. I'll try anyways.

First, to Robbie, whose love saved my life. The truth always sounds like hyperbole where you are concerned, but it is true nonetheless. You showed me that I was never drowning, I was just treading water very inefficiently. Through your humor, patience, encouragement, and unconditional love, I learned how to swim on my own again. While I never want to swim without you by my side, you showed me that I could, and I will forever be grateful for the trust you helped me find in myself. Thank you for providing the hum necessary for my creativity, for being the voice of reason in a mind full of viscous versions of myself, for giving a home to every jagged edge of me, and softening them with a love that feels like a thousand answers to questions I was never forced to ask.

To my mom, whose love was the gentle shove between my shoulders to keep going. You overcame dyslexia and the abandonment of childhood teachers to read me Stephen King's short stories before bed as a kid. You were the narrator of every story of my youth and showed me the power, privilege, and delight of storytelling. It was your love of reading that led me to write stories to begin with. You read the first story I wrote at the age of seven, and you were the first to read this story decades later. You are, and always will be, my reader. And I will always, always write to and for you.

To my dad, whose love understood all of me even before I understood myself. Growing up in rural Montana in the aughts was not an ideal environment for a strange tomboy. But you showed me that strange was good, and I listened because you were my strange dad. You introduced me to horror movies, and aliens, and ghosts. You encouraged my imagination, even if that imagination led me on ghost-hunting missions instead of princess tea parties. I never had to ask if it was okay to be something other than a girl, because you never treated me like one to begin with. You always saw the whole of me, and you always made it okay. I'm so proud to be your kid.

To Holly, whose love has always come when it was needed most, even from thousands of miles away. As the years pass, and friends fall away, you are the constant. From the age of fourteen, we have been weird, monster-loving freaks, always on the hunt for our Edward Cullen. I'm glad we never found him, but without those years of ghost hunting and horror watching, and haunting Montana forests for our vampire boyfriend, I would not be the creative I am today. You gave a home to the weirdness in me, gave humor to all my pains, fed me crackers when I couldn't feed myself. Your love was the constant in a decade of self-hatred and doubt. Thank you for always reaching out your hand.

To my mutt, Freddie, better known by his litany of nicknames that I will not embarrass him with now. Thank you for being the constant companion at my hip as I put these words to page, for staring up at me with love and wonder as the tears fell, and for demanding pettings and walks that were, in fact, very therapeutic for me.

To the people who have supported this book in small and huge ways. To Lolly a.k.a. L.V. Oaks, my indie publishing confidante and angelic friend. You gave me the courage to bring this story to life myself, and have been there every step of the way to offer encouragement and advice. Thank you for your constant friendship and support. To my editor, Cait Millrod, for stitching together the loose threads of this story in a way that made me feel truly understood and seen. Your quiet encouragement has brought these characters to life in ways I only dreamed of. To Mollie Helck, my alpha reader and cheerleader, and to Anastasia Poliakova, my incredibly talented and patient illustrator. This book would not be what it is without each of you.

Last, to the internet community that came together around this story and around me. Your love has given me wings. I thought I could be happy quietly existing as my true self, surrounded by books that other people had made. But you showed me that there was more work to be done in the great *out there*. You showed me that there was an audience for my strange mix of scary and swoony, that it wasn't crazy to write horror stories for hopeless romantics like myself. Your words of encouragement turned this idea into a novel, and me into an author. Thank you, forever, for your strangeness and kindness.

About the Author

J.C. Hemstreet grew up with a flashlight to their chin, telling scary stories in the dark of a hallway closet or a backyard tent to anyone who would listen. Their fascination with the macabre and cryptid only deepened with age, as authors like the Brontë sisters and Daphne Du Maurier steered them toward the haunting, dark side of romance. Now, Hemstreet is on a mission to bring horror to the hopeless romantics by crafting stories that bridge the gap between spooky and swoony. Hemstreet lives in San Francisco with their husband and rescue mutt, where they work as a transactional attorney when not emersed in fantastical, monster-filled worlds. You can connect with Hemstreet on Instagram (@bookswithjc) or at their website:

www.jchemstreet.com

Printed in Great Britain
by Amazon